DARK AND TWISTED TALES

Book Two

Copyright © 2023 by Jay R. Wolf

First Edition: All Rights Reserved.

No part of this book may be reproduced in any form or by any electronic or mechanical means, including information storage and retrieval systems, without written permission from the author, except for the use of brief quotations in a book review. This book is a work of fiction. Names, characters places and incidents either are the product of the authors' imagination or are used fictitiously. Any resemblance to actual events, locales, or persons, living or dead is purely coincidental.

ISBN 978-1-960411-03-7 (eBook)

ISBN 978-1-960411-04-4 (paperback)

Published by Night Muse Press

Cover Art by Maria Spada

Character Art by Kalynne Art

Editing by Nastasia Bishop in collaboration with Strardust Book Services

Formatted by R. L. Davennor

NIGHT MUSE PRESS
EST. 2020

ALSO BY JAY R. WOLF

The Dark and Twisted Tales series:

A Sea of Unfortunate Souls

The Dark and Twisted Tales series novella:

A Cage of Cursed Souls

CONTENT WARNING

This novel contains graphic depictions of violence, death, torture, mental illness, and adult language. It is intended for a mature adult audience.

The seas are full of dangers, so continue at your own risk…

To my boys: Jaxson and Luca.

Without your constant chaos this would have been done so much sooner!

And yet I still love you the most times infinity.

1. STORMY SEAS

Arie

WHY DID THE SEA HAVE TO BE SUCH A BITCH?

Darkened clouds loomed above the *Black Betty*, roaring with anger as high winds threatened to tear me from the mainmast. Shivering, I wiped stinging rain from my eyes to no avail. My whole body was just as fucking drenched as my face. Through the strands of plastered hair, and the stinging bits of saltwater obscuring my vision, I refused to let up.

Brine filled my nostrils as I searched for my gift. The rumble of the storm and the shouts of my men dissipated, leaving only the blood pounding in my ears and the hammering of my heart to be heard. Sparks of magic pricked my skin as a surge of power sprouted from within. It rattled in its cage, banging and pleading to be let out. I held out a hand and called the gift to the forefront of my mind. The force of strength curled from my toes along my legs until reaching my core. I reveled in the release of power as it flowed from my grasp.

The magic answered with a deafening crack.

A flash of lightning lit the sky in a deadly strike. I clung to the mast, waiting for the rain to cease or clouds to dissipate. Instead, the waves continued to crash over the *Betty* in anger and the clouds darkened more than I ever thought possible. In all my life at sea, I'd never known it to resist my gift.

I peered down at my crew. Dread and defeat covered their faces. Keenan, my quartermaster and best friend barked orders from the bow while both Nathaniel and Hector worked on tightening down sails.

Giles, our sailing master, was at the helm; even from here I could see his white-knuckled grip and fear laced in his eyes. I'd seen him scared before, which seemed odd for someone who sailed pirate ships, but this was something else entirely. He'd been acting strange since our fight with Ursa. It left me wondering if something had spooked him and now the ruthless pirate I'd come to know over the years was afraid of his own shadow.

I looked around at the rest of my men. Those who weren't trying to keep things upright had clutched onto various posts and rope to keep them from going overboard. All of these men, even those of the *Marauder*, were counting on me, and I …

I failed them.

I shifted my gaze to the clouds, to the moon that peeked through as if to mock me.

A LAND OF LOST SOULS

What in sea's sake had I done to deserve this? What had I done to piss off the goddess that she'd send a never-ending storm? She'd been the one who showed up during my battle with Ursa, who spoke to me and guided me when I needed it. Of course, I wasn't exactly sure why she helped me. I was a sea witch, a magic-wielding mermaid, and the best monster hunting pirate captain in the seven seas, but what use was I to a *goddess*?

Why did it feel like this was some sort of punishment?

"I got rid of the Leviathan for you, you worthless salty bitch!" The wind tore my words away, only fueling my rage. Visions of my mother transforming into the sea monster flooded my mind as I raised my head toward the churning clouds. "And this is how you repay me?"

The storm answered with another *boom* of thunder.

Apparently, the goddess didn't appreciate being called a salty bitch, but if she wasn't going to help then this mission was over before it even began.

And wasn't that just wonderful?

Far below, a voice broke through the pandemonium of the storm. I ignored it. Didn't they realize I was busy trying to save them all?

A tinge of power tingled at my fingertips when another sound rang out over the storm, interrupting my focus.

"Arie! You need to get down from there."

Damnit. "Can't you see I'm a little busy here?" I stole a glance downward just as a flash of lightning illuminated the owner of that rich, urgent voice. *Hook.* He stared up at me, his dark brow pulled together in anger and ... something else. Was that fear? Worry?

I shook my head. It didn't matter. I wasn't coming down, not when energy brimmed within me. I had to keep trying.

"Damnit, Arie. Get down here and do something productive. Obviously, your magic isn't working."

Productive? Anger rushed through me. What in sea's sake did he think I was doing up here? Sightseeing? Admitting defeat wasn't exactly in my repertoire of abilities, even if he had a point. What more could I do for a storm that refused to cease?

"And what exactly do you expect me to do, Hook?"

"We have to figure out a different strategy."

I gritted my teeth. Hells, if he wasn't right. I'd been up on this mast for too long, but how could I admit defeat? How could I look at the faces of my men knowing I'd let them down?

I searched the deck for a shaggy head of blond hair through the sea of men, but Pascal was nowhere to be found. He was the one who wanted to take this voyage to Neverland, not just to get him home, but to save it from the one who'd tortured him. Hook and Pascal had given me bits and pieces that they'd remembered. How Pascal had been the leader of a band of misfits and Hook had been one of them. How Neverland was a beautiful island with magic all of its own.

Neither of them really knew what to expect upon our arrival. They weren't even sure they'd have anything to go back to. Wendy had cast Pascal aside and once he was gone, chaos would ensue. Pascal stated the Lost Boys he left behind were no match against her. All we knew for certain was that Wendy would have done everything in her power to destroy what Pascal had built there.

However, when I'd agreed to take the two of them back, I sure as hell didn't agree to die while doing it. If it weren't for him, I'd be somewhere warm, preferably with ale in one hand and a man or woman in the other. I let out a snarl and climbed down the mast, not because Hook asked me to, but because I had a wizard to find. He was the only shot I had left. If he couldn't tell me why my magic failed me, we were all doomed.

A wave crashed over the top of the ship as I landed on the deck. Hook wrapped his arms around me and held onto the mast, keeping us upright. The wave engulfed us in its icy grasp, and I held my breath—and Hook—for dear life while I prayed to the goddess to spare my men. Take me and spare them. They didn't deserve this.

As the wave subsided, I opened my eyes to find Hook inches from my face. I inhaled. Mint, musk, and something … earthy. It reminded me of home.

His dark eyes bore into mine and my cheeks flushed with warmth. He stood far too close for comfort, and I fought against the desire to reach out and touch him. I could feel a sheen of sweat forming on my skin, despite the fact that I was still dripping from the onslaught of rain.

"Finally decided to listen to me?" Hook's low rumble sent shivers down my back.

Without answering, I shoved him aside and made my way across the slippery deck. It rocked beneath me as I used whatever I could to keep myself upright. Hook said something else, but his words weren't my concern just then. If anyone knew how to stop this godsforsaken storm, it had to be Pascal. Because if not, I worried none of us would make it out in one piece.

"Arie!" Frankie grabbed my arm. Her blond hair was rid of its natural curls. "There's something wrong with Pascal."

"You mean more than usual?" Keenan said. I whirled around to find him standing next to Hook. His pale and dirty face hardened. "*Betty* can't take much more of a beating, Cap. We need a plan."

"Which is exactly why I'm looking for Pascal." I turned to Frankie. "Where is he?"

"Below deck." My sister's normally bright smile faded as she took in the storm. Most would be frightened of a storm at sea, but not Frankie. What had she gone through that a storm such as this didn't frighten her? She hadn't really been afraid of King Roland during her captivity either, which bothered me too. Someone without fear could be dangerous.

But now wasn't the time to worry about her past.

"All right, I'll go check on him. You go see if Hector and Nathaniel could use an extra pair of hands."

Frankie gave a stiff nod and raced off to find her mentors.

"I'm coming with you." Hook took a step toward me, and I stuck my hand out and regretted it the moment his chest met my palm. Heat found its way back to my cheeks and I quickly lowered my hand. Probably too fast because his lips quirked up.

Get a grip, Arie.

"You need to be out here helping us stay upright." He stared at me, as though he didn't hear my words of objection. I let out a sigh and rolled my eyes before turning around and taking off toward the bunks.

In the distance, Frankie barked orders to one of Hook's men. A small, skinny man—whose name I couldn't remember—looked as if he'd seen a ghost.

Leaving her to it, Hook and I made our way below deck. The roar of the storm faded, but the moans and groans from *Betty* grew louder down here. I winced. Keenan was right, we needed something to happen in our favor, and soon.

We found Pascal sitting against a wall in the bunks. Lanterns, the ones still sitting on the walls, had faded, casting the room in a dull glow. Pascal's knees were tucked close to him, and his unkempt hair covered most of his face. The last time I'd seen him this way was after a kingsman had tortured him.

His entire body twitched upon our approach.

Sunken cheeks, dreary eyes, and what appeared to be dry tears had me practically sprinting to him. I don't know when I started to feel this motherly instinct toward Pascal. I had the strongest urge to find a blanket, wrap him up in it, and sing to him until whatever bothered him finally left. Instead, I dropped to my knees and waited for him to speak.

"Hi, little dove."

He'd mostly stopped calling me that name since getting his memory back, but there were times where his mind drifted and slipped back into the days of being the king's wizard. He'd call me little dove, crack a wicked smile, and speak without a care in the world.

"Pascal, you all right?" Hook asked.

His gaze met Hook's and he frowned. "Things have gotten complicated, I'm afraid."

"What are you talking about?"

Pascal sat up, but rather than reply he simply rocked back and forth, swaying in time with the ship's movements. Hells, I didn't have time for this.

"Pascal, if you haven't noticed yet, there's a damn storm threatening to kill us, and we still haven't reached Neverland. Tell us what's got you all worked up, or help us fix this mess, because I'm all out of options." At this rate we'd be going to Davy Jones's locker before the sun rose. Something had to give.

Pascal simply shook his head.

"Pascal, damnit, either tell me what the is going on or I swear I—"

Just as the words left my mouth the rocking of the ship slowed, and the faint shouts of the men on deck shifted to cheers. Did this mean the storm was finally over? It didn't answer the question of why my magic didn't work on it, but my body wanted to vibrate with excitement over its ending. That was until I realized Pascal was still visibly upset. I'd expect a bit more excitement at the very least. But rather than jump for joy, tears rolled down his cheeks.

"I had no other choice. It had to be done. It had to be done, or we wouldn't have made it. I had no choice. You believe me, don't you?" Pascal's frantic words were heightened by the fear in his icy blue eye, and the other seemed far more clouded than normal. He wiped away tears and turned until he faced the wall.

"What are you talking about?" Hook said and sat on one of the empty bunks.

"Neverland is angry. Angry at me for leaving—for abandoning it for so long. I thought it would be overjoyed to see my return, but instead it wanted me out. It wants me gone." His voice lowered. "*You don't belong here anymore, Peter."*

He ran his hands through his hair, pulling at the strands.

"Neverland should be angry with Wendy, not us," Hook said.

My hands curled into fists at the mention of Wendy's name. The villain in Pascal's own story. I hadn't managed to get much out of Hook or Pascal in regard to what she did other than the torture she inflicted on Pascal. But that was enough to make me want to show her the real meaning behind torture.

There was, however, a member of the Brotherhood on my ship. Surely Jameson and his brethren knew a few tips on torture. When we finally defeated Ursa, I'd thought the assassin would have went on his merry way, but he'd asked to stay and while I wasn't so sure about having him come with us to Neverland, especially when he'd kept himself scarce and useless, he had at least managed to stay out of the way. It still didn't stop me from having others keep an eye on him. Perhaps now he could come in handy.

"I shouldn't be here." Pascal shook his head. "I should leave. You go to Neverland and save it. I-I can't…"

"Pascal, the sun will rise soon. Why don't you come up with us, and we can sort all this out with the crew." I held out my hand.

Though rather than take it, his eyes grew wide again, and his face paled.

"*No*," he hissed. "I can't. I had no choice." He paused for a moment and lifted his gaze to the ceiling. "No, you know what will happen. This is a bad idea."

He wasn't speaking to either of us, at least it hadn't appeared that way. I looked at Hook who shrugged at the wizard's odd behavior.

Then again, was it odd for a half-crazed man to talk to himself?

"We're not going to get anything from him right now, Arie. We may as well leave him to his thoughts and come back when he's a bit more himself."

Leaving him now in this state was a mistake, and I wasn't going anywhere until I got answers. I sat until my back rested on the wall next to Pascal. "I'm not leaving until he's all right. Go up and make sure everyone's good. I'll be up momentarily."

He hesitated, but only for a moment before he nodded and headed back to the rest of the crew.

Pascal and I sat there in silence, save for the creaks and groans of the ship, and the shouts of men from above. I swear only days ago we were sailing toward Scarlett's Lagoon in search of the Leviathan. Back when Pascal was nothing more than the king's wizard, a man feared from Khan to the Enchanted Realm.

What was he now?

His memories had come back, and he'd expressed a dire need to return to his home, but this journey had done something terrible to him. If only I'd known him before all this, before the torture and the chaos he'd inflicted, before my own pain and loss. Maybe we'd have been friends.

All I saw now was a broken and defeated person with nothing left to lose.

I didn't know what to say to make all this better for him. So, I sat and waited until he was ready to talk first. My ass grew numb, and pins and needles shot down my legs. I shifted, and he huffed a laugh and turned to meet my gaze.

"You don't have to stay down here, Arie. I'll be okay."

"If that's what you want, but I have a rising suspicion you want to tell me what's going on. If I'm wrong, I'll get up and leave you to sulk alone."

I didn't want to leave, but if he needed space and time to gather his thoughts, I'd do it. The storm may have dried up, but there was still a lot to do before our Neverland adventure, and I suspected we'd reach the shores soon.

Pascal regarded me for several minutes before he frowned and dug his hands into his pockets. "Have you ever heard of the god, Pan?"

"The gatekeeper to the Celestial Plains? I've heard the name a time or two." Unsure of what this had to do with his current problem, I settled in for what appeared to be the beginning of a history lesson.

"He's the creator of Neverland and all its inhabitants—all besides the mermaids who belong to the Goddess of Sea and Sky, as you know. He made Neverland a safe zone of sorts. Blessed the land, the waters, and the people with magic. There isn't a single leaf or drop of water without it. That's why it's not on any map, why most people don't know it exists. To keep from being tainted with the outside world—to keep its magic pure and the Celestial Plains safe—he made it nearly impossible to gain access to."

I knew about what a blessing from a god could do, but this was news to me. Having never heard of Neverland outside of fairy tales, I guess now it made sense why no one knew it was a real place.

"Because of this, there's only certain ways one can enter Neverland."

He hadn't mentioned anything before when we were working out our plan to get to the island. Why was this only coming up now?

Pascal turned away from me. "Pan only allows those he deems worthy to enter the land. Those of innocent hearts and the purest souls. Do you know who those people might be, Arie?"

Sure as hell wasn't me, but rather than say so, I nodded. I'd gotten the impression back in Atlantis. The Lost Boys, the ones Pascal saved, were all children.

"I spent a lot of my time searching for lost souls. Those who were abandoned or abused by those meant to protect them, or who were on the run from the dangers of this world. Innocent and pure of heart."

He started repeating himself again and I grabbed his shoulder for reassurance. I had a feeling I knew where this was going, why Pascal was having a hard time getting back to Neverland.

"Unfortunately, my father has decided I'm no longer worthy of entering Neverland."

Father?

I stilled. The strength, the affinity for magic, healing, all of it made sense. Pascal wasn't just a wizard: he was a fucking *demigod*.

"Pan is your—"

"Yes. My full name is Peter Orion Thaddeus Pan."

What a name.

"So where did the name Pascal come from?"

"It was the alias I used whenever I left Neverland. No one besides the Lost Boys and other beings on the island knew my real name. When I woke up in Khan under the king's rule, it was the only name I could remember. Though, now I almost prefer it. Anything to rid myself of my father."

Hurt. That's what I'd been seeing. Not dismay or defeat. He was hurt. Had something else happened before this? Pan was refusing him entry to his home, but this look, this pain, it was much deeper than I thought. Hadn't Pascal said only those of innocent souls could enter Neverland? There was nothing innocent and pure about Pascal anymore. Not after what the king had made him do, the pain and torture he inflicted on the people of Khan.

How did he expect a group of pirates to get into Neverland then?

"If it matters, I prefer Pascal as well."

He smiled, but only briefly before the hurt and pain returned. "Anyway, the second way to get into Neverland is with the use of fairy dust. But no one aboard this ship has any or I'd feel it. The fairy dust is magic which masks its user. It keeps them from being detected by the magical barrier. They can pass through whether they're innocent or not. A lot of people don't know about the dust. It's what I'd use to get a few of the Lost Boys in. Again, a story for another time."

Fairy dust, magical barriers, and a god. I wanted to laugh, but really it wasn't any different than what I'd seen and dealt with. Deadly monsters, killer sirens, talking fish, a king at the bottom of the sea. If anything, Pascal's story fit right into my world of crazy.

"So how are we getting in then?"

Pascal rubbed a hand over his face before turning to me. "I had hoped my father would help with that problem, but it turns out he wouldn't let that happen. Not without a bargain."

A terrible feeling dug itself into the pit of my stomach. What had he done?

"So, I asked my father what I could do, what I could present to him that would allow me to return home." Pascal paused and wiped tears from his cheeks.

What would Pascal have that a god wouldn't? If Pan is Pascal's father, surely he has the same, if not more, power than his son.

"I'm so cold and alone and empty without it."

My body broke out in goosebumps, and I shivered. Did Pan take his soul? He didn't seem to be the same wizard I'd known before.

"But it's the only way for Pan to travel through the realms as he sees fit."

Pascal's voice lowered to a whisper as he rocked back and forth. He held out his hand, and in the small of his palm was the tiniest vial of yellow sand. No, not sand, dust. It sparked and popped inside the vial.

Fairy dust.

"It will get you and seven others safely to Neverland's shores. Once you're there you—"

"Hold on, you're not coming? Isn't this the whole reason we're here, Pascal. You can't stay here, you have to come with us."

Pascal shook his head. "I can't. Not without ... I just can't."

He wasn't making any sense. He'd given up everything to get back here. Now he was going to sit back and do what?

"Does this have anything to do with why you're so upset? What did you have to give up, Pascal?"

Tears welled in Pascal's eyes as they drifted up to meet mine.

"My shadow."

11. BROKEN

Pascal

MY FATHER'S FACE FLOODED INTO MY MIND. Golden hair, and deep blue eyes stared back at me, judging me with a lift of his brow and a wrinkled nose.

You should have stayed in Khan.

I leaned my head against the wall and shivered, though it had nothing to do with the cool wood against my skin. I let the memory of my father's disappointment linger a bit longer. *I'm sorry, Father. I'm so sorry for what I've done, for the disappointment I've brought you. Please find a way to forgive me. I'm … I'm …*

An ache wrapped itself around me, crushing my lungs with its icy grasp. I clutched my tunic and gasped for air only to be met with resistance. Was I dying? I pressed my other hand to my wet cheek. What was this? I shifted until my knees pressed against the floor and I felt my body shake with each heavy breath.

A knock rapped at the door, but I couldn't move, couldn't suck in enough air to breathe let alone speak. Seconds later, a pair of soft gentle hands warmed my cheeks and lifted my face. Thick red curls and a gentle smile greeted me.

Arie.

Blood pounded in my ears, drowning out Arie's words. I didn't want to hear what she had to say. I didn't want her comfort, or her pity. I opened my mouth to tell her so when a tinge of power rolled over me. It crawled over my skin and seeped into my bones, something sharp digging in. I cried out as each strand of darkness snapped in half, replacing my panic with … relief.

She feels so good.

The voice inside my head moaned with Arie's touch. The same voice I'd heard upon getting my soul and memories back. The one who never seemed to want to shut up.

I resent that.

Ignoring … myself … I leaned into Arie's touch allowing every bit of her comfort to wrap itself around me. Her magic came from two different and strong places. From her father, a mermaid and king of Atlantis, and from her mother, a sea witch. She could control storms, speak to the sea, and somehow, she managed to free thousands of souls from her mother's clutches without killing herself in the process. But to me, her magic was so much more than that. Her presence alone had the ability to calm the storm in me. The one that had been brewing since the moment Wendy sunk her filthy claws into my mind.

Whatever power Arie had over me wasn't something to be taken lightly. Neither was the power my father now held over me.

"Are you all right?"

I stiffened at her words. How could I be? Without my shadow I'd be forced to remain indoors while the sun was out. I'd never be able to feel its warmth on my skin or the way the lights shine against the seven falls. And how would the Lost Boys feel when they found out I'd given it up? I'd already made a mess of my life and I wasn't sure if I was ready for their disappointment. I'd done too much damage in Khan, hurt too many people. But I had to. I had to stop the one responsible no matter the consequences it brought me.

The memory of my two lives clashed together as one when I woke in Atlantis, and I ... I remembered *everything*.

The Lost Boys, Neverland, the Fae, and *her*. All of it flooded back the second my soul returned. Even now as the *Black Betty* swayed in the depths of the sea and Arie's aura beamed with bliss, I remember what had been done to me, and worse, what I'd done as King Roland's wizard.

Wendy's bright eyes and short, wavy blond hair crashed into my mind like a battering ram. I'd experienced a lot in my many centuries of life, but Wendy had somehow managed to surprise me, something I hadn't expected was possible anymore. And then, when she was done with me, she threw me to the sharks. King Roland was his own personal hell. I hated the man, even as his wizard, but I lived to serve.

Gooseflesh rolled down my arms and I shivered.

No. I live to be free.

"The sun is setting—I figured you might want to eat before our meeting with the crew."

Arie dropped her hands and turned to pick up a platter I hadn't seen in my moment of panic. An array of fruits and cheeses sent my stomach into a rumbling fit.

"I'm staying here."

The bunk creaked under her weight as she sat opposite me. She crossed her hands over her chest and stared down at me but she didn't speak, and didn't plead with me to go with her.

"What exactly does losing your shadow mean, Pascal?"

"Did you know that the gods don't have shadows?"

Arie didn't speak, just shook her head as if waiting for me to get to the point.

"It's complicated, but now that Pan has mine, he can go anywhere in the Seven Seas he wants. He's no longer bound to Neverland and the Celestial Plains. But that means I'm forced to roam only when the sun has set. Without my shadow, the sun will burn me and my human body."

Arie paled a little. "You're serious?"

I nodded. "It's how humans are protected from its rays. Rhian, the father of the gods and the god of the sun gave it to humans as a gift. So, you see why I can't go with you to Neverland."

Rather than question me, she simply sat there and waited. I had nothing more to say.

"Is there anything else?" I asked.

"No, but I'm not leaving this bunk until you eat. You're a damn skeleton, Pascal. Eat, or I'll force it down your throat."

I wouldn't mind if she forced something else my way. The voice purred.

What is wrong with you? Arie is our friend, so shut up and go away.

Well, that's not very nice of you, Peter.

Neither is drooling over the pirate queen. I'm not interested in—

But I am.

Ignoring the voice yet again, I reluctantly plucked a grape from the platter of food and popped it into my mouth. I groaned at the dulcet taste on my tongue; a delectable far too good to let go to waste. From strawberries to melons to different types of cheeses, all of it was euphoric on my tongue. I hadn't realized how famished I'd been until that moment.

"How do you have this kind of food on the *Betty* anyway?" I asked.

"The cook has a few tricks up his sleeve," she said before changing the subject. "Pascal, I know you think you should stay behind, but we … I need you to come with us. The sun won't be a problem. We can head to Neverland when the sun goes down and seek shelter when we need to. But we need you. You know Neverland better than anyone, and the Lost Boys will know who you are. Do you really think they will accept a band of pirates in their home?"

She had a point. Pirates had always been considered the scum of the Seven Seas to us Lost Boys. I remembered telling her so when she first asked about what to expect upon our arrival. A warm welcome wasn't exactly what I'd pictured. Not only that, but I'd left them so long ago there was no telling who remained on the island, and for all I knew, Wendy could have killed them all.

Wendy.

The thought of my torturer crashed into me once more and I tried to force the images away, but they refused. No matter how hard I tried to block out those last few nights of being in Neverland, it was all I could think about.

There was so much blood, so much pain and anger. The boy I'd once been was ripped away, piece by piece as Wendy did her worst, leaving nothing but a hollow shell behind and—

Me.

I shuddered at the voice in my head, the one reminding me I wasn't alone anymore. The one I now shared my soul with. The one who'd done so many terrible things. I hadn't the faintest idea how to wrap my brain around the fact that there were two versions of myself mixed together in some tainted version of a soul, but somehow it happened.

"Pascal?"

I jumped at her words. "Just show them the jar of fairy dust."

She sighed and leaned forward to rest a hand on mine. "Look, I know you're hurting, and we don't have to talk about any of this if you don't want to, but you *have* to let me know. I want to know how to help you. You're a son of a god, a man who fought by my side while we killed the Leviathan. It may be hard to believe, but I'm on your side." She'd said that name with distaste. Not that I could blame her. Ursa had tricked a lot of people into believing the Leviathan was just some monster. Arie's victory over her mother had been one of the most amazing things I'd ever witnessed. But that didn't change my desire to never leave this ship again.

"Just let him be, Arie. He isn't going to come with us." Hook appeared through the door, his broody eyes scrutinizing Pascal. I stifled the urge to tell him where to stick his prosthetic and instead turned my focus back to Arie.

"The crew is going to want to know what happened to you and why the storm stopped. At the very least can we tell them what's going on?"

I sighed. "Yes, that's fair, and I'll come to the meeting, but I won't leave this ship."

"We'll see," was all she said before leaving.

The pale crescent moon shone like a silvery claw in the night sky, illuminating some of the crew's familiar faces. I peered up at the blanket of stars that stretched well beyond the horizon, stars that would become the only familiar thing I'd ever see in the sky. Without my shadow I'd never be able to leave the confines of darkness. Not unless I wanted to cross into the Celestial Plains, and I sure as hell didn't want to see father anytime soon.

Arie's voice roared over the crowd of pirates. "We made it through the biggest storm in the history of men and the only things lost were a few barrels, a ripped sail, and some crushed boards. Everyone is relatively in one piece, and I call that a victory!"

Cheers rang over the *Betty*.

"All right, all right, settle down," Arie laughed. "We have far more pressing matters to address."

I tuned out Arie's tale about what had happened to me, what I had to give up, and whatever else she deemed necessary. Though I had a much harder time ignoring the concerned looks, raised brows, and murmurs.

My eyes panned over the group of pirates. The ones who'd started to accept me, who greeted me when we crossed paths or offered to share their ale with me. Finally, a burly looking man strode up beside me and rested his arm on my shoulder. He leaned in close, his hot breath on my ear, and a dank stench of ale assaulted my nose as he spoke. "You don't have to worry about your Wendy problem. Once we're done with her, we'll make sure your daddy pays the pirate price for taking what rightfully belongs to you."

Our lovely, red-bearded giant was always the one for violence.

"While I appreciate that, my father is a god. He'd kill you with nothing more than a snap of his fingers. He's not called the God of Death and Ruin for nothing. The Celestial Plains has been his home for eons. A strike from your ax will not kill him, and I don't think he's ever known the feeling of fear."

Nathaniel threw his head back and laughed. Heads turned as the pirate slapped his knee and wiped tears from his cheeks. "Oh, Pascal, you kill me. Sorry to rain on your sunshine"—his voice melted into a deep rumble— "but everyone's afraid of something. You and Arie deserve better than the lives you've been given, and I'll be damned if the crew of the *Betty* sits idly by while more atrocities happen to the both of you. We'll get your revenge, just as we will Arie's. These are words I give to you, wizard, from now until my last breath."

I raised a brow at his words—at his vow. Why did he care? Why would he pledge his life to helping me when I'd done nothing for him. I was pretty sure I'd tried to kill him. Or was that Hector?

"That's not necessary—"

Just then, a roar of anger cut through my objection.

"You can't be serious."

"We won't stay behind."

"This is outrageous."

I don't think they're happy about staying put.

While I agreed, perhaps I could ease their minds.

"We can't all go to Neverland. Those of you who try to find—or trick your way in—will die. Neverland doesn't accept anyone without fairy dust unless they have an innocent soul. Arie has just enough to get eight of you onto the island without issue and—"

"Then let me be one of those who go!" shouted a pirate I didn't see.

"And me!"

"Enough!" Arie yelled. "I appreciate those eager to put their life on the line. But I've already made up my mind. Now shut up and listen for a minute. I don't need to remind you of what happens when you don't."

A hush fell over the sea of grimacing faces. Yet, those faces melted back into pride as Arie continued her speech.

She pressed a hand to her hip where I knew she kept her dagger—

Slayer.

Right. Where she kept Slayer.

A girl from Bellavier didn't ride the ranks of a ship by being soft, and the men who stood around me obviously knew more than I did about the pirate queen. It made sense that she'd have to show herself to a group of men. What did she do to those who didn't listen?

Maybe she gutted them. I wouldn't mind seeing our little dove in action again. She's not our little dove.

"So, let's get right to it, then." Arie's lips pursed as she hesitated. Her gaze flickered from one pirate to the next as if searching for what to say. "Nathaniel. Hector. Will you accompany me on my journey to Neverland? Fight by my side and risk your life for this mission?"

Both men stepped forward.

"Aye, Captain. From now until the end of my days." They spoke in unison.

Arie nodded. Next to her, Keenan fidgeted with his sleeve, his hardened expression gave away nothing, but there was something in his stance that gave him away.

Perhaps he's mentally begging her to pick him.

My thoughts exactly.

Well obviously they're your thoughts. Keep thinking that and people will think you've gone mad again.

I needed to get this damn voice out of my head.

"This next person is because they know the land. Before anyone has an objection, I suggest you keep it to yourself." Arie's shoulders stiffened as she turned. "Captain Hoo—"

"Yes," Hook said.

Arie relaxed a fraction, but something sparked in her eyes. She turned back to face the crowd. "And this next person I'm choosing because I promised to never again leave them on the sidelines. Frankie."

"I'm all yours, Captain." Frankie stood between Hector and

Nathaniel, her hands placed at her back and her feet planted at even length apart. A stance I'd seen many times in my trips to the Enchanted Realm. *Curious.*

Keenan whirled around to Arie; his mouth opened but she held up a hand.

"I know. It's a risk, but one I must take. If we're ever to fix the problems we have, I must bring my sister with me."

"But, Captain, surely I'm a much more suitable warrior to bring to unknown lands?"

"Excuse me?" Frankie bit out.

"Maybe," Arie interjected. "But you are the only one I trust *Betty* with. You need to stay here—it's the only way I can leave without worrying about my ship being set on fire or sunk to the bottom of the sea."

I knew what Arie really meant by those words and the ones she refused to say. For a while now Arie had a weird feeling about Giles. On this trip alone he'd managed to get us lost and had nearly killed us when he wasn't able to sail through a storm. Arie managed to get control over the situation, but ever since then she'd kept a close watch on him. Him and Jameson—the brotherhood assassin. So, it made sense when those two were the next two choices. Giles because he needed off this ship, and Jameson because she knew keeping her enemy close was a far smarter decision than leaving him here where he could be left to his own devices.

The quartermaster crossed his arms and scowled. "I don't like this."

Arie sighed. "I know."

Keenan nodded before retreating somewhere in the crowd. Hurt came and went on Arie's face before telling everyone her next pick. I didn't care who she picked; all I cared about was getting back to my bunk. I rubbed a hand over my chest, over the full ache that festered there. Emptiness. Raw and ... hollow. Tendrils of darkness crawled beneath my skin and wrapped my muscles and bones in its blackened grasp.

I dropped to the floor, gasping for breath as men scurried back.

"That settles it." Arie pushed through the crowd and dropped to her knees beside me. Her voice lowered to a whisper. "Pascal, I'm sorry, but you have to come with us. It's the only way to get your shadow back and to finally put an end to your nightmares—to Wendy. Whether you want to accept it or not, you're my last choice. I know what the consequences of not having your shadow are. You're coming with. Is that clear?"

I shook my head.

Arie sighed, and her voice dropped to a whisper. "Look, I'd appreciate it if you came. But, if what you want is to stay here, I will respect that."

I couldn't do this. What good was I when I'd be forced to remain inside at all times? How could I be of any use?

Do you want to take down Wendy?

With everything I had.

Then we have to help. You are the only one who knows the truth behind Wendy and what she's capable of. Think of what she'd do to Arie if she got the upper hand.

Arie was far too strong and smart to get caught by Wendy.

Are you willing to take that chance?

"Pascal?"

I peered up to Arie and swore.

No, I wasn't willing to take that chance.

Defeated and unwilling to argue further, I did nothing, I said nothing. Because Arie was right. I'd never get my shadow back or bring justice to Wendy by staying on this ship. And I'd rather die in Neverland than on this ship with insufferable pirates.

I cleared my throat. "We'll have to go now or we'll never make it to the Tiki Tree before sunrise."

A lightness consumed me as we lowered ourselves into the rowboat, my pulse racing with each passing second. We were here. I was going home. Yet, I couldn't bring myself to smile or celebrate. I couldn't afford myself such a luxury when none of this felt right. Not without my shadow.

I didn't look at the island until we were hauling the rowboat to shore, and only then did I allow myself a second to take it all in.

Home wasn't as I remembered it.

My leather boots sunk into dark sand as I sauntered up to the tree line. Well, what was left of it anyway. Dark and bleak trees stood leafless and rotting. Some bore burn marks along their trunks while others appeared to have lost their leaves akin to the first signs of winter.

I fell to my knees and dug my hands into the sand. Each grain filtered through my fingers, but somehow it felt different than it once had. No pulse of Neverland's heart beating to the same rhythm as my own. No whispers of the wisps or call of the fae. We, the land and all its occupants, were always one mind. One soul.

Our soul isn't one anymore, remember?

I cursed, pushing away the annoying voice and returned my focus to Arie.

She'd said something to me. What was it?

"Pascal?" she asked.

Remembering her words, I said, "The way h-home is that way." I pointed toward the dying forest and swallowed the sob threatening to escape.

Home.

Everyone stared at me, their looks loaded with questions I didn't have the answers to. My gaze panned until it found Hook—*Ulrich*. My brother and friend. A boy who had found his way from the island to commanding a pirate ship. All this time he'd been right there. I'd seen him in Khan, spent days upon days with him on Arie's ship, and not once did I realize the captain and my friend were one in the same. Not until my memories returned, anyway. I'd know his broody look anywhere. Though now he'd grown from the scared little boy I saved to a fearsome pirate captain.

He'd been one of the first to join me in Neverland—a Lost Boy. Both him and his brother had fled a terrible situation, and I'd brought them to safety. Now here he was returning the favor. If only Clayton would have joined us.

"We will figure this out," Hook said with his hand outstretched. I grabbed it, pulling myself to my feet.

"Any idea how we're going to find where we're going in the dark?"

Hector muttered.

"We don't need the light to find our way." Hook walked up to stand next to Arie and handed her a canteen.

"Is that so?" Jameson asked.

"Yes, and even if we get lost, all Pascal has to do is ask. Neverland tells him everything," Hook replied.

I sighed. A true statement for a time long past. Now, I wasn't so sure. The island felt different than it had the last time I stepped foot on its soil. There was no spark of energy running through me, the wind bore no whispers, and the trees were far too dead to speak. There was nothing but vast emptiness. A hollowness dug itself into my soul, pleading with me to fix whatever was broken. But how could I fix a broken island when I couldn't fix myself?

"What the hells is that supposed to mean?" Jameson asked.

"We can talk about this more once we're not so exposed," I said. There were a lot of things I hadn't wanted to divulge to everyone just yet. It was better to keep people at a distance, to keep them oblivious to the truth I buried deep down in order to protect the ones I loved. That, and there was no telling what lurked within the forest anymore. It was better this way.

Keep telling yourself that.

I nodded to Hook whose gaze seemed to be more interested in Arie than the trail ahead. I'd known him for so long and never once had I seen such a look on him. The one where all the stars aligned and bright lights lit the sky. The question was, did Arie feel the same? Did she realize his smile grew when she walked in the room, or how he stole glances her way when she wasn't looking?

Anger flickered inside me, though it felt nothing close to my own. *Well, we sure aren't going to be the ones to tell them. Our little dove needs to focus on the task at hand.*

Are you jealous?

Internally I shook my head. I was being ridiculous. This other voice, whatever was going on, I couldn't let it get to me.

I pushed past the crew until only the sand stood between me and what awaited beyond the dead trees. I gulped in as much air as my lungs would allow and welcomed the brine lacing my tongue.

This was it: each step would take me closer to home and closer to the boys I'd abandoned so many years ago.

We didn't abandon them. She *gave us no choice. I'll gut her and throw the pieces to the Never creatures for what she did.*

Now that was something we could agree on.

"Does anyone else get the feeling like we're being watched?" Giles asked.

"Who knew pirates were afraid of water *and* the dark." Jameson muttered.

"I'm not afraid of—"

"Shut up you two." Nathaniel hissed.

Dead grass and shriveled leaves crunched under my boots, breaking the otherwise quiet woods. The farther in we got, the more I noticed the acrid smell that seeped from the ground and crept up to my nostrils. I scanned the trees, searching and praying for birds to flutter from their limbs, or rabbits to dart between their trunks, but only the pirates behind me were left to keep my mind at ease.

Scarlett's Lagoon had been like this. Was there a monster lurking about, waiting for the right moment to attack?

With that thought, gooseflesh trickled down my arms, and I shivered. Someone was here. I whirled around and nearly collided with Hook.

"What's wro—"

"Arie, watch out!" Frankie cried.

A blur vaulted past me, knocking Arie to the ground before she had a chance to grab her dagger.

Long dark hair sat in braids against bare and broad shoulders. Dark red trousers and leather boots were the only thing covering them. Black ink wove in swirls around the letters "LB" along their left shoulder blade. My heart skipped, and my stomach leapt to my throat. I knew that tattoo. I had the same one in the exact same place. Slipping my hand over the tattoo, I winced at the raised and scarred skin. Flashes of flickering red entered my vision, and burnt flesh filled my nostrils.

So much pain. So much blood.

Spots entered my vision as everything around me darkened.

Easy. We can't break now.

"Get off her, Ace!"

It was Hook who brought me back to the present. When had he moved? He stood with Ace pressed against a tree, his hook ready to puncture his jugular if Ace dared to move an inch. Jameson stood next to him; something dark came and went in his eyes. I was glad to see his bird was nowhere in sight—that thing just didn't seem human and looked at me as if it knew me personally. Giles, on the other hand, had paled and stepped away from the commotion.

Next to us, Nathaniel held Arie back as she fought to free herself. "Let me go, Nathaniel," she said through gritted teeth. "Let me go so I can introduce this jackass to Slayer."

"Who's Slayer?" Ace ground out, his voice much lower than I remembered it.

Something wasn't right. Ace was … older. When I left, he was merely a boy. Skittish and afraid of almost everything. He'd been abused and prodded and sold like cattle by his father. Dark scruff lined his jaw, and he stood several inches taller. Had he left Neverland in search of me too? Or could this be something else entirely?

There was time to speculate about that later.

I glanced at Arie and winced. If it were possible for someone to die on a single look, we'd be mourning a life rather than having a reunion. My gaze trailed down to her clenched fists. Other than her apparent anger, she seemed otherwise intact.

"Wait, how do you know my name?" Ace asked.

"Yeah, Hook. How *do* you know his name?" Arie thrashed once more in Nathaniel's arms. "Nathaniel, if you don't let me go right now, I swear to the gods—"

Nathaniel threw his head back and laughed. "Sea's sake, I love a feisty woman. And only if you promise to be good."

Arie nodded and ripped herself from his grasp.

"I know your name because it was I who gave it to you." I stepped around the captain and lowered his hook from Ace's throat. He took a step back, leaving me to face the current leader of the Lost Boys—the one I'd left in charge before going after Wendy.

Fierce blue eyes pierced through me. His rounded jaw, high cheekbones, and crooked nose were an odd pairing, but it didn't stop Frankie from staring. I caught her on the other side of Arie, her gaze fixed on the boy I'd once called brother.

I returned my focus to Ace and waited for his face to change, or a drop of his jaw. But nothing faltered or gave away he knew me at all.

It's the scars. It's always the scars.

I traced a hand along the deep gashes on my face. Each ridge or bump were reminders of the torture inflicted. Of the pain and suffering *she* caused. Every part of my being urged me to find her. To bring her the same fate she once brought me. My fingers stopped below the milky eye that clouded only parts of my vision. Thanks to magic. Without my powers I was certain I'd have lost vision completely.

"*You?* You're not Peter Pan. And you"—he turned toward Hook—"are lucky I'm alone. If you ever point that thing at me again, I'll kill you with it."

Behind me, Arie snorted. "I'd pay money to see that."

"You came here from Khan." I lowered my voice to a whisper. No one else needed to know the troubled past Ace once lived. "I rescued you from a drunken mother and an abusive father who whipped you and then sold you," I continued, and as each word left my mouth, Ace's face grew paler. His eyes widened and jaw dropped before a single tear slid down his cheek.

He wiped away the wetness and flung his arms around me. "I-I thought … but it's really y-you … how?"

Ace stepped back, turning until he found Hook. While Hook had aged since we'd last been home, I still saw the same boy lurking behind the pirate façade. He'd been so scared, no matter how tough he tried to be. During his time as a captain, had he ever found out the truth about his past? I was never going to tell him, it wasn't up to me, but I'd make sure he found his way back when the time was right. He deserved to know the truth about what happened to him. To learn about the VonWhite family.

"Ulrich?" Ace gasped. "I-I can't believe it."

"It's Captain Hook now." Hook laughed and raised his hand.

I don't remember how he got that.

Neither did I.

Hook nodded. "It's good to see you, old friend."

"I-It can't be. You're dead. You're both supposed to be …"

Hook shook his head. "Not dead, just lost."

What had Wendy said to my family while I was away? They thought we were dead? They had to have known better. I opened my mouth to inquire more but was interrupted.

Arie surged forward. "He tried to fucking kill me and you're all going to pretend it didn't happen?"

I'll kill him for you, little dove.

"Shut up," I hissed.

"Excuse me?" Arie stomped toward me, her face now inches from mine.

"Not you."

Arie gave a stiff nod and shot Ace a look of indignation. "How many more of you are there lurking about waiting to attack?"

"As I said, I'm alone."

Arie opened her mouth, but Hector beat her to it.

"There's nowhere to hide in these trees, Captain."

"Yet somehow he managed." Anger flickered in Arie's face again. I remembered that look. The one with distrust and the desire to bring her pet dagger out to play.

Watching the anger in Arie's eyes reminded me so much of my own. I knew what it felt like to be attacked, to feel powerless in an unknown place. Neverland was new to her, but it wasn't to me.

We'll protect her.

Once again, I agreed with the other me.

"I told you someone was watching us." Giles's grip on his sword tightened as he stepped back.

"They have a point." Jameson shrugged as he walked closer to Arie. "Where did you come from?"

I ignored the other pirates and turned to Arie. "Ace travels alone. It appears it still rings true after all these years. There's no one else here."

"And you know this because Neverland told you?" she asked.

I nodded, not willing to divulge any more information just yet. I wasn't even sure I knew the real reason why Neverland and I had such a bond. I'd been born here, and my father was its creator, but even then, I wasn't so sure what gave me the power to know what it wanted and felt at any given moment.

"I-I don't understand." Ace rubbed his face. "How are you here? How did you survive? We were told—"

"You were told wrong," I snapped. "Now, can we please stop this nonsense and get back to the Tree?"

Ace glared at Arie. "You want to allow pirates into our home?"

"Ace, we don't have time for this."

The Lost Boy's eyes widened, feral and ... empty. "You're right, we don't want to be caught out here where the Neverbeasts roam. I'll bring you home, Peter, but it may not be the welcoming you're hoping for."

I wanted to pry further, to demand he tell me what happened while I was away, but we needed to get back before my shadowless frame dissipated with the morning light.

III. LOST AND FOUND

Arie

THIS WAS NEVERLAND?

Slender pines stood naked with their bare arms outstretched, and their leaves crunched under my feet, expelling the silence.

Silence.

I stopped and listened. Nothing—not the whisper of wind through the branches, nor the trill of birds, or the murmur of rivers. I saw nothing but a desolate wasteland of dry trees and dirt. Even the scent of pine needles and earth was absent. There was nothing about this that reminded me of the lush, magical kingdom I had read about in stories—with greenery that seemed to go on forever, sparkling rivers, and soft beaches of golden sand.

This ... this place reminded me of what I'd read about the Dread Woods. A place far from here where nothing but rot and death fill the land. Gooseflesh trickled down my arms and I shivered. I'd never been to those woods, only heard the rumors and read the texts, but I couldn't shake the impending doom lurking over me. The same unrelenting dread those woods were famous for.

I drew my gaze upward to the dark fluffy clouds that rolled in. Another storm? I felt no static in the air nor smelled the first hints of rain. Was it the same storm I'd been unable to stifle? We'd be sitting ducks out here in a storm, and I didn't trust my magic enough right now. Not when it had failed me so terribly at sea. I knew now that it had more to do with Pascal than myself, but it didn't stop me from wondering if my magic would be useless in Neverland too.

"Don't worry," Ace said, his gaze fixed on mine. "It hasn't rained here in quite some time."

He frowned, wrinkles tugged at tired eyes, then he blinked, and the hardened shell returned. "At least not around these parts. I suppose that's just more of Wendy's work at play."

Across our path was a huge charred trunk of a redwood, as if it were the fallen mast of a tall ship struck down by lightning. Ace placed his hand on it and hummed. He sang a nasal, wordless tune that resonated in my bones.

"What is he doing?" Frankie asked.

"He's sending the tree's soul to the Celestial Plains. Must mean it hasn't been this way very long," Hook answered as he swayed in time with Ace's song. It almost felt wrong to listen, as if I were invading something meant to be private.

"Trees have souls?" Frankie asked.

Hook chuckled. "Everything has a soul."

"Wicked."

Hells, we didn't have time for this. I looked to Pascal whose gaze flickered between the path forward and the sky. I'd since lost track of the moon beneath the clouds. How much longer was it until sunrise?

Ace let go of the trunk, patted it twice, and thankfully returned to the path ahead.

The crew trailed after him. All except Pascal. He'd been strangely quiet since our arrival. I'd grown so accustomed to his insistent yapping since he came aboard the *Betty*. This new silent dead inside Pascal … the one who decided to isolate himself … he scared me. Not in the 'I'll murder you in your sleep' way, but more like the 'you don't know what I'm going to do next' kind of way.

"You okay?"

Pascal shot me a look. His bright eyes fixed on me. Something flickered in them, and they widened. He shuffled away a few paces and rubbed his face.

"F-fine."

Not saying more, I stepped toward him, grabbed his arm, and tugged him forward. We had to keep going.

"Come on, let's get you home."

Pascal had been a monster once, a pawn maneuvered by strings only the king had the ends to. I wanted to sail back to Khan and end the king where he slept. But I—nor anyone else—could blame him for making Pascal the way he was. King Roland hadn't broken him down until he was already a shell of his former self. The king hadn't taken away the man's soul and ripped it into pieces. According to Hook, that was Wendy's doing.

Now his strings were cut and his shadow gone. What would something so vile do to a person? From what I'd been told, Peter had been a soft sort with a big heart and a kind soul. What happened when his lost soul found its way back to a hollow shell?

Burning anger rippled through me. No one, not even Pascal, deserved any of that. I bit my tongue to keep from snarling. I slid a hand over Slayer and the blade practically vibrated beneath my hand.

"Is this place always so quiet?" Giles whispered from behind.

"It never used to be," Ace replied.

"I heard Neverland used to be a magical kingdom with creatures far different than anyone had ever seen before," Jameson said.

"How do you know anything about Neverland?" I asked.

But the assassin simply shrugged and muttered something about knowing a vast number of things.

I opened my mouth to say something more when Pascal interrupted. "So, where is Wendy?"

Ace spun around but continued walking backward. "She's where you'd expect her to be, but now isn't the time. There are things you need to know first."

Magic grew thick in the air. I tasted it on my tongue. Earthy and gritty, the same scent from Scarlett's Lagoon. The same unease washed over me as it did then. I turned to Pascal whose gritted teeth and clenched jaw sent a bout of worry through me. We didn't need him to lose control. I tugged on his arm. "Pascal, take a moment and think. You need rest and food before searching for her." I lowered my voice and my arm. "Breathe, my friend. We're all allies here."

Pascal sighed and patted my hand.

"She's right," Ace said. "Taking on Wendy right now isn't a good idea. It's been a long time since you've been away, and a lot has changed. When you left, Peter, Neverland left with you. Well, the one we used to know anyway."

Pascal scanned the rotting forest as thought something might pop out at any moment. For all the powers I had as a witch, telepathy wasn't one, but in that moment, I would have given anything to know what he was thinking.

Hook was no better, as his attention never wavered from our surroundings. He kept watching as if something was going to jump out and attack at any moment—all besides the times I'd catch him staring at me. His lips curled into a smile, and butterflies fluttered inside me. I swallowed the feeling down as quickly as I could and shoved my hands in my pockets before returning my focus back to Ace.

"She caught Marcus, another Lost Boy, and tortured him, then let him go so her Neverbeasts could finish him off. We found him in pieces the next day. In a way that reminded me of a cat playing with the mouse it'd just killed. None of the meat was eaten, just torn and spread around in some sort of warning."

"Vicious bitch," Hook snarled. "When I get my hands on her—"

"Umm ... if I could interrupt," Giles called from behind me.

Sweat dripped down his brow and a hint of fear lingered on his face. We really were going to have to talk with him before all this was over. Having a crew member be this terrified rose far too many questions. This was becoming more than just being afraid of sailing a ship. "What are Neverbeasts?"

Beside me, Pascal stopped moving. He ran a hand over the long raised scar along his face.

Ace regarded Pascal for a moment before speaking. "They're Wendy's pets. The beasts are intelligent and more deadly than other beings in Neverland. They may be creatures who answer the calls of the moon, but it's Wendy who controls them. They don't eat, hunt, or sleep without her permission."

Hells, to have control over something so deadly ... I shuddered. In all my studies during my hunts, I'd never come across such a creature.

"Do they only reside in Neverland, then?" I asked. Which would make sense why I hadn't heard about them before. Maybe they came from the Dread Woods?

Ace shrugged. "I've never heard of them outside of Neverland so it's possible, but I've also never been to the Enchanted Realm, and from what I've been told, there are a lot of dangerous things roaming the forest."

"Damn, I'd like to get my hands on one of those." Nathaniel rubbed his hands together as though the beasts were a grand prize worth searching for.

I turned to him, and pointed a finger pointed. "You so much as think about bringing home a creepy creature from this island and you'll be sleeping with the fish."

Nathaniel laughed, a deep belly laugh that warmed me all the way to my toes. "Fine, fine. I promise to be on my best behavior."

As if he had a best behavior.

Frankie looked up at the darkened sky. "How much farther to wherever it is we're going?"

"Not long," Hook answered. "Home is just—"

"Silence," Ace hissed. He pulled a knife from his belt and knelt on the ground. He tilted his head to look at the vast emptiness. Did he see something? As the question left my mind, chills ran over my skin and the hair on the back of my neck stood on end. I withdrew Slayer and dropped to the same position as Ace. What was out there?

I knew monsters. More so the ones at sea but I knew them, nonetheless. Vile creatures with a ravenous hunger for prey.

But I wasn't prey. *I'm Arie fucking Lockwood.*

A shape amidst the shadows moved against the still trees and a pair of gleaming red eyes revealed themself in the ragged moonlight. I opened my mouth to cry out but blind terror ripped the sound away, leaving me rooted in place. Terror washed over me and seeped into my skin, coating my bones in its inky blackness.

"What in seven seas is that?" Frankie's voice trembled.

I tried to turn to look at her but I couldn't bring myself to stop staring. Blood pounded in my ears, drowning out Ace's words of warning. Around me, the others backed up several paces, but I remained frozen.

Golden specks shimmered in its eyes and peered at me and begged me to come closer. A fog drifted over my mind, easing the panic and erasing the terror.

My cheeks warmed. A warmth that cascaded down my limbs until it consumed me whole. I wanted to reach out and grab hold. To wrap it in my arms and call it mine.

I wanted—

Something ... no, *someone* barreled into me.

Leaves crunched beneath me as we tumbled to the ground. Pain tore through my arm and specks flashed in my vision. I struggled under the big boulder holding me down as a flash of darkness soared over the top of us. The big boulder cried out in agony as the fog lifted from my mind.

"Arie, *shit*, are you okay?" A very pained sounding Hook—not a boulder, but close enough—scurried off me, grunting and groaning in pain as he held out his hand.

"Are you?"

Hook nodded, but his face held a grimace that told me otherwise. I stood, brushed off my pants, and turned to find whatever attacked us gone and the rest of the group staring at us.

"Why didn't it attack us?" Hector asked.

"Didn't it?" I stepped around Hook. His shirt was torn in three long slices but his back had got the worst of it. His raw and red skin was already visibly swollen around the wound, and black, inky blood dripped down his back and seeped through his shirt.

I reached in, and someone grabbed my hand. Ace whistled between his teeth and shook his head. "Don't touch that."

I ripped my arm from him and hissed, *"Don't* touch me."

"Yeah, mate, I wouldn't do that if I were you." Nathaniel stayed where he was, but his hand shifted to his dagger. "At least not by two-handed boys; maybe if you had a hook—"

"Shut it, Nathaniel," I hissed, but there was no denying the obvious red my face turned. Or the fact that my words sent Nathaniel and Hector both into fits of laughter.

"Sorry," Ace muttered. "But this is poison, and anyone who touches it without the proper treatments will end up the same way Ulrich will unless we get back to the tree."

What was he talking about? He wasn't poisoned, he was nearly mauled by what I assumed to be a Neverbeast.

"Neverbeasts are poisonous?" Frankie asked.

"That one is, and it wasn't sent here to attack." Ace turned and looked at Pascal. "She knows you're here now. We have to get back to the Tiki Tree. *Now.*"

Next to me, Hook coughed and wheezed. His pale and clammy skin worsened with each passing second. Every few paces, Ace would turn around and ensure the pirate was still upright. Concern laced his features, and my disdain for him lessened ... slightly.

It was obvious he cared for his people, and to him, Ulrich was one of those people.

Finally, we emerged through a thicket of trees and what came into view was not at all what I expected. There wasn't a house, or a cottage, or a small hut. Hells, there wasn't a building at all. A massive oak tree towered over us. Red and orange leaves dangled from thick branches and vines covered in pink and red flowers. The tree's radius was massive and far bigger than anything I'd ever seen before with large roots that rose from the ground, intertwining with one another. Dozens of glassless windows and balconies were scattered all along its trunk that beamed with a golden glow into the descending night.

This place was so much better than I expected—Pascal and Hook had given very little information about their lives here. My brain refused to believe anyone in their right mind wouldn't want to talk about how amazing Neverland was.

Then again ... *was* Pascal in his right mind?

We stopped in front of a massive door. The letters 'LB' were carved into the oak followed by swirls upon swirls all connected to one another. Identical to the tattoo I'd seen on Ace. It swung open, and a young man stood on the threshold. Bright gray eyes shifted from one person to the other as he took us in. His brown tunic and pants were covered in dirt, and twigs and leaves stuck out from a head of blond hair.

"Ace, what's going on? Who are these people?"

"Chuckles, get inside and tell Doc to meet us in the war room. We have a patient for him. And be quiet about it."

Chuckles's gaze landed on Hook who leaned a little bit more into Nathaniel's grip. Without another word, he retreated inside.

"We'll need to go around back. I don't want the other Lost Boys concerned about what we've got going on. I'm not so sure they'll enjoy the idea of several strangers being brought into the house without a moment to discuss what happened." Ace stole a glance in Hook's direction. "And we don't have a lot of time left."

My throat tightened. Was Hook going to die? He'd saved me, shoved me out of the way and taken the brunt of the beast's claws. Tears welled in my eyes, but I blinked them away. I refused to cry. He still breathed, still walked, and still cracked that stupid grin of his when he caught me looking at him. No, he was going to be fine. He had to be.

Ace led us around the large tree until another door came into view. This one, much smaller and less pretty than the other, opened upon our approach and Chuckles reappeared. "He's grabbing his things and said to take the patient's shirt off, but no one is to touch the wound."

"Wait, how did he know what was wrong? He hasn't even seen Hook?" Giles asked.

"Doc knows things." Ace shrugged and gestured for us to enter.

"Knows things?" Hector raised a brow. "That's not cryptic or anything."

The room we entered should not have looked so ... big. Long intricate tapestries hung along the walls and stretched several feet to a vaulted ceiling. Hundreds of candles and lanterns hung along the various posts casting the room in a bright glow. Several shelves of books sat against one of the walls while another bore weapons of all shapes and sizes. Daggers, axes, swords, and maces. An open drawer beneath the weapons stored what appeared to be scrolls and other odds and ends. At the center of the room sat a large mahogany table covered with maps, scrolls, and a half-eaten sandwich.

Nathaniel set Hook down in one of the wooden chairs, and with

Hector's help they removed his shirt. I caught a glimpse of his broad shoulders and muscular back, and the same 'LB' tattoo I'd seen on Ace. The captain rested his head on the table, his breath coming in short and painful gasps. Dark shadows had formed under his eyes, and his body shook. I pressed a hand to his head and panic swept over me. He was burning up.

I stood up, about to demand someone take action when a door next to the bookshelves swung open and an elderly man stepped in. Elderly? Pascal had said all inhabitants of Neverland were boys. But Ace and Chuckles were closer to Frankie's age, and Doc appeared to be someone's grandfather. The man's long white beard and hair didn't exactly scream 'child' to me. He carried a black bag in the crook of his arm as he hobbled over to Hook.

He clicked his tongue and adjusted the glasses on his face. "This one came into contact with Chimera."

Chimera?

Frankie must have thought the same thing because she said, "You mean the fire-breathing, three-headed monster? The one from the legends?"

Doc laughed. "No, there is no such thing. At least not in these parts. No, Chimera is the name of a lieutenant in Wendy's band of beasts."

"Her two lieutenants are the biggest and deadliest of all her creatures, "Ace continued. "They've been with her the longest and in exchange for their *servitude* they've been given abilities. Chimera can poison with his claws and speak telepathically with Wendy. He was probably out there scouting and now that he has seen all of you, he'll probably report back to her." He fidgeted nervously. His gaze flicked to Pascal who had taken up a spot near the back of the room. "The Maiden, on the other hand, has more of a vicious bite than a poisonous one. She's used as Wendy's stealth and guard. The one who does most of the dirty work."

Pascal shot out of the chair he'd been sitting in, and his face paled. Ace bolted over to him and the two spoke in hushed tones. Their whispers didn't carry far, so I couldn't be sure what they were saying, but the more Ace talked, the calmer Pascal got. Maybe I wasn't the only one who was able to calm down our wizard.

"We can discuss the dangers of Wendy later." Doc collected himself and gestured to Nathaniel and Hector. "Help me get him somewhere more comfortable. The next part of this will be unpleasant."

The pirates hesitated, and I gave a stiff nod. Doc may be willing to help our Hook, but even us pirates didn't dare trust someone with one of our own. Which was why I'd stay a few paces behind Doc and ensure everything went smoothly. They lifted a —now unconscious— Hook into their arms and followed Doc.

Pascal and Ace stayed behind, though I couldn't help but recall the sheer terror on Pascal's face. What had caused such a reaction? The beast? When it came to Pascal, I never knew what set him off.

Darkness swallowed us as we entered a hallway. A draft of cool air sent gooseflesh down my arms, and Frankie nudged me. "This place is giving me the creeps."

"Years ago, you would have said this place was the most beautiful and magical place you'd ever seen," Doc said, pushing his glasses farther up on his nose, then he opened another door.

Nathaniel and Hector entered first, laying Hook down on the only bed in the room. This was an infirmary? Atlantis's infirmary had hundreds of beds lined in neat rows with equipment that beeped and windows that let in what light Atlantis had to offer. Here, someone had nailed pieces of wood over the windows, so the only thing that offered light was a single lantern, which flickered upon our entrance.

"Now, all of you get out while I tend to the patient." Doc turned and started shooing us out, but I didn't budge. There was no way in hells I was leaving Hook alone. He may have known these people, he may have spent years with them, but now he was mine. *Mine.* The sound of that warmed me to my toes, and I bit my lip from the urge to curse.

Hook was a crew mate. He wasn't mine, just a part of my crew. No more. No less.

"I'm afraid I have to insist."

"It's fine, captain," Nathaniel said before I could protest. "I'll stand guard."

The thought of leaving Hook didn't sit well with me. I had no idea what kind of shape he was in, but I had to believe he was in good hands. After all, what could I do for him that a doctor couldn't? But Nathaniel would stand guard and I'd send Hector to watch over the rest of our crew's back and ensure Jameson didn't go off on his own. I wasn't sure bringing Jameson along was the smartest decision, especially when he'd seemed far too eager to join when I'd asked him to accompany us. But there was something about him that always had me on guard. Perhaps it was nothing more than the fact he was an assassin.

I retreated back to the war room where Pascal and Ace sat at the table along with other faces I didn't recognize. All except Chuckles who looked much paler than Pascal had moments ago. His hands were locked in a white-knuckled grip with the young man next to him. A man with golden eyes. A Fae-Kissed Lost Boy. The one gift a fae can give a human without repercussions from the Elders of the Enchanted Realm—a gift of sight. My gaze dropped back to their hands. He turned to Chuckles; their expressions softened and a smile tugged at his lips. A tightness tugged at my chest, a longing I hadn't felt in a very long time.

"Everything's going to be okay, Pibbs. I promise," Chuckles murmured.

Next to Pibbs sat another man with bushy brows and a pointed nose. He looked from Frankie to Hector and then landed on Giles who had taken to sitting on a chair on the far end of the room. Until finally his gaze met mine and dropped instantly while he shifted awkwardly in his chair. Maybe he wasn't very fond of strangers. Or was it pirates? Good to know, I wasn't very fond of rude men.

"Arie! Perfect timing." Pascal rose from his chair and gestured me forward. I sat in the empty chair next to him. "How's our mutual friend?"

"Doc's looking in on him now," I said.

I tried to push aside my feelings of worry and focus on my surroundings.

"If it's true, and he was attacked by Chimera,"—Pibbs shook his head—"I'm afraid there's not much that can be done, and time is limited."

"What do you mean not much can be done?" I snapped.

Ace pursed his lips. "Doc can only clean and treat the wound, not the poison. He can stall it for now, but there's no telling how long it will keep Hook alive. Pretty soon his body will shut down, he'll convulse, and—"

I waved a hand at Ace. "Okay, okay I get it. But what will keep him alive? There must be a cure, right?"

My chest tightened, and if I didn't have several strangers staring at me, I may have allowed the tears I'd been holding back to fall. Though, they obscured my vision anyway.

"I'm afraid there's nothing in the tree that can help your pirate."

For sea's sake he's not my *pirate.*

Anger spread its way through me, mixed with fear and the unknown. My hands shook, and my heart raced harder than it ever had before.

"So, is there something outside of this tree that can help?" Frankie chimed in, to which I was grateful. I wasn't sure I could handle diplomacy right now.

Ace sighed. "It's complicated."

"Complicated how?" Hector asked.

Pascal butted in before Ace could answer. "Where *are* the fairies?"

"That's part of the complication. When you left, Neverland's magic began to weaken. Trees stopped speaking, the nymphs were forced to return to the Enchanted Realm, and the fairies ... Well, they became valuable. Wendy started capturing them and before long ..." Ace shrugged.

Pascal slammed his fist on the table. "And none of you tried to get them back?"

"Of course we did," Chuckles said. "Her Neverbeasts were far too strong for us to do anything about. You've been gone a long time, my friend. There's much to be discussed."

"First, I think we need to know what he's been doing this entire time." Pibbs let go of Chuckles's hand and shot out of his chair. "Where were you? Why did it take you so long to get back to us? We were yours to protect. You brought her here, you are why—"

"Pibbs! That's enough." Chuckles tugged on his shirt and pulled him back into his seat. "You know this wasn't his fault, my love. How could anyone know Wendy would turn out like this? Her soul was tainted long before she came to Neverland and you know it."

Pibbs lowered his head and sighed. "Sorry. Sorry, Peter."

Pascal shook his head. "There's nothing to be sorry for. You're right, a lot of this is my fault. However, there's things you don't know as there are things I don't know. Now is the time to get everything out in the open and figure out what's next."

"Who cares about any of this? Hook is in there and we have absolutely no idea if he's going to live or not and none of you seem to give two shits."

"Arie," Pascal warned. "Take a second. We're trying to get to the bottom of this."

"Take a second?" I snapped. "According to Ace, Hook doesn't have time to waste."

"I'm afraid she's right." Doc stepped through the door and stalked over to the table. He placed his bag down before rummaging through and finally pulling out a vial of black liquid.

"Is that what I think it is, Leonard?" Ace asked.

Doc handed the vial to him. "It is."

The two of them examined the liquid while the rest of us waited in silence.

"Anyone care to enlighten us on what that is?" I asked, irritation growing within me.

"The poison in his system is moving at a faster rate than I've ever seen before. He has hours, maybe days if I can continue to treat the wound."

A chill washed away everything else in the room, leaving me with nothing but ... dread. I'd known it wasn't going to be good but hours? Days?

I wanted to lash out at Pascal, to make him do something. He was a wizard after all, but I also knew Pascal wasn't himself no matter what kind of show he was putting on for the others.

"But you don't have the means to cure the poison. Is that right?" I did my best to keep my composure but the blood boiling in my system threatened to undo me. "So, he's just going to die, and you all want to sit here and talk about what exactly?"

I can't listen to this for another second.

"Arie," Pascal tried to grab for me but I stalked off before he could.

Deciding where to go, I let my feet take me as the protests of the others trailed behind me. I needed to see Hook. To know that he still breathed and his heart still pumped.

I'd go back to the ship. There had to be something in my books that talked about poisons. But the ship was hours away. How long did Hook have before he succumbed to the poison? How long did I have to save him? After all, I always paid back my debts and the last thing I wanted was to be in his.

My hand drifted to the doorknob then stilled. The lump in my throat grew ten sizes. This was stupid. It's just Hook. I opened the door to find him upright and leaning back against the wall. No doubt the cool wood against his dressings eased the pain a bit, though I suspected that had more to do with whatever medicine Doc had probably given him. His lips curled upward displaying his teeth.

"Arieeee." His emphasis on the 'e' sent a smile to my face.

He looked slightly better than earlier but not anywhere near out of the dangerous waters. He was pale, though a hint of pink had returned to his cheeks. Dark circles shrouded his eyes, and each breath brought on a terrible wheeze. Sweat and dried blood mixed together along his bare skin and pants.

"You should be sleeping." I closed the door behind me and sat on the edge of the bed.

"Probably, but *shhh*, listen, do you hear them?"

Knock, knock, knock. Chirp. Knock, knock.

Birds? Woodpeckers perhaps?

Hook tilted his head upward to the window and grinned. "I've missed the sound of pixies."

Pixies?

He began humming along with their incessant knocking. The tune wasn't exactly a tune at all—the knocking sounded no different than someone banging on a door. The meds given to Hook were much more potent than I thought.

"On a scale of 1 to 100, how coherent are you?"

Hook's brow furrowed as he scanned me from top to bottom. His face sobered when he stopped at my face, and heat rose to my cheeks.

"I'd say at least a … wait, what was the question?"

I chuckled. "Seems like Doc gave you some strong medicine."

Hook's mouth dropped open. "Doc's here? Of course he is. Doc's medicines always do the trick." He coughed, a raspy, deep cough. I swallowed down the lump in my throat and sat on the edge of the bed next to him.

"Apparently not this time."

"Oh?"

I sighed. How was I going to tell this man he was dying? Would it be kinder to lie? I wasn't sure I was ready to watch the smile on his face fade.

"What is it?"

"Well …" I paused. "The Neverbeast that sliced you up was also poisonous."

Hook leaned his head back and closed his eyes. "And I guess it's not easily cured?"

"Do you know of anything on this island that might …" My voice trailed off.

"That's more Doc's expertise. I'm sure he's already working on it. Nothing for"—another coughing fit—"us to worry ourselves about."

"Nothing to worry about? You can't be serious? Hook, you're d—"

"Ulrich."

"What?"

Hook opened his eyes, sat up, and scooted away from the wall. He winced and groaned, but I didn't dare touch him. His clammy skin brushed against mine as he leaned into me.

"Call me Ulrich."

"But—"

He turned his head until his eyes locked onto mine.

"I wanted to tell you before, and now that things aren't looking good, maybe now is the perfect time. I hate the name Captain Hook. I only agreed to it because people feared the name. When I came into port, I didn't have to worry about rival pirates or shopkeepers raising the prices of their goods." He paused and gave a faint smile, one that did weird things to my stomach. "You can call me what you want, but I do prefer Ulrich."

I nodded. "I think I can do that."

What the hells, Arie? He wanted me to call him by his real name. Something seemed too personal about that and yet I'd agreed to it. Without a second thought? We sat there in silence, staring at one another. My throat ran dry, and my hands shook in my lap, but I remained still. I lowered my gaze to his dressings; they'd have to be changed soon.

"You're very pretty, you know," Hook said.

My body froze. This was simply the medicine talking. Nothing more.

"I—"

"*Shh.*" He pressed a finger to my lips. "Don't pull an Arie and tell me to shut up. Just take the compliment." His words slurred while his gaze fixated on his finger on my lips.

"You know, there's something else I've been wanting to do for a very long time."

"Is that so?" My words were muffled through his warm finger.

The air around us was thick and heavy with anticipation as we sat face-to-face in the cramped room. Ulrich's gaze was piercing, and his presence was both intoxicating and intimidating. His finger left my lips to brush a strand of hair behind my ear, and my body lit up like the lantern on the table next to us. This was Hook—Ulrich. A man who'd arrived on my ship and turned my entire world upside down. He wouldn't hurt me. Then why did every instinct tell me to run? My heart thumped and blood pounded in my ears, but I remained still. Unable to bring myself to do anything except gawk at him.

Did I want this? Did I want him to be this close? I wanted to say something, anything that would break the tension, but nothing came out. All I could do was sit there in awe as I took in every inch of his face.

Hook cleared his throat. "Can I …"

A flutter of heat surged through my body as Ulrich moved closer. His scent, a mixture of mint and musk, seemed to fill the entire room. My lips parted in anticipation. His mouth finally touched mine, and my entire body seemed to awaken all at once; sparks ignited under my skin, and a wave of warmth washed over me. His hunger was palpable, his grip firm, and his intensity undeniable as I felt myself being pulled into his embrace. My toes curled, and my fingers dug into the sheets as the sweet taste of him overwhelmed me.

A part of me didn't want to admit the attraction I felt for him. We were rival hunters, sworn enemies. Sure, we'd come to an agreement when he had boarded my ship, and we'd become cordial over time. And yet now something felt different. After sacrificing himself for me, there was no way I'd be able to deny it.

But then he pulled away and left me gasping for breath.

My mind returned to me as Ulrich inched his way farther back onto the bed.

I cleared my throat and slid off the edge, my knees weak and protesting my weight, but I couldn't stay in here for a second longer. Whether it was the tonics he'd been given that left him doing things he normally wouldn't, or something else, I couldn't be sure. For all I knew this was a reaction from the drugs and not his true feelings. Though, I knew for sure that I needed to get out of here before things got more intense. And after that, I was almost certain I wanted ... more.

"Goodnight, Arie." Laughter lit Ulrich's words as I scurried out of the room.

IV. MISSING

Pascal

I SHOULD HAVE GONE AFTER ARIE. Should have calmed her down and ensured she was all right. I'd been so focused on Wendy and what she'd done since I'd been away that I hadn't taken what she was going through into consideration. Perhaps once this meeting was done she and I could work together. I wasn't about to let my friend die by Wendy's beasts. I had to believe there was still a chance for him.

While I didn't have the magic to make this right, perhaps I knew someone else who did. Doc had said he only had hours, maybe days, but I also knew Doc to be a bit irrational about how long someone had to live. After all, he hadn't expected me to live as long as I did. Perhaps he was wrong about Ulrich too.

I brought my focus back to the task at hand. Arie had presumably gone to check on Ulrich, and the rest of the pirates had been ushered out of the room. I suspected they'd be unwelcome in a council meeting.

The Lost Council members were scattered around the circular wooden table. Its once jagged edges were now smooth and worn from countless meetings held around it—many of which I'd been present for. How many had I missed since being gone? I sank into one of the chairs, and my gaze settled on the wood in front of me—a tribute to Jack, his name carved into the table's surface. The letters formed beautiful, delicate loops and curves that seemed almost too fragile for this dark place. I ran my fingers along the grooves, and tears threatened to spill over. Jack used to be so full of life, always the first one to pick up any instrument and make music with it. Jaina had a special talent for scaling the tallest trees and scouting ahead of the rest of us. But now they were both dead. Hot rage surged through my veins, so strong I fought to hold myself together.

"How?" I rasped out.

"Devoured by Wendy's beasts," Ace answered with a sad voice. His anguish was palpable and instantly mirrored by my own anguish and anger. A dull ache crept inside me at the thought that my absence had cost so many other young lives.

How many Lost Boys and Girls were left? Guilt tugged at my insides for not being here to protect them from Wendy's wrath.

I should have listened to the members of the council and killed her right then and there, but a part of me wanted to give her a chance to explain herself. I needed to know why she'd turned on me after everything I'd done for her. I never once asked for anything in return other than her loyalty. Even after she betrayed me, I had foolishly hoped for a change in her. I had begged her to stop and to realize how many people she was hurting. But she didn't stop, and she didn't care. Instead, as a way of showing her appreciation, she'd tortured me and threw me to the biggest wolf of them all. She murdered people I cared for and had taken the twins I loved so dearly; they were the first ones to inhabit Neverland after me, and now they were gone.

I looked around the room at the council members before me. Ace, once a small boy full of naivety and mischief, was now their leader, standing tall and composed next to Bucky, a boy who once was hard-shelled and emotionless but now sat across from me, his face unmarked by the characteristic lines and dark circles of worry that hung over nearly everyone else's faces in the room. Chuckles, Pibbs and Viscera were all there too. Just six of us council members left.

I glanced outside at the stream of dull light in the distance. I bit my lip and dug my fingers into my palms. We needed to hurry this along before the sun rose.

"And where is Wendy during all of this?" I asked.

"Peter, I don't—"

"Ace, please. I need to know."

"She's on Lily Cove," Chuckles said.

Inwardly, I seethed. Red-hot fire surged through my bones at the thought of Wendy on Lily Cove. Why of all places did she have to go *there*? She had a place gifted to her, an entire villa on the east side of the island. It was meant to be a home for all the girls on the island, but most of them refused to go. I didn't realize until much later why that was or what they feared. I'd been too caught up in my own world to pay attention. I'd been too focused on the world to realize what was happening right in my own backyard.

Wendy had been a plague to everyone she'd ever encountered. And I'd been the one who brought her here.

"Taigra would have skinned her alive if she were still here." Viscera dug a small blade under his nail and gave a sly grin. "To think if she wouldn't have said yes to you, Peter, she'd never have—"

"Viscera!" Ace hissed.

My lips drew into a thin line, and a tremor shot through me. I gripped the arms of my chair until my hands shook and my knuckles grew white.

Taigra.

The name sent a jolt of pain through me. I closed my eyes and dug through the many years of memories. Faces of Lost Boys, men and women in King Roland's court, and pirates on Arie's ship flooded through my mind, but not hers. I remembered the dark hair and dark skin, but the features were lost to the time we'd been apart.

We should make Viscera pay for that, the voice rumbled inside my head, pulling me from my despair. Its anger was nearly as potent as my own.

Maybe, but now isn't the time.

And when is a better time than now? You never used to be like this. We took what we wanted, did what we pleased. We were the king's wizard.

And we're not anymore. We're shadowless and unprepared.

It took all my strength to stay rooted in my seat and not sprint out of the room and into the darkness. Instead, I mustered what I could and continued.

"And what has she been doing in Lily Cove?" I loosened my grip on the chair.

"Gathering followers, gaining territory, slaughtering our people. You name it, she's probably doing it," Bucky said.

"What have the Lost Boys done to counter these attacks?"

Silence grew thick in the air as all the attention trailed to Ace. His face paled as he fidgeted with a string on his tunic. "We've tried many things. Attacks, traps, late-night ambushes; it's never enough. We keep losing too many people to her beasts. They're far more dangerous and deadly than anything we've faced before. They can be killed, but it's not easy."

"I—"

Arie barged into the room, and her face flushed as she approached the table. She hadn't been gone too long but still long enough to see that something seemed … off.

Something's wrong. The pirate hurt her.

Or it was something else. I smirked at her, and her eyes darted away. *Yes, definitely something else.*

"Arie. Come, sit. Chuckles, will you pour my friend here some ale?"

Chuckles's mouth dropped open as he glanced between me and Ace. I knew the rule; no one that wasn't on the council could sit at the table, but Arie was an honorary member of this council whether they liked it or not. She was too valuable to not have a say in what goes on here. After what she did to Ursa, her own mother, she deserved to be at this table.

"I don't want a drink, I want to know what we're doing about"—Arie cleared her throat and dropped into an empty chair—"Hook."

"There is nothing that can be done," Doc said. "We don't have the capabilities and—"

Arie slammed a fist on the table. "Bullshit. What aren't you telling me? You said earlier it's complicated and that it had something to do with the fairies. What does that mean?"

Doc rubbed a hand over his face and turned to me. "Peter, I—"

"Please, call me Pascal."

The Lost Boys around the table stared at me, some muttering and others gasping at my request. Confusion written on their child-like faces.

"You want us to call you ... *Pascal?*"

Peter. A name given to me, whispered to me on my name day by my father. A man who was once proud of his son. Until I returned broken. Rather than greet me back, he'd scorned me, refused me entry to Neverland unless I gave up the one thing holding me together. I'd never see the sun again, never feel the warmth on my face. Because of my father, I'd never again see the light of day. So no, I never wanted to be associated with him again. Ever. Plus, I'd gotten used to Pascal.

You mean to me?

I cleared my throat. "Yes."

Doc continued. "Very well, Pascal, I think it would be unwise for anyone other than the council to be in this meeting. There's much to discuss and—"

"You're right, there is much to discuss, and all of that has a time and a place." Arie pulled Slayer from her side and placed it next to her on the table. "Are you really telling me everything going on now is more important than saving a life? I'm not going to ask you again. What aren't you telling me, *Doc?*"

"Bloody fucking pirates." Doc's eyes widened and he scooted back in his chair.

Ace gritted his teeth. "Watch your tone, pirate. There is more at stake than just one life."

"And *pirates* have no say at this table." Viscera shot out of his chair and veins bulged in his neck. His pale lips pressed into a thin line. Viscera was one of the original boys and a pain in the ass. Not admired by most, but his soul was as lost as the rest. I'd always known him to have a temper, and that the temper was always worse around strangers, especially pirates. Not that I could blame him. After all, pirates had killed his parents. Though, something else seemed off with him. I tried to remember, to pull on the memories I'd lost, to recall what had happened to him before I left, but nothing came to mind. "Scum, murderous, evil pirates in our home. I thought you were better than this, Peter? I'd never expected you to collude with the *enemy*."

Arie grabbed Slayer, and I gripped her shoulder, but it was Frankie who jumped out from the shadows. Where had she come from? I was certain she'd gone to get cleaned up along with Hector. Though, from the looks of her, she'd never left the room. *Interesting.*

I ground my teeth to keep from smiling as Frankie's icy glare dug into Viscera. "You should be thanking the pirates for bringing your leader home and coming to aid you against Wendy. From what I've heard you need all the help you can get. And his name is Pascal, you twat."

Arie snickered beside me, and Viscera's entire body shook as he scurried away from Frankie. A breath hitched in my throat as I caught a glimpse of Frankie's eyes. Pitch black and shadow-like. Specks of light flickered in the darkness. She blinked away the darkness until her normal color returned.

I believe Frankie has some explaining to do.

I agreed with the voice, but that wasn't up to us. Judging from Arie's reaction, she'd noticed her sister's eyes as well.

"Apologize to the girls, Vis. They may be all you say they are, but you and I both know they are necessary," Ace said.

"What the hells is that supposed to mean?" Arie snapped. "And we're wasting time. How about we worry more about the pirate who has been poisoned and less about shit we can't control?"

The council members stared at Arie; a woman who had an uncanny ability to shut up an entire room of people with a simple glare and exchange of words.

Viscera grumbled under his breath as he gathered his chair and sat back down.

"Enough." Doc raised his voice, something few saw from the old man. "We have matters to discuss here, and if you can't handle that then there's the door."

Arie took a step forward, but Frankie grabbed her arm and whispered into her ear. Whatever she said worked because Arie sat back down in her chair.

Ulrich needed to be saved, but we also needed to know more before we began searching for answers that may not even be there. I pinched the bridge of my nose. Where were we? I thought about what needed to be said. Should I start with what happened to me? About what I'd done?

What would they think? What would—

They'd think of us as a survivor. Someone who made it through weeks of torture, someone who had to behave while taking orders from a tyrant king who'd used us as a pawn. They'd look at us as they always had.

My breath was sharp and heaving as I fought to catch it.

"What else can you tell me that we need to know?" I asked. "The others that live in Neverland, what of them?" Surely Wendy hasn't taken over everything. An eerie feeling crept its way through me. On a normal day, fairies buzzed around the Tiki Tree, mermaids and nymphs and the occasional pixie visited our home with goods to trade. It didn't matter the time of day, or night, there were always creatures muttering about in this place.

The room went silent, and Ace rubbed a hand over his face. "They're all gone."

"Gone? All of them?"

"Yes, Pe—Pascal, they're gone. Wendy either captured or killed them."

If Wendy took all the fae, if she had them trapped or worse … something pricked at the back of my neck. "What of Tinkerbell? Is this why you say things are complicated?"

"Who's Tinkerbell?" Arie asked.

Ace ran a hand over his face. "She was the last fairy we had at our disposal. It's also why we have no way of healing Ulrich. Fairy dust would counteract the poison, but last week …"

He trailed off, his gaze flickering to the rest of the Lost Boys.

"What about last week, Ace? Where. Is. She?"

"We don't know," Chuckles said. "Teddy and Tink went searching for more fairies but only Teddy returned. He spends most of his days looking for her, but he hasn't had any luck. He's here somewhere in the tree if you need to speak with him."

"You're telling me all it takes to heal Hook is some of this fairy dust. The same dust that brought us here? But not just that, you also don't know where any are?" Arie snapped. "Unbelievable."

"Yes, so you can see why this matter is complicated," Doc answered.

I drummed my fingers along the table to keep myself grounded. Every muscle twitched at the thought of what Wendy could be doing to Tink. "I'll speak to Teddy as soon as I can. What else do we need to know?"

"I know, how about a way to fix Hook." Arie muttered under her breath.

"Arie, please. Give us just a little more time to figure this out, okay?" I asked. My gaze flicked back to the window. The light was brighter than it was a few minutes ago. How much time did I have? How much time did Ulrich have?

Arie glared at me, her face shifted to a dark red as she threw her hands up and turned around to stand next to her sister in the shadows.

I knew how she was feeling. I wanted nothing more than for Ulrich to be okay. But right now information was the most important thing to surviving Neverland. I could have retreated to my room the moment we arrived here, but that would only make me out to be—

A coward? A man with no ball—

Possibly. But it would also confirm what Wendy said all those years ago. My mind drifted to a time I'd rather forget.

Wendy's short blond waves hung over her face as I looked up at her from my back. We'd spent days playing this game. She wanted information and I'd refused to give it to her.

"You are a sorry excuse for a son of a god. And here I thought you were something special. She told me so. The Mistress was certain you were the one, and yet here you sit. A pathetic little boy who's too scared to do what needs to be done."

Wendy lowered herself until her lips were inches from my ear. "After I'm done with you, there will be no Peter Pan left in Neverland. Only his memory, and I plan to ruin that too."

Chuckles's voice roused me from my thoughts. "Because of Wendy's beasts, the nymphs who survived had no choice but to leave the island and return to the Enchanted Realm."

I could only imagine how desperate they must have been to return to a place they had once fled. Centuries ago, they had been violently driven out of their homes by humans who were determined to build, expand, and take control of their land. Trees were ripped from their roots, homes were destroyed, all for the sake of human progress. If the nymphs were truly gone, it explained the decay that now surrounded us. Without their blessing ... I shuddered at the thought.

Ace's voice shook as he described the destruction of Neverland. The once vibrant waters had turned a murky green, dried riverbeds now cracked in the scorching sun, and dozens of trees had reduced to little more than scraggly twigs. Most devastating of all was the absence of the fairies—they had been the ones to bring life back to the island, but without them, the darkness was consuming it.

The realization of my own role in all of this hit me like a physical blow: it was my absence that left this island defenseless. I was taken and tortured against my will. I'd been betrayed by someone I thought

I could trust, and in that moment, I'd lost everything—my life, my home, and my soul.

And I had.

I had been the one to bring Wendy here, and whatever had happened to this beautiful island was my fault. Even though I was lost and uncertain how I could get back, part of me almost wanted to stay away because being here was nothing more than a reminder of my mistake.

"We fought so hard to keep them safe …" Ace's voice shook, his hands balled into fists at his sides, and dark rage shimmered in his eyes as he glanced back at me. "Without fairy dust and without your presence, our magic is depleting, and Neverland is dying."

"It's why we've aged," Pibbs said, his voice heavy with grief. He ran a hand through his hair and glanced away, trying to hold back the tears. "Neverland is nothing without its creatures." He paused. "And its soul."

My father had always told me that a place such as Neverland lived and died by its magic, but for it to have turned on its own people? To have taken away their youth and to leave them aged simply due to my absence? A wave of shame and guilt engulfed me as I buried my face in my hands.

Then fix it. We're the gods damn wizard of Khan, with an arsenal of magic and power that has struck terror into men and monsters alike. We've spread darkness through an entire country. Yet here we stand, powerless to stop a girl from trampling on our home. We can't keep going on this way. Either take control or surrender the reins to me.

Could we do that? Was it possible? I shoved such a thought far from my brain. It was a voice, nothing more. I was hallucinating, imagining things. Right? I swore under my breath and lifted my head to scan the faces around the table and stopped at Arie. Fierce, cunning Arie. Of course. I smiled.

"What about this is amusing to you?" Viscera snapped.

"Nothing is amusing about the destruction of our home," I said, keeping my gaze on the pirate queen. Her lips pressed into a thin line while her arms crossed. Yes, Wendy may be feared on this island, but Arie Lockwood was known across the Seven Seas. Had taken down a monster beyond anyone's imagination. She'd tamed a crazed wizard and got a deadly pirate captain to fall for her without realizing it. The boys may have lost the battle, but the war was just beginning, and I had the ultimate weapon.

"However, what *is* amusing is the advantage we currently have. Wendy may know that I'm back, but she doesn't know I brought bloodthirsty pirates with me. I say it's high time we use that and strike her where it hurts." A light beamed within me. This was it. This was how I got revenge. This was how we *won*. Wendy's fate was set, and she'd finally get a taste of her own destruction. "Tell me more about what she's planning and doing. Surely our scouts are still around. I want to know *everything*."

Ace's gaze met mine. "Patience, my friend, first there's something else needing address."

"All right, go on."

Ace hesitated, his gaze barely able to stay on my own as he opened and closed his mouth. It was almost painful watching him stumble over his words.

Matches the way most of our victims look when we're done with them.

I shook my head and shoved away the mental images flooding my memory. All the blood and screaming and stench of death.

"Oh, for sea's sake, get on with it," Arie blurted out.

I sighed; she was certainly not winning over these Lost Boys.

Can you blame them? She's fierce and strong and more than they could ever be.

Internally I rolled my eyes and brought my focus back to the council.

Ace's glare burned into Arie, then redirected itself to me. "Where's your shadow?"

Arie's figure went rigid. I placed my hand on the hollowed emptiness in my chest, a reminder of the sacrifice I'd made—that my father had demanded. The knowledge that without it I wouldn't survive weighed heavily on me. There was no telling what the loss of my shadow would do to me, but my death was inevitable unless I got it back.

Then we had better find a way to get it back.

I lowered my hand and peered over to Ace. "How did—"

A gust of frigid air rushed through the room as a figure stumbled in, panting heavily. Their tattered cloak clung to their body and concealed their face. Ace ran over and yanked the hood from their head, revealing a red-haired boy with freckled skin and sunken cheeks. His face was flush, and exhaustion radiated off of him, but I recognized that face.

Teddy.

"What is it?"

Teddy grabbed Ace's arms and shook his head. "I found her, Ace. I found Tink."

V. A Fairy Heist

Arie

TEDDY SHOOK WHILE TEARS STREAMED DOWN HIS cheeks. All color had drained from his face, and he whimpered every time Ace asked him a question. He could barely speak, let alone explain what happened while he was gone. His black cloak was shredded along the bottom to reveal bloodied bare feet. Though he didn't seem to notice. Either that or he was in shock. His bright red hair clung to his dirty face and his fingers fidgeted with his cloak.

"When did you leave? I thought you were in the tree." Ace wrapped an arm around the boy and pulled him into a hug. "You shouldn't have gone out alone at night."

"I had to find her, Ace. And I did, but it's too late. No one can get to her now."

"What do you mean?" Pascal had stood from his seat and was already approaching the two boys. He'd seemed a bit more himself since being surrounded by his family. Whatever was going on in his head didn't matter so long as he kept it together. By the sounds of it, Wendy was a monstrous bitch with a god complex who needed to be brought down from her pedestal. Lucky for me, I enjoyed hunting monsters.

Teddy spun out of Ace's hands at Pascal's words. He stopped and his mouth dropped at the sight before him.

"P-Peter?"

Pascal nodded. "It's Pascal now, and we have time to catch up later. Tell us where Tink is."

Teddy, unbothered by Pascal's correction, ran to him. He wrapped his arms around Pascal, crushing him in a hug. "I can't believe it's you."

Pascal embraced the hug, his brows furrowed and his lips pursed together.

I turned away, letting them have their moment, and it also gave me a chance to think. If there was a fairy alive, it meant Ulrich had a chance to live. Hope wrapped itself around me at the thought. All I'd have to do is figure out where the fairy is and how to bust her out, and then get her back here before anyone—including Wendy—found out. Hells, maybe it meant the rest of my crew could join us. We'd have better defenses and more experienced fighters.

"You said Tinkerbell is alive but no one can get to her. Why is that?" Pascal asked.

Teddy's voice shook with his answer. "N-Neverbeasts. They

have her surrounded."

I swore. Of course. Wendy wouldn't leave her captive unattended, but how were we going to get the fairy out? I didn't know the land, didn't know much about Neverland at all, but these Lost Boys did. If they brought me to where Tink is, maybe I could get her out.

"Where is she being kept?" I asked.

"Arie, did you not just hear what he said?" Pascal shook his head. "She's surrounded by beasts. We'll have to come up with a plan, a way to get her out."

"Screw your plan," I snapped. "I'm done waiting around. We need to save Ulrich before it's too late. Where is she?"

Teddy stared at me. "Who are you? I don't recognize you. Hang on, Ulrich is here too?"

"She's a friend of mine," Pascal chimed in before I could say anything. "You can trust her just as much as you trust me."

Teddy sighed. "Fine. They're keeping her in Crocodile Creek territory. In Skull Caverns. I was able to catch a glimpse of her before the beasts showed up, and I managed to get out of there before any of them saw me."

Ace paced behind Teddy and Pascal, a hand pressed to his lips while the other balled into a fist at his side.

"How do you suppose we get in there?" Pibbs asked.

"I don't know," Pascal replied, "but it might be better to wait it out until morning and come up with a plan. We don't want to rush in there unprepared. For now, everyone needs to get some sleep. Chuckles, will you show our guests to their rooms? Give the girls Jaina's room and the boys can take Jack's."

"Excuse me?" I whirled to Pascal. "You hear a fairy is alive, one who obviously can help us, and you want to wait? You can't honestly think I'll sit around and wait."

Pascal sighed. "We'll wait until morning—hopefully most of the beasts will be away and we can canvas the area. It's better if—"

"We aren't pirates," Ace interrupted and glared at me. "We don't just jump into things without preparation. Doc will take care of Ulrich as he always has."

"To hell with this." I threw my hands up and stormed out of the room.

I didn't give two shits about waiting until morning. Ulrich's life hung in the balance, and I was going to do all I could to save him. Leaving to bring back the fairy also gave me hope of getting the rest of the crew onto Neverland. All they needed was a bit more fairy dust.

So, while the crew and the Lost Boys made their way to their rooms for the night, I acted.

Gripping Slayer with a determined strength, I slid a finger down the side of the blade before fitting it snugly by my side. My pistol was loaded and ready. Extra daggers and knives strapped around my body and hidden in my boots gave me extra security in this foreign environment. Every weapon was primed and ready; I was not taking any chances.

The door to the war room was open and the room unoccupied as I entered. The smell of old parchment and dust filled my nostrils.

Surely there had to be a map of Neverland somewhere in here. Dozens of scrolls sat on the desk closest to the door. I picked up one and unraveled the ribbon before unrolling the parchment. Symbols with the same swirls and designs as the ones on the Lost Boys' tattoos and the door to the tree. Neverland's own language, symbols that I wouldn't be able to read without help.

I wasn't sure why I thought I'd be able to find a map and instantly be able to find my way through Neverland.

I sighed and slipped Slayer from its sheath. Perhaps I could *convince* a Lost Boy to decipher it for me. Though after a while of searching, none of the scrolls gave me what I wanted, and the bookshelf proved utterly useless. At this rate I was better off grabbing Teddy and forcing him to show me where the fairy was.

I stormed out of the war room to do just that when I collided with ...

"Frankie?"

She was shrouded in a black coat. Its hood pulled over her head, casting a shadow over her face. Black pants and a shirt clung tightly to her with knives strapped to various parts of her body. She was ready for a fight.

"I believe that's what they call me, yes," Frankie said.

"What are you doing out here?"

She placed a hand on her hip. "I could ask you the same thing."

I caught sight of her new clothes and weapons and raised my brow. "Where did you find those?"

Frankie shrugged. "I took to exploring and came across some unoccupied rooms."

Leave it to my sister to explore places she shouldn't be exploring.

"I also found this." Frankie held up a piece of parchment. The exact piece I'd been searching for: a map of Neverland.

I gasped. "I could kiss you!"

Frankie's nose wrinkled. "Please don't." She turned around to head toward the front door. "I think we can convince one of the Lost Boys to—"

"We?"

Frankie shot me a look. "Yes, Arie, we. If you think—"

"Going somewhere?"

Both of us jumped and whirled around to find Ace at the top of the winding stairs. I was still in awe over how massive this tree was. Rooms on several levels up along the trunk of the tree, stairs that wound around each door. Dozens of lanterns floated above us casting the room in dim light. If I wasn't in a hurry to save Ulrich, I might have taken to exploring as my sister did.

"How did you sneak up on me?" Frankie frowned. Was that anger in her face? No one enjoyed being snuck up on, but it was nothing to be angry about.

"What are you two doing?" Ace descended the stairs, his eyes fixed more on Frankie than me.

"Gallivanting through the night like a couple of harmless pirates." Frankie gave Ace a bright smile, one I've seen her use quite often on our fathers.

"We're going to save Tink. Care to join?"

"You two can't go out here alone at night. I told you, it's far too dangerous. We need to wait until morning. There will be Neverbeasts crawling all over that place. You won't last a second."

"Ace, I'm sure you run a tight ship here, and I'm sure these Lost Boys are better off for it. But I'm a captain of a pirate ship, a hunter, a sea witch, and a mermaid wrapped up in a pretty red-headed bow. I can handle myself."

Of course, I wouldn't admit to him that I was afraid. That beast that attacked Ulrich had shaken me. The dark shadow that nearly took off my face and ate it for lunch. Ulrich had saved me, and I'd rather face a hundred of those things than sit idly by, waiting for something to happen. I was a woman of action, and I always would be.

Ace went rigid on the last step. "You're a mermaid?"

Shit. Was I not supposed to tell him that? Pascal hadn't warned me. "What of it?"

Ace looked at Frankie and frowned. "We may have a chance after all. Look, if you really want to do this, you're going to need someone who knows Neverland. I'll come with you."

Frankie shook the map in the air between the two of them. "I found a map. I think we can handle it ourselves."

Ace crossed his arms and leaned against the wall. "That map is outdated and doesn't show you which territories are okay to travel through. Plus, I don't think either of you are fluent in Nevlian."

"Nevlian?"

"It's Neverland's native language and takes a long time to master. So, I guess you'll need a guide."

I wanted to object, but before I could, Hector waltzed down the stairs.

"If he's going then so am I."

"For sea's sake, too many people will draw attention." I rubbed a hand along my face. Who was I kidding? After years of doing this, you'd think I'd have learned to sneak out the back door before anyone noticed what I was doing. "Fine, but that's it. Let's leave before anyone else decides to volunteer."

We walked out into the darkness, and I inhaled, pulling as much clean air into my lungs as I dipped into my senses. The silence of the night lessened as I found the center of my power. It thumped and boiled beneath the surface and begged to be used. I'd failed to stifle the storm at sea, and I'd failed to stop that beast from attacking Ulrich.

Now was the time to make it right.

"Which way?" I asked.

Ace pointed. "This way, and stick close."

Neverland's woods were far different than the woods in Bellavier, my home. Or what had once been my home. The last time I'd been there I'd found out who my birth father was, and hadn't that been one hells of a surprise. Not just a father but a damn king of Atlantis. An ache wrapped itself around me and tugged. I missed home and my fathers. Their deaths had yet to be avenged, and if it weren't for Pascal's reassurance that being here would help me find them, I'd never have agreed to come. Of course, I wanted to help him, but my mission hadn't changed since I left the ports in Vallarta. I needed more information on this Brotherhood and why they decided it would be a good idea to kill the two people who'd done nothing more than love me and Frankie.

I was so lost in my own thoughts I barely heard Frankie's question.

"How do we know Wendy isn't going to be there when we arrive? Or out here for that matter?"

"We don't, but Wendy's main focus will be on Pascal now," Ace replied. "She will have most of her beasts scouting trying to find the treehouse, but the way we're going should heighten our chances of not being seen. She has no idea that we know of Tink's location. With luck, if we keep off the main trails, we'll make it there and back without trouble. Though getting Tink out is going to be the hard part."

"How *are* we going to get her out? Isn't she guarded by those things?"

Ace turned to Frankie. "The powers of a mermaid."

I stopped walking. "What?"

"I'll explain more later. We need to get to Crocodile Cove before it gets too late."

"No. You'll explain now." Ulrich didn't have this kind of time, but if I was going off to a cave with beasts crawling all over, I had to be able to trust the people at my back.

"Mermaids have abilities that will help us get her out. Now, if you don't want Ulrich to die, we need to move."

Not a single part of me wanted to let that statement go, but he was right. Ulrich was waiting for us, and I wasn't about to let him die because we took too long. No matter how much I didn't trust Ace right now. I'd spent most of my life watching my back and today was no different. I trusted Ace far less than I could throw him, but I'd be ready if he tried to cross me.

"How long have you lived in Neverland?" Frankie asked.

"I don't really know." Ace shrugged. "Time doesn't work the same way in Neverland as it does the outside world. It ceases to exist, really. That, and I don't really remember much before coming here."

I shot him a look. "What do you mean?"

"Pascal's magic. He helps us forget the tragedy and pain we experienced as a kid. I have some memories, the ones that were too tragic to be taken away, but he helps us heal and move on. When I got here, I stopped worrying about time and the outside world. I made new memories."

While I understood the desire to take a child's pain away—understood a little too well—I never imagined wiping away someone's memories. The fact that Pascal had taken those and gave all those boys new lives … warmth and respect flooded through me. How could Pascal, a man who killed and tortured people, be the same man who saved countless innocent lives? I knew the answer of course—Wendy. Yet, something about it left an awful taste in my mouth.

"There were a lot of us for a while. The entire tree practically burst with lost brothers and sisters."

I hadn't meant to ask, but the words flowed out before I could stifle them. "When did Wendy arrive?"

Ace rubbed his face, one that appeared much more tired than it had a moment ago. "A while after I did," he huffed. "She tricked him."

"What?"

"I didn't know then. No one did, not really. I don't even think any of them still know the full extent of it. But I do."

"What in sea's sake are you talking about?"

He rambled a bit more before his eyes fixed on me. "Pascal received word there was a girl in need of his help. He said her mother begged him to take her away from an abusive father. To take her to where she'll always be safe. And so, he did. If only he'd known then that it was all a ruse to get Wendy to Neverland so she could enact her plan. So she could harm those we loved."

He bit out that last bit as anger flashed in Ace's face and he hacked and slashed a sword on a nearby bush sending leaves scattering to the ground. He cursed and hissed and threw the saddest tantrum I'd ever seen. I grabbed Frankie by the arm and pulled her back while we let him take his anger out on the poor bush. Frankie gave me a look, but I shook my head.

After a few more hacks, he lowered his sword. He sucked in deep breaths. Slowly, he turned around. His cheeks were a deep red, and he refused to meet our gaze. Frankie left my side and placed a hand on his shoulder.

"Feel better?"

He nodded. "Sorry ... I just—"

"Why are you telling us this?" I asked.

Ace eyed me wearily. "I don't know you. I don't trust you. But for whatever reason Pe ... Pascal does, and I trust him. So, if you're really here to help us, and I want to believe that's true, then you need to know about Wendy."

I nodded. He had a point. Also, for some odd reason, it felt good to hear him say he didn't trust me. Because he shouldn't. Pascal may vouch for every last boy on this island, but that doesn't mean they've earned my trust, nor my respect. Though, I understood what I saw in Ace's face just then. The anger, the desire to end the corruption plaguing his people, his home. That I could respect.

"She was loved by everyone. Everyone except the Lost Girls. They didn't always feel that way, but something changed and none of them would tell us why. I didn't understand until later it was because Wendy had manipulated everyone. She could twist your words and turn everyone against you without a second thought."

"What about Pascal?" Frankie asked.

Ace scoffed. "They were best friends. He protected her from everyone. Well, everyone except Taigra."

I'd heard that name before but never anything about her or who she was to Pascal. Perhaps this was a better conversation when he was here to tell his tale. It almost felt invasive to ask. Rather than delve deeper into waters unknown, I changed the subject.

"How much longer?"

"We'll come up to Skull Cavern soon," Ace replied.

"Does this mean we're already in Crocodile Creek?" Hector asked, and I jumped. I'd almost forgotten he was here. Sometimes he and Nathaniel had this odd ability to blend in with the shadows until no one realized they were there. It made them two of the best scouts I'd ever known.

Ace nodded. "It used to be exactly as the name suggests. A place where crocodiles roamed. Until the Neverbeasts hunted them for food."

The rush of running water off in the distance sent a need deep inside me; a need to be back out on the open waves, to feel the sea breeze on my skin and taste the brine on my tongue. I always missed the *Betty* anytime I was away. Even more now that I was in some strange place with strange people.

We walked the rest of the way in silence until the trees thinned and a large rock formation came into view. Skull Cavern was exactly what the name suggested. Off the coast of Neverland stood the biggest rock formation I'd ever seen. Two gaping holes glowed a vibrant yellow while the entrance opened wide ready to swallow us whole. Tall jagged rocks stuck out from the water all covered in thick green moss. Gooseflesh rolled down my arms and legs. Frankie must have been feeling the same as she stepped closer to me.

"All right, Mr. Man-with-a-plan, how are we getting over there?"

I turned around to find Ace patting down a tree.

"Has he gone mad?" Frankie whispered, though not quiet enough apparently.

"There's a secret compartment here some—ah, there it is."

Beneath our feet, the forest floor shook, and something rose from the depths of the sea. More rocks? No. As it rose higher, I realized it wasn't rock but wood, and each piece connected to each other by some sort of vine.

It was a bridge.

Broken or missing wooden planks sat in a row, swaying back and forth with the wind. It stretched from the edge of the water and into the mouth of the cave. While it didn't appear to be the safest passage, it beat having to swim.

Ace left the trees and stood beside me. I peered up to see the slight furrow of a brow, and a jaw so clenched it made *my* teeth hurt. Did he worry about what waited for us in the cavern? Or was something else bothering him?

Ace cleared his throat. "Come on, we're going to have to keep it quiet until we find Tink. It's night, so the beasts should be out patrolling, but I guarantee there will be some guarding Tink. Though, I'm hoping we can get through the tunnel network without running into any of them. I may have a way to buy us some time, but there's no telling what will happen when we walk through the entrance."

Boards creaked and moaned under my feet as I followed Ace. He continued rambling about the best way to maneuver through the cavern, and since I hadn't the slightest idea where these tunnels led to, I figured the least I could do was listen.

The air dropped in temperature the second we made it to the other side. I rubbed my arms to ward off the chill, but even then, my long-sleeved tunic and trousers weren't enough to fight the eerie feeling creeping up my spine. The same trepidation I'd experienced entering the Leviathan's lair. I just hoped I wasn't going to run into more piles of the dead.

Though here there were no stalactites or stalagmites to be seen. Nothing but rocky walls and sandy floors. Ace disappeared into the darkness and returned a few minutes later with a torch in hand.

"Let's get in and out before they realize we're here. It's going to be a tight fit so stick close and be as quiet as you can."

Ace, followed closely by Hector, led the way down a winding path and not once did he stop as we passed several other pathways and openings. The path we took narrowed the farther we went, and Ace's pace never let up. If he didn't slow down, we were going to lose him, and the last thing I wanted to do was get lost in a place crawling with Neverbeasts.

In front of me, Frankie halted and placed her hands on her knees. She gulped in breaths of air. *Hells*, I'd almost forgotten. Frankie was claustrophobic.

"Ace. Hector. Hold up."

Ace whirled around and his face softened a fraction. "What's wrong?"

"She doesn't deal well with tight spaces."

Ace nodded and held out his hand. "It's not much farther. Grab my arm and I'll guide you through. I promise I will get you out of here, okay?"

Frankie nodded and grabbed hold of his arm. It said a lot about Ace's nature that Frankie willingly allowed him to escort her through. Without skipping a beat, the Lost Boy had offered his aid, and something warmed within me. Maybe he wasn't so bad after all. And yet I still didn't trust him.

He finally stopped as the small passage widened enough for Frankie to breathe without passing out. He pulled the pack off his back and rifled through until pulling an instrument from one of the pockets.

"Pipes?" Hector asked.

"Not just any pipes. A panpipe. This particular one happens to be blessed by Pan himself."

"Okay, I'll bite." I raised a brow. "What do you need that for and how did you know to grab it?"

"With hope, the Neverbeasts will probably be asleep. If not, this will ensure they do sleep. It doesn't work for long, and sometimes not at all, but it's the only chance we've got," Ace said.

It wasn't exactly the most reassuring thing I'd ever heard, but

Frankie seemed a bit more relaxed than I did. She pulled out her pistol and waited for orders. The same readiness our father Viktor always had. Another burst of warmth built in my chest.

All these warm, fuzzy feelings are going to be the death of me.

The smaller room pooled us out into a much, much larger one. The top of the cavern stretched hundreds of feet into the air. Torches hung along the walls, illuminating the large and … not so empty space.

I fought to breathe. Dozens of black figures lay sleeping in small groups around the room. Dogs. They looked like black—freakishly big—dogs. None of them moved or even acknowledged our entrance.

At the center of the room was a small metal cage and an even smaller figure lay in its depths—*Tink*. She laid in the center, flecks of dim golden light flickering around her. I was too far away to make out much, but it didn't matter, we just had to get her out of the cage and past a herd of Neverbeasts.

Piece of cake.

"Hector," Ace whispered. "You be their guard. If this doesn't work, we're going to have to fight our way out of here."

Hector gave Ace a salute and moved in position behind me and Frankie.

Ace pressed the pipes to his lips and skipped them over the instrument with such finesse and ease. Warm tones echoed against the cavern to heighten the magic the pipes created. It swirled around me in beautiful waves, sending chills through every part of my soul. I nearly lost myself to its rhythm when I remembered why we were here.

I had a mission.

Pulling myself from Ace's trance, I gestured to Frankie and

Hector and readied myself.

If someone were to ask what a pirate captain did for fun, it certainly wouldn't be traipsing through a maze of murderous death-puppies.

I gripped Frankie's hand and hers tightened against mine as we took quick, calculated steps. I held my breath, praying to the gods to get us safely to the cage without accidentally stepping on a tail or kicking an outstretched snout. I'd gotten this far in life, but I swear if I was to be eaten by Neverbeasts, I was going to come back and haunt the shit out of Ulrich. I may be out here trying to save his ass, but I didn't want to become dinner.

Tongues lopped out of mouths, paws twitched with restless dreams, and a few let out soft snores. They reminded me of the pack of wild dogs I used to see in Bellavier—only much, much bigger. Malakai and I spent time putting out food for them so we could watch how they moved, how they worked together, but most of all how they slept. Their backs toward each other in a group, none of them too far from another. Then he'd tell me how important it was to work with others the way wolves do in a pack. Everything Malakai and Viktor told us always turned into some sort of lesson. Did these beasts feel that same way? Were they a pack, or were they nothing more than ruthless creatures forced to do Wendy's bidding?

Either way, the gooseflesh on my arms and legs told me I needed to stop thinking and get out of Skull Cavern.

Iron bars, only centimeters apart from one another, stood between me and the fairy. That, and a rather large lock on the door. There was no way I'd be able to get close enough to unlock it, and blasting the lock open wasn't an option either. I had to figure something else out.

"Any chance you know how to pick a lock?" I whispered to Frankie who was already pulling pins out from her hair.

I crossed my arms, but Frankie kept her focus on the cage. I looked at Hector, but he just shrugged. She bent the pin into a straight line and got to work. Where in hells had she learned how to pick a lock? We'd spent so much time apart; I barely knew the girl kneeling in front of me. There hadn't been much time for us to talk since reuniting and most of the time Frankie avoided it. I hadn't a clue why, but I also refused to press the matter. Maybe it was time to have a long chat about what she did during her search for me.

"There," Frankie said as the lock clicked. The door opened with a creak, and I winced. A few beasts stirred and one turned on its back, but none of them woke.

Tink lay motionless as I neared the cage. The iron burned against my skin, and I gritted my teeth. Now wasn't the time to let iron affect me. The fairy was so small and frail. Would she break into tiny pieces if I touched her?

I lowered myself until my face was closer to her. "Tink? Tink, we're here to get you out of this place. Can you hear me?"

The fairy's gossamer wings fluttered at my words.

"We're going to have to figure out a way to pick this lock." I turned around to search for something when Frankie pushed me aside.

She pulled out a pin from her hair I hadn't noticed and got to work. It didn't take long for the lock to click open and my mouth dropped.

"What the hell, Frankie?" I whispered.

Frankie stuffed the pin back in her hair. "Just get her and let's get out of here. I don't like this."

I nodded and turned back to Tink. "I'm going to pick you up, okay, stay still."

At my touch, the fairy shot up and scurried away from my grasp. Her bright yellow eyes widened in horror as her gaze met mine. I whispered soothing words until she realized neither me nor Frankie were the big bad Wendy. I stared down at Tink. Her dark matted hair sat just below her chin, and her beautiful warm skin reminded me of those I'd met from the tribes to the eastern seas. A place where the sun always shone and pleasure spread far and wide.

"Wh-who are you?" Tink's voice was light and high-pitched but soft enough that none of the beasts heard her. Either that or whatever Ace was doing kept them from waking. I'd have to get me one of those pipes before we left the island.

"We're friends. If you come with us, we can get you out of here." I held out my hands and smiled. I wasn't so sure I'd convinced her, but she gave a stiff nod and walked over to me. It wasn't until then I noticed her wings. Translucent and full of vibrant color that sparkled against the cavern's lights, they were remarkable, but something wasn't right. Both wings had long jagged slits splitting each wing in half.

"Your wings," I cooed. "Did Wendy do this?"

Tink stopped short of my hands and peered up at me. She gave a stiff nod before climbing up and resting in my palm. She looked so frail and tired. Was this how Wendy made Pascal feel? Weak and cut off from the world. Fairies, from what I knew, survived in groups.

How long had Tink been without her family? An ache crept in my chest. I'd been without my own family for so long but managed to find a new one with a bunch of weird misfits, but they were mine. Tink needed to heal, but in time maybe she'd find herself a new family too.

We reached Ace without waking any of the beasts. That was until Ace's pipes stopped working. I looked over to find him shaking them as if they were broken. The hair on the back of my neck stood on end, and a tingly sensation rolled over my skin. I had just enough time to tuck Tink into my arms and roll away before something charged at me. I hit hard against the ground as Hector and Frankie cried out.

Around us, Neverbeasts started to wake. Fear wrapped itself around me in a firm grasp as they rose to their feet, shaking off the sleep and turning toward us. The beast that attacked turned and stalked closer. A freakishly large and scary looking beast. None of the others appeared that big. The beast's hackles rose as it bared its teeth at Ace. Bright red eyes stared at him, never wavering even as he pulled out a sword. Frankie aimed her pistol at the beast, but I wasn't so sure those would have much effect against it. Not with how large it was.

I thought about grabbing Tink and the others and taking our chances outrunning them all, but I wasn't sure I'd make it a single step. We were sitting ducks waiting to be devoured by the biggest damned dog I'd ever seen. Well, Neverbeast anyway.

"N-nice p-puppy." Ace's voice trembled.

The beast snarled and snapped its jaw.

"I don't think it wants to be called a puppy." Frankie took one step back and another until she stood next to me.

How were we going to get out of this? I knew absolutely nothing about these creatures. What kind of weaknesses did a Neverbeast have? Were they fast? Could they swim?

I didn't have time to figure out what I was going to do before the beast leapt. Ace dodged, rolling out of the way. Unsheathing Slayer, I jumped in front of Frankie and waited for the other beasts to make a move, but all remained where they were. Why weren't they attacking? Was this big one their leader? Were they waiting for the right moment?

"Arie, you said you were a mermaid, right?" Ace asked as he lowered his stance in preparation for another attack.

"What?"

"Are you or are you not a mermaid?"

"I am."

Once again, the beast lunged, and Ace dropped to the ground. His sword came up in time to slash its underbelly. It cried out as it tumbled across the rocky cavern floor. The other beasts roared their anger.

"Command them to stop," Ace yelled.

"I'm sorry?"

"With all the strength you can gather, tell it to stop."

"I'm not going to—"

"Just do it," Ace snapped.

The large beast scurried back to its feet and ran toward us. There was no way this was going to work, mermaid or not. I didn't control the damn things, but Ace seemed sure of himself, so I held out a hand and pulled on whatever magic I could. A static buzz rippled through me as I said, "Stop."

Nothing happened.

I closed my eyes and dug into the well of magic brewing beneath my skin. It coursed through me, tugging on the strings that held me together. I bit down on my lip and held my breath as the charge built and I cried out.

"Stop!"

The beast's paws dug into the rock. Its hind legs lifted over its body until it landed hard on its back to lay at my feet. My heart thumped, and blood pounded in my ears. I let out the breath I'd been holding. I'd fought sea monsters with less fear and yet something about this thing scared the living hells out of me.

The rest of the beasts sat on their asses and stayed where they were. *I can't believe that worked.*

They all stared at me and waited for my next command. Was this how Wendy worked her magic on them, how she controlled them? Before I could think about what I was doing, I lowered a shaking hand until it pressed against the dark and long fur of the beast. Soft like silk, its fur curled around my fingers and welcomed my touch. Its gaze met mine, a weary gaze that told me I'd better do whatever it was I needed to do. The problem was, I had no idea what to do here. Ace hadn't given instructions or a guide on what I was supposed to do, and I'd only had my mermaid powers for a short time.

Once more I closed my eyes and let the magic course through me. It built and curled and twisted until every bit of me brimmed with power.

I let out a slow, deep breath, sending the magic into the beast. My limbs burned as we both cried out.

My breath caught in my throat and my lungs constricted as darkness consumed me. Decay and rot entered my nostrils as the magic continued to sear my soul.

Finally, the magic dissipated, and I fell back and away from the beast. I gulped in breath after breath. "What the f-fuck was that?"

"I have no idea." Ace grabbed Frankie and tugged her away from the now unconscious beast. "But we need to leave."

It was still night when we emerged from the cavern. The air had dropped even more in temperature, and the waters had calmed to an eerie stillness. Behind us, roars of anger echoed out of the cave. We didn't have much time before they would try attacking again. I peered down at Tink who clung to my hand. She rose to her feet and cleared her throat. "I can help. All of you need to grab ahold of each other."

Frankie clung to my arm with Hector beside her, and with my free hand I grabbed Ace's shoulder.

"Good, now don't let go." Tink shook, sending flecks of light into the air. It landed on us just as blackness took over my sight and the howls of the beasts ceased. From one blink to the next, we left Skull Cavern and stood in front of the treehouse.

VI. FAITH, TRUST, AND FAIRY DUST

Arie

TINKERBELL'S SMALL FRAME CLUNG TO ME AS WE ENTERED the treehouse. Soft rays of morning light filtered in through the few windows it had to offer. By now Pascal would be somewhere dark, or possibly asleep and awaiting nightfall. Could Tink help him get his shadow back too? I didn't know much about what a missing shadow would do to someone, but from Pascal's panic back on the *Betty*, it wasn't good.

"I'm going to go lay down for a bit before everyone wakes up." Frankie waved and trotted up the stairs to one of the bedrooms. Hector trailed after her, leaving me and Ace to deal with Tink.

"Want me to set you down?"

Bells rang again as Tink's gossamer wings fluttered, sending bits of golden flecks everywhere. Was that the dust everyone spoke about? She shivered in my hand, and I lowered her down onto one of the couches. Only then did I realize that brown tattered rags covered her. Bare feet stuck out beneath the rags, and gooseflesh covered her exposed arms. Ace furrowed his brow at Tink and slipped into another room and came back with a small, fairy-sized blanket. He wrapped it around her and lowered himself until their faces met.

"It's good to see you, Tink." Ace smiled, and he sat on the floor next to her.

"You too." She gaped at the treehouse, and her eyes flickered from one side to the other until they landed back on Ace. "Tell me, who is this girl and how was she able to do what only mermaids can?"

Ace and Tink both looked at me, and I grinned. "Because I am one."

Tink's jaw slacked. "That's impossible. All the mermaids on Neverland are dead."

"Well, it's a good thing I'm not from Neverland, then."

She stared at me, assessing me and what my words meant. I didn't even know what it meant. I thought the only mermaids were the ones in Atlantis. I never would have guessed in a million years that Neverland had also been their home. Did King Rylan know about this? Had he visited Neverland before? He hadn't mentioned anything when I told him where we were going. Then again, we didn't exactly have a lot of time to discuss much of anything before I left.

"Then how did you get to Neverland?"

Ace's gaze darted from mine to Tink's. "Peter got her in."

Tink's wings fluttered and buzzed. "Peter's home?"

Excitement brimmed in the air as she dropped the blanket, sending flecks of golden light shimmering from her back. Though the splits in her wings kept her grounded, it didn't seem to stop her from rising a few inches off the ground.

"Thanks to her." Ace gestured to me.

"You saved him?" She gawked at me, but only for a second before she bowed. "I never thought I'd see one of your kind again, and to have one save me and Peter. You have my eternal gratitude, Light One. It would be my honor to give myself to you. To bond our souls as one as it has been done since the beginning of time."

"I'm sorry … what?"

Ace glanced up at me. "Bonding to a fairy is the highest honor a mermaid could receive. It's how Neverland has survived all these years."

"Ace is right. The magical bonds between the fairies and the mermaids mean a great deal to the magic on Neverland. A link granted by the God of Life and Death, and the Goddess of Sea and Sky. Fairy dust and the mermaids' magic, together they are the bond that holds the realms in place. Neverland is the sacred bridge between Plains," Tink continued.

"You mean between this world and the afterlife? Like some kind of purgatory?"

Ace contemplated my words before answering. "You could say that. Except all souls pass through here—the bad *and* the good. Without Neverland and its magic, the souls would seep into this world, causing a magical imbalance. It would also mean easier access to those who still have their souls to enter the Celestial Plains. Which means if

Wendy succeeds at taking all of the magic and fairy dust ..."

I stilled. Was Wendy after souls? What had Ursa said? *'You may have bested me, daughter, but you will not stop her.'* I wasn't so sure my mother had been talking about Wendy, but now ... a girl from Neverland? I didn't believe in coincidences and this sure as hells didn't feel like one. Shivers coursed through me.

Had Ursa known about all of this when she started consuming souls? She'd made it quite clear that my powers were what she needed to succeed in her plans, that the mermaid side of me was special, she just didn't tell me that my magic was part of the magic that held the damn key to hold the realms in place. Perhaps this was why she wanted my powers all along—to enter the Celestial Plains.

"Are you okay?" Ace asked.

I hadn't any idea how to answer that so I simply nodded. My problems weren't his to figure out.

Tink sighed. "Wendy has succeeded in much more than we realized. Why do you think she was capturing the fairies instead of killing them? Once she figured out how to wield our fairy dust, it was only a matter of time before she figured out how to open the other side. She knows what will happen. The only thing I don't know is why. What does she gain from this?"

Seven *fucking* seas. Ursa *wasn't* working alone, and now it was far too late to get answers from her.

"So does this mean Wendy is a witch? I thought only witches could harness souls."

Tink shot me a look. "How do you know that?"

"I'm also a sea witch."

"You're a mermaid *and* a witch?"

"And the best bloody pirate captain a crew could ever have." Nathaniel and all his red-headed self barged into the room. Bags under his eyes and a handful of some sort of baked good.

"Why are you out here?" I asked.

In other words: *why are you not watching over Ulrich?*

"Doc sent me to ask Tink for her help, and I have Giles standing watch. Though now that I think about it probably wasn't a good idea."

Apparently, it wasn't just me that had noticed Giles's odd behavior back on the *Betty*. Though, that didn't mean he couldn't be trusted to watch Ulrich's back.

"Leave it to Doc to know I'm back. What does he need, and I'm guessing you're with her?" Tink pointed at me.

Nathaniel nodded and a sadness washed over his face as he peered at me. "Hook's not doing well."

My heart sank, and my chest tightened. I was moving before anyone could say another word. My feet led me in the right direction while my brain scrambled with worry.

I flew past Giles and barged in the door. Doc stepped out of my way, and I pressed my hand to Ulrich's and met clammy skin. Warmth rolled off him, and I fought against the will to pull my hand away. His red and swollen eyes were shut, and his sunken cheeks and pale skin made him damn near unrecognizable.

I swear to the gods, Ulrich, if you die on me, I will spit on your grave.

Anger mixed with fear coursed through me, and I blinked back tears as someone else stepped into the already cramped space.

I bent down until my lips brushed his ear. "If you die after all the trouble I went through to save your ass, I'll find a witch to bring you back just so I can kill you myself."

I swore and spun around to find everyone watching me.

"Is everyone just going to stand there or are you going to help him?"

Ace set Tink down next to Ulrich, and the fairy's wings flickered from yellow to a deep crimson. She walked up to his head and placed a hand on his cheek. A glow emanated from her fingers but faded just as fast.

"I'm too weak, my magic far too drained to do him any good."

Ace, Tink, and Doc stared at me once again, and I threw my hands up. "Well, what am I supposed to do? I don't have the ability to heal someone from the brink of death."

"You don't," Tink said. "But if we were to bind our magic together it would give me the strength I need to cure him."

Was binding myself to another soul worth saving Ulrich for?

"What does this bond entail exactly? How does it work?"

Ace took a step closer to me. "Being bonded to a fairy is no different than the magic that courses through you. Think of it as an added superpower. Your magic is the only thing that's linked. You can siphon power from her, and she can do the same from you."

Tink nodded. "Our energy will be connected. When you deplete yours, I will feel it and vice versa. It won't stop or impede you much, it simply makes you feel tired and groggy. We would be able to communicate through our bond when in close proximity. You'd feel when I was sad, and I'd feel if you were hurt. We could locate one another, though that one tends to be a bit tricky, especially for newer bonded partners. And it would only be a general direction rather than actual coordinates."

"And currently, it's the only way we'd be able to save Ulrich," Ace said.

"What's the catch?"

"What do you mean?"

"You can't tell me this is all sunshine and rainbows and expect me to believe that. There's something you're not telling me."

Ace and Tink exchanged glances.

"Tell her," Doc sighed. "For this to work there must be full transparency."

Ace nodded. "Not only would your magic be bonded, but your souls would be too. If one of you dies, the other one does too. It also can never be reversed unless a blessing is given from the gods."

What? My mind spun and my head throbbed with this newly given information. I'd heard too much about souls and links and whatever else was going on. I needed to think, a chance to breathe without someone looking at me as if I had all the answers. I barely had the ability to keep myself and my crew alive, but to be bonded to someone whose death could result in my own ...

Doc must have recognized my hesitation because he walked closer to me and placed his hand on my shoulder.

"I never thought I'd see Ulrich again," Doc murmured. "I knew him long before anyone in Neverland did. He was a wild child, a real thoroughbred. It's been dull and meek without him and Peter here. But now they're both here because of you. Ulrich has always been a fighter and that won't change, but he's going to need help to survive this."

"You knew Ulrich before he came to Neverland?" I asked.

"Of course, my six brothers and I took him and his brother, Clayton, in when they were little."

Clayton. Hells I didn't even think about Ulrich's brother. Perhaps one of us should get word to him. While he'd abandoned Ulrich to stay in Khan, I was sure he'd want to know if his brother was ill.

"I've cared for this man for a very long time. It may not have appeared as such when we spoke earlier, but he's as close to a son as I'll ever have. I tried everything in my arsenal of medicines to cure him but even then I knew only the fairy dust would save him."

The emotion coming off of Doc's words hit me like a brick wall and I blinked back the odd desire to cry.

"So, you're his foster family?"

"I—we were, yes. And now it appears he has found a new one. Are you willing to let your family, a member of your crew, die, Arie? I suspect not considering the way you look at him." Doc held up his hand before I could interject. "Don't try to deny it. All I want to know is if you'd risk your life for him the same way he did for you?"

The same way he did for me. The same way we always seemed to do. I'd save him, he'd save me. It was like a game we'd started. While we'd become civil lately, most of the time we clashed—two captains on one ship had started to take its toll—but I did trust him, and he wasn't completely awful. After all he'd...

He'd kissed me.

A kiss that still lingered on my lips.

I sighed. Ulrich was a pain in the ass, but he was *our* pain in the ass—a member of the *Betty*. Doc was right: I did care about Ulrich and what happened to him. I strolled over to the bed and sat on the bed next to Ulrich and took his hand. We'd been rivals, enemies even, and now that we'd grown closer, I knew I couldn't let him die just because I was scared.

"Yes." I said. "I'll do it."

Bonded in life and broken in death,
Together as one until our final breath.
My power is yours and yours is mine,
From this day forth until the end of time.

An unrelenting wave of energy and magic surged through me, etching itself into my bones and coursing through every vein with an unstoppable force. My eyes widened as they tried to take in the magnitude of what was happening.

Tink's small frame sat in my hand as we recited the words that Doc gave us—binding us together until death, our power forever intertwined.

As soon as we finished, the room began to shift and swirl as the effect of the bonding settled in. For better or worse, Tink was now bound to me and me to her. She had promised to save Ulrich, and I wasn't sure his life was worth this huge risk, but so far it hadn't hurt me.

An unyielding bond between two souls, between two strangers. If Malakai and Viktor were here, they'd be telling me to open myself up and let in the good. And from what I could tell, from the feeling of Tink already in my mind, she was good.

Pure and unimaginably good. Everything I wasn't. I'd killed, and destroyed, and abandoned far too much for my soul to be anything but tainted. Could she feel it, even now as we stood here and the bond settled in? Did she know what kind of person I was?

Tink glanced over at me, a frown on her face. "You're worried?"

I sucked in a breath and did my best to calm my emotions but it didn't help. "Aren't you?"

"Yes, can't you feel it?"

A tinge of something tugged at my insides, something that felt unfamiliar. While it did feel much like my own worry, this felt foreign.

"I think so but I'm not sure how any of this is supposed to feel."

Doc cleared his throat and clapped his hands together. "It will take time for it to completely settle. You will both experience different things with this bond, but lean into it. Let it guide you and fill you with power and certainty." He gave us one last look before leaving us alone.

Tink turned to me and smiled. "You must really like him."

I narrowed my eyes. "What?"

"Ulrich. For you to accept this, to agree to it—he's a lucky man."

"Ulrich is a member of my crew, a good man and someone who saved my life. He was only in this predicament because of me. I'm just returning the favor."

Tink laughed, and for the first time I caught a glimpse of her in her full form. The fairy's wings had healed, and there were no more faint lines of stress or worry. The bond had seemed to have helped her too. "That's a mighty big favor for someone who's just a member of your crew."

I opened my mouth to object, but Tink fluttered down from my hand and followed after Doc before I could. I ran out after them. "Hold on, I'm coming with you."

Doc turned around and shook his head. "While I understand you wanting to see Ulrich upon his healing, he will still need much rest, and by the looks of it so do you. There is nothing you can do at this point," Doc said as he approached me. "You have already saved him by allowing the bond to take place. Now is the time for you to take care of yourself and get some rest as well."

A crushing wave of exhaustion hit me. I'd been high on adrenaline since we had arrived in Neverland, and while I knew Doc was right, I still couldn't keep Ulrich's sickly frame out of my mind. I needed to make sure this worked and then I'd go to bed.

"While your concern is appreciated, Doc, I can take care of myself." I looked over to Tink. "Unless there are any real objections to me being in the room?"

Took shook her head. "Come on, Doc. She's just going to follow us anyway."

Doc let out an exasperated breath and led the way to Ulrich's room. He opened the door, and I nearly gagged at the smell. Dread ripped through me as I pushed past Doc and Tink to find Ulrich. His breaths came in gasps and wheezes that began to ache. Sweat laced every bit of his body along with the sheets beneath him. His body shook, and he barely had the strength to look at us upon our entry. My eyes traced along his frame until stopping on his chest. Black veins trailed from over his shoulders before moving downward and stopping at his ... heart.

"Oh my." Tink buzzed past me and up to the bed. "This is much worse than I imagined. The poison has reached every bit of him. I-I'm not sure he can be saved."

Burning rage boiled within me. "You said this would work. You said the bond would save him. And now you're telling me it's too late? No." I shook my head. "I will not accept that. Fix him."

Tink shot Doc a worried glance, but he merely shrugged at the fairy.

"Fine, but know that he may not—"

"Just do it," I snapped.

Tink fluttered up to Ulrich and knelt down, placing her hands on the end of his blackened veins. A faint humming surrounded the room, growing louder in intensity as a warm and gentle light emanated from her fingertips. The light encased Ulrich until he was surrounded in its pale embrace, growing brighter until I had to shield my eyes from it. I prayed to the gods for Ulrich's recovery as Tink continued to work her magic.

I'd asked the gods so many times to save people, to bring back the ones I loved, and while most of the time they didn't answer, there were occasions where they did. And this time I needed them to answer me. I needed them to bring Ulrich back to me, because if they didn't ... if he died here ... the thought left me as Ulrich cried out.

"He's in so much pain. I don't know if I can muster up enough energy," Tink grunted as she pushed more of her light into him.

My hand settled on Ulrich, and warmth spread up my arm into the rest of my body. A low hum resonated in my soul as I braced myself and focused on sending the warmth out of me and into him. But instead of soothing energy, something else surged through both of us. Everything around me grew dark, and dread washed over me as I felt the poison radiate from deep within, threatening to consume us both. Was Tink feeling this too?

"Arie, that's enough."

I cried out as pain tore through me, but I couldn't stop my hands as they roamed over Ulrich's skin. Someone spoke again, their words lost to the pounding in my ears. Spots covered my vision, and my head throbbed against whatever the poison was doing to us—to me.

My body fought against whatever this was, but it wasn't enough. Moments later my world spun, and everything turned to darkness.

I slept in a dead girl's bed.

After I'd fainted, Nathaniel had been summoned and had brought me up to Jaina's room, one of the twins. I'd been so out of it that by the time I reached the bed I was out within seconds. Though it didn't last long, not when my dreams reminded me of the death that surrounded me. Ulrich's near death, the death of my fathers, the fact that the girl who owned this room was dead. So much of it that I'd tossed and turned and woke up with a start.

A cool draft wrapped itself around me as I peered out the small window nearest the bed. Soft rays of light filtered through the canopy of trees. I couldn't tell what time it was or how long I'd been up here.

I slipped out of the bed, realizing I was covered in some sort of oozing gunk, and made my way to the opposite side of the room to a bathing chamber. To my delight, someone had already filled it with warm water. Once bathed and feeling a bit more myself, I stepped out and through another door that led me into one of the biggest closets I'd ever seen. Obviously not the way out. Rows upon rows of clothes hung along massive walls ending at a vaulted ceiling. How had Jaina gotten up there? My eyes fell on a ladder with wheels at the bottom that stretched up as high as the hanging clothes.

Hopefully she wouldn't mind me borrowing some of them. I ruffled through until I found something suitable then walked up to a mirror that hung along the far wall, almost as big as the one in the basement of my home. Though, this one didn't appear to have any hidden messages for me. Or mermaid kings.

King Rylan. *My father*. My biological father. Malakai and Viktor would always be the men who raised me, but it was hard to deny the man I'd met a few months ago. I found myself enjoying his company, his words and wisdom. Even though we'd been together a short time, it felt as though I'd known him my entire life. When I finally completed my mission, the first thing I'd do was sail back to Atlantis.

What really got my attention though was the entire arsenal of weaponry between the clothing. Everything from swords and daggers to bows and crossbows. A large double-edged ax hung above the shelves right under a shield with two swords crossing at the center.

I liked this girl ... *a lot*.

I was just undoing the straps to my waistcoat when a rap on the door pulled my attention back into the main room. The door opened with a creak, and Frankie appeared from the other side.

Her blond curls cascaded down bare shoulders to meet at the top of a cropped dark blue shirt that exposed her navel. A slit up a blue skirt showed every bit of her tanned leg, and light shades of paint on her eyes and cheeks softened her features.

She looked more grown up than she ever had. Too many years were missed between us, and all I wanted to do was sit here and listen to her tell me about everything she'd done. She'd traveled far and wide to find me before being captured by King Roland. She hadn't even told me how that had happened—she really didn't tell me much of anything. Most of our conversations were short and more focused on the jobs that needed to be done on the *Betty*. Sometimes, no matter how hard I tried to think otherwise, my mind believed that Frankie preferred Hector's and Nathaniel's company to my own. But it wasn't as bad as the beginning when all she did was ignore me. Silver linings I guess.

"Oh good, you're—damn. Tink said there were some complications, but look at you!"

"I'm fine," I said, waving off her look of concern as she looked at my black-ooze-infested clothes. "What did Tink say happened exactly?"

"Apparently instead of trying to help heal Ulrich, you were siphoning the poison from him to you. She managed to stop the process, but whatever you did worked because she said the poison is gone."

"So, he's okay then?"

Frankie shrugged. "I haven't seen him yet, but Ace said he's got something to tell everyone. Oh, and have you seen Jameson?"

When was the last time I'd seen the assassin? I'd been so caught up in saving Ulrich I'd forgotten to watch his movements.

"No, and I don't like that he's keeping himself scarce. See if Nathaniel and Hector know where he is. I'll be down in a moment."

Jameson had been far too quiet for my liking since arriving in Neverland. Assassins were known to stay in the shadows, but he had no reason to while we were here. Not unless he was up to something, and wasn't that just the icing on my shit cake of things to worry about.

Frankie shut the door behind her, and I retreated back to the closet. I settled on a plain, flowy green shirt and a pair of black pants that seemed to be made out of material I'd never seen before. I threw them on and stuffed my feet in my boots and hooked Slayer to my belt. I made my way to the big mirror and frowned at the reflection. I never considered myself anything special. My big frizzy red hair, deep green eyes, and crooked nose weren't exactly the epitome of beauty. My damp hair hung in loose waves against freckled skin. Though it was no longer covered in dirt and grime thanks to the wonderful tub in Jaina's bathroom, it still wasn't perfect. But I enjoyed the way I looked; plain, boring, with a fierceness underneath that would strike at any given moment.

With one last look in the mirror, I turned and made my way out of the room. Voices surrounded me as the main room buzzed with Lost Boys. Well, what was left of them anyway. I'd only met a few, and according to Ace, there weren't many of them left. What Wendy and her beasts didn't do to them, Neverland did. Death and disease and starvation. It was hard to live on an island that was dying.

Even though Tink was back, and life seemed to flutter back into the quiet emptiness I'd felt upon our arrival to the treehouse, they still bore grim faces. One of them peered up at me. A smile came and went on his face, but it never reached his sad eyes. How long had they been like this? How long ago had Wendy ripped away the happy thoughts from these poor, unfortunate boys?

"Ah, Arie, there you are!" Ace gestured for me to take a seat next to him on one of the couches. Frankie sat on his opposite side fidgeting with her skirt. "Are you doing all right?"

I nodded. "Where's Tink, and is Ulrich okay? I want to see him."

"That won't be necessary." A deep, groggy voice melted within me as Ulrich appeared through the doors of the war room. He stepped out with a cane in one hand and Nathaniel a few paces behind him as he limped his way in. Color had returned to his cheeks and with every wincing step it was apparent the meds had worn off.

Heat rose to my cheeks as his gaze reached mine. Was he thinking about the kiss? Did he even remember it, or the spark that went off like dozens of lightning bugs? Why the hells was that the first thing that popped into my mind? I'd nearly died twice trying to save him, and my stupid hormones decided to think about a damn kiss. I dropped my gaze and cleared my throat. "Glad to see you're moving around."

"I'm told I have you to thank for that." Ulrich reached for my hand and brought it to his lips. Warmth spread through me in waves. "So, thank you."

I pulled my hand back and shifted nervously as everyone stared at us. "You'd have done the same for me." I turned to Ace. "You had something you wanted to talk about?"

Ace clasped his hands together and grinned. "I do, yes, please take a seat."

"Shouldn't we wait for Pascal?" Frankie asked.

"Tink went to check on him and fill him in. He's been refusing to leave his room since the meeting. Not sure what's up with him." Ace shrugged.

Everyone, including myself, ignored Ulrich's grunts and groans as he sat on the couch next to me. Nathaniel lowered his head in between us and whispered, "I'm going to go find Hector and do a perimeter sweep to see if I can find our assassin, unless you need me here?"

I shook my head. "Stay safe."

Nathaniel gave a grunt and walked off.

Beside me, the pirate captain lowered his voice, his breath hot on my ear. "That's twice you saved me, Arie. Do it again and people might start to think you actually like me." He leaned back against the couch and rested his head against the back of it. "I won't forget it."

Shivers coursed through me, and images of Ulrich's lips on mine flooded my memories. His soft yet firm lips pressed into mine sending a shock wave of sparks through every part of me. I looked down at them and fought against the desire to kiss him right then and there.

I opened my mouth to respond, but words evaded me.

Damn him.

How had a single kiss turned me into a blithering idiot? If it weren't for the necessity of this meeting, I'd have bolted the second I had the chance.

"As you all know, Tinkerbell is back," Ace said, and cheers rang out from the group of Lost Boys. A dozen or so of them sat in various spots around the room. Some on the floor, others on couches and chairs.

"We have these two women here to thank for that." He grabbed Frankie's hand, and then mine. Ulrich's grip tightened on his cane, and I wiped my unoccupied hand over my mouth to hide my smirk. "They risked their lives to save Tink, but more importantly, we found out some really good news."

What was he talking about? What news?

"Arie is a mermaid."

Gasps and murmurs cut through the room, and heads whirled in my direction.

"What does this mean?"

"Are you sure?"

"We can finally be free."

A whistle tore through the frantic voices. I plugged my ears and scowled at Ace.

"Sorry about that," he murmured. "Mermaids were killed off or left because of Wendy. She knew what threat they brought to the table. By now she knows that Pascal has returned and with him a band of pirates, but what she doesn't know is that this pirate is much more than that."

I was having a hard time wrapping my brain around that fact. I'd been able to control the seas and speak with sea life. I had the ability to shift into a mermaid and breathe underwater. I was the daughter of a king and a witch. Now I had the ability to stop Neverbeasts? How much more power could one person have?

A young kid—the smallest of the bunch—stood from the floor. Hazel eyes shifted from me to Ace and back again. "Does this mean we stand a chance?"

"It's possible. If we can convince Arie to stick around for a while and help us out."

Once again glances came my way. I'd overseen taking care of and looking out for pirates for so long that a few boys wouldn't be that much of a challenge. But I barely knew what I was up against. I wanted to tell them they weren't my problem. But that was a lie. I'd promised Pascal I'd help him and in turn that meant I had to help these boys. This just meant I needed to know more about Wendy.

"I promised Pascal I would help as much as I could, but in return I need information too. So yes"—I looked at Ace—"I will help, but I need all there is to know about Wendy."

"Pascal and I can sit down with you later tonight and discuss matters more privately."

I nodded. That was fine. I could wait, but I wasn't so sure Wendy would. By now her beast would have told her we were here and that we had Tinkerbell. She'd find some way to retaliate.

"Are we not worried about Wendy finding out we have Tink?" Frankie asked.

"She can't get into the treehouse," Chuckles said. "Once you've been banished the magic won't let you in. That also works for the surrounding area. Plus, she shouldn't be able to find it."

Pibbs continued, "There's a ward that makes the Tiki Tree invisible to those who've been banished from it. She can probably feel its location, but they wouldn't be able to penetrate the barrier."

"Not yet anyway." Ace stood from the couch. "The magic is

dwindling, and once it's gone so will the ward and so will any chance of us surviving. But now we have Tink, and we have Arie."

"Which means we should celebrate," called out another Lost Boy.

"Celebrate?" I huffed. "What in *hells* is there to celebrate?"

The Lost Boy's eyes widened, and he shrunk down into his chair.

"We celebrate when the war is over, not after the victory of a rescue," I snapped.

"Oh, *come on*, sis." Frankie jumped from her seat next to Ace. "Have a little fun. We should enjoy the small victories. Ulrich and Pascal have returned to their home, thanks to you. Tink was saved and returned to her home, thanks to you. Ulrich is better … because of you. If we don't find time to celebrate these little things, we'll never be able to see the bright side. So, let's have a little party before the shit starts."

I waved a hand. "Fine, but there better be alcohol involved."

VII. NEVER SAY NEVER

Pascal

BOLTING UPRIGHT, MY BREATH CAME IN GASPS AS sweat covered every inch of my body. The nightmare of Wendy's torture dissipated, and reality came crashing back. I was still in the treehouse, still in my own bed. There was no Wendy demanding to cut me limb from limb until I gave her what she wanted.

It had been the same recurring dream since my soul returned. Every night, the same reminder of what she'd done. The same pain and fear. I thought I'd be safe from her now, but I was wrong. Even my dreams weren't safe anymore. Wendy was still out there, searching for me. I had to stay one step ahead of her, and the only way to do that was to stop her at her own game.

A LAND OF LOST SOULS

A light tapping on my bedroom door pulled me from my thoughts, and I moved from my bed to open it. A small figure with delicate gossamer wings and a shining, twinkling body hovered in front of me. No sooner had I recognized her than I gathered her into a tight embrace, letting tears fall freely.

"It's good to see you too, Peter. Or should I say, Pascal?" Tinkerbell gasped into my shirt. I released her from my hold before I could suffocate her entirely. The sound of twinkling bells filled the room, replacing the tension that hung thick in the air only moments before.

"You're back ... but how?" I started to ask but stopped when realization hit me.

Arie.

Sweet, wonderful Arie. Of course she wouldn't sit idly by and wait for the right time to save Tink. Afterall, there wasn't ever a good time when dealing with Wendy. She knew of the risk, and she still went and saved Tink.

"Your pirate friend is quite lovely," Tink said, her eyes glowing with admiration. "And a mermaid at that."

I nodded, a smile on my face. "She's something."

Something magical.

Tink flew past me. She moved slowly, and her wings seemed to flutter much slower than they had in the past. Wendy had done her worst to my old friend.

Wendy seems to be doing a lot of that lately.

"Have you seen Ulrich?" I asked.

Tink nodded. "He'll be just fine."

Relief flooded through me. "Good."

Neither of us spoke for a while. I kept my gaze away, unable to look my old friend in the eye. Not that I could keep anything from her. She probably already knew what I'd done outside of Neverland. She was a resourceful fairy with an uncanny ability to see into my soul. But that didn't mean I'd make it easy.

"I wish you would have let me come with you," Tink said.

Guilt seeped into my bones, into every part of me that knew exactly what she meant. Cryptic words or not.

"Wendy would have captured you too. She would have killed you the same way she did …"

I couldn't bring myself to say her name out loud. *My Tiger Lily*.

"None of this is your fault, Peter. Not Wendy, not Taigra. None of it."

I scoffed. "Isn't it? I'm the one who brought Wendy here."

"Yes, but you're also the one who saved countless Lost Ones from terrible fates. Don't you remember what Taigra—"

"Don't go there, Tink."

Tink's light turned to a shade of red. "No, I will go there. I will because you need to hear this. Taigra wouldn't have wanted this for you, she didn't die so that you could lose yourself to whatever's going on in your head right now."

"She stood up against Wendy and lost, Tink. I stood up against her and lost. What do you expect me to do now?"

"Fight. Keep fighting until there's nothing left to fight for."

Silence fell over us for a while until Tink let out a small laugh.

"Do you remember that bet Pibbs and Taigra had going on?"

A smile crept to my lips, and I shook my head. "You mean the one that was rigged? Everyone knew Ace would win, and yet somehow he managed to get attacked."

I recalled that day. Taigra and Pibbs had a long-running stand of bets that always seemed to go in her favor, much to Pibbs's dismay. Everyone in the entire treehouse knew Ace was the most silent of us all. He was meant to sneak in and take the pixie's sacred flowers without them noticing and had done a damn good job of it until something woke them up.

"That's because Taigra made sure to rig it. Who do you think spooked the pixies?"

I threw my head back and laughed. "I still remember the look on his face as the pixies started attacking him."

"He had to jump into the lagoon just to get them off." Tink fell back on the bed with laughter and tears in her eyes.

"Taigra had sworn up and down it wasn't her, but we all knew. Even Pibbs who had to take over her cleaning duties for two weeks."

We sat there for a long time, reminiscing about the past and the better times before everything went to hells and back. Every story and memory was a knife to my heart. My head ached knowing that Taigra would never be here to thwart someone's bet or prank one of the other Lost Ones, and yet it was so full with her memory.

But it was all gone in a second.

"You should have told us what you were doing that day." Tink's voice lowered, and anger lined her words. "You should have worked out a better plan. We could have stopped Wendy together."

I hadn't wanted to believe Wendy's transgressions. She'd been dealt a terrible life before I'd met her—sold and used by powerful men. I'd taken her in and given her a better life, and in return she became my best friend. So, when rumors found their way to the treehouse that Wendy had taken every Lost Girl and tortured them to death, I didn't want to believe it.

But you believe them now.

I trailed a finger down the scar that marked my face. Recalling my dream and Wendy's torture. Recalling Taigra's lifeless body in a pool of dried blood.

I think I believed even then that she was evil—perhaps I just needed to see it for myself, and look at what that cost me.

So get up and do something about it.

I huffed and shook my head. Tink shot me a look, but I ignored it.

"I did what I thought was best, and yes, I know now that it was stupid. The past is the past, let's just leave it at that." There were more pressing matters. For starters, figuring out what Wendy's next move was. "Tell me what you know about what she's doing now."

Instead of commenting on my weird behavior, Tink went on about how Wendy managed to capture her while out on patrol with some of the Lost Boys. She'd spent days locked away in a dark room before Wendy finally came to see her. But worst of all was what Wendy was doing with their dust.

"She wants to use the dust to locate the door to the Celestial Plains. I don't know why or if that's even possible, but it will be nothing short of disastrous if she succeeds."

She thinks collecting fairy dust will allow her to open the door? The *door?*

Panic surged through me, and I dropped to my knees.

She found out. Wendy figured out how to open the door to the Celestial Plains. I'd been tortured and beaten, and my soul nearly destroyed to keep that a secret from her, and yet she still figured it out. There was only one way to open the gates if you didn't possess the blood of a god—and that was power. Enough power to make the gate believe you were a god. Fairies were meant to harness the dust. A pure-blooded human wouldn't be able to hold it without it being disastrous—or deadly. Unless she had figured out a way to harness the fairy dust. Wendy had been left to her own devices since my departure from Neverland, and now she had what she needed to get there. There was no telling what other powers she had at her disposal. The fairy dust did much more than just grant the person power, it was a way to enter and leave the island. It had resources that would aid her in getting anything she needed.

Fuck. This was all my fault.

You had no choice. You did what you had to survive. We both did.

I always had a choice. *I was weak.*

"We have to stop her, Tink."

The fairy hesitated for a moment. "What does she want? Why is she doing this? It's the one thing none of us were ever able to figure out. She's deranged and unhinged, but there's a determination in her unlike anything I've seen before."

"I don't know anything for certain. But I do know she's been looking for the door to the Celestial Plains since the second she stepped foot in Neverland."

Tink hummed. "That doesn't surprise me but does she honestly think she can go up against Pan? The second she'd cross the bridge he'd end her."

The sound of my father's name sent a surge of anger through me. My father who rejected me, who stole the glue that held me together. Wendy was no match against him, but I wasn't so sure her plan had anything to do with confronting my father. It was the one thing I never could figure out. Through all her torture, I'd only ever found out what she wanted rather than the why. What in seas sake could Wendy possibly want with Pan?

"I don't care for her reasons, only that she's stopped."

Tink paced along the floor, her bells chimed, and small amounts of dust covered the rug. "All right, well there's not much we can do from here. Why don't we go out and join the others; they're celebrating my return as well as yours and Ulrich's. It'll be good to get out and mingle for a bit, don't you think?"

I shook my head, knowing the sun still beamed in the sky. Knowing I'd possibly never see it again sent a ping of anxiety through me. I needed my shadow back. I needed it back before all was lost.

"What's wrong?" Tink asked. "When has Peter Pan ever turned down fun?"

You have to tell her. You have to show her. She's the only one who understands what this means.

She'll know about you ... about us. Hells this was getting difficult.

She's going to find out one way or another. Do you think it can be kept from the one who knows you best?

No, of course not. But even the thought of exposing the darkness within me was too much to bear. Allowing my long-lost friend to peer into the ugliness I'd committed, to face the pain and death I had caused, filled me with guilt. She would never look at me the same. It was bad enough my father had done what he did, but to open myself so blindly to Tink wasn't something I could do. I'd done far worse and deserved none of the light that beamed within this treehouse. I had no hope that she would ever understand the monstrosities I'd committed under King Roland's thumb. The thought of her disgust when she finally learned the truth was unbearable.

Rather than allow her to see into my soul, I stammered through my story, only telling her the bits needed to be heard. How my father's voice had cut through my mind as we neared Neverland, and how he'd demanded my shadow to enter. My voice cracked and tears escaped despite my best efforts to stop them.

My father's words tore through me once again.

You should have stayed in Khan. Neverland is better off without you. Why would I let the one who abandoned his people back into his home?

By the time I was finished, Tink was on my shoulder, her head against mine as she hummed a soft tune in my ear. I wasn't sure how long we sat there, but the only sliver of light in the room had grown dim. I cleared my throat and wiped away the tears.

"I won't begin to understand how you must be feeling. Not having your shadow is terrible, and I couldn't imagine how you've managed to get this far without it, but it's not the end of the world.

You've survived much worse and you will survive more of it in your lifetime. We will get your shadow back, but you must know none of this is your father's fault."

I stiffened. "What are you talking about? I heard him. He was in my head. The things he said to me and the storm …"

Tink slid down my arm and landed on the ground in front of me. "Your father hasn't left the Celestial Plains in years. He locked himself behind the gates and swore to never return once Kai left. Do you not remember that? You were the one who told me."

Hells, how could I have forgotten about Kai?

The Goddess of Sea and Sky. The one my father loved above all others, the one he could never have. He'd spent his entire existence loving her. Though she couldn't handle the infidelity. My father loved the idea of loving the goddess, but he had a much harder time being faithful to that love. It was why she left, and once she did, there was a change in him.

Well, you did lose your memory.

He became more reserved and locked himself away. But he'd come out to speak to me and demanded my shadow. Hadn't he?

"If not him, then who? Who could disguise themselves as my father and take my shadow without my knowledge?"

My gut wrenched at the image that popped into my mind. Wendy was a witch, but she wasn't fae. She didn't have the ability to change her appearance. Did she? And what about the storm? Bile rose in my throat, and I ran to my bathroom, narrowly missing the sink as I threw up.

No. No, no, no …

Does this mean what I think it means?

Yes. She now has the means to enter the treehouse undetected.

But how did she even know we were coming?

Tink had started up her pacing again. "I think that maybe we need—"

A blood curdling scream interrupted her words, and I launched myself from the bedroom and down the stairs before Tink could say anything more.

VIII. SEVEN FALLS

Arie

THERE WAS NOT ALCOHOL INVOLVED. At least not anything potent enough for me to forget … everything. Ace had sworn they had plenty, but it wasn't nearly as strong as what I had on the *Betty*. Instead, I'd taken to tracking down Nathaniel and Hector who usually always had a flask or two on their person, but they hadn't come back from finding Jameson. Worry crept over me, but I swallowed it down. Rather than dwell on them just yet, I took to finding Giles.

He sat alone, fidgeting with his glass before he noticed me coming. "Hey Cap."

"Giles, I've been meaning to speak with you. How are you feeling?"

He shrugged. "Okay, I suppose."

"So, you want to tell me what's been going on with you since our battle against my mother?"

Giles hesitated, and his cheeks flushed before speaking again. "I think things have just gotten more complicated than what I signed up for. But, y-you don't have to worry about me, Captain. I'll be okay."

I heard the worry in his words, the subtle notion that he was in fact not at all okay. I'd known Giles for quite a few years and his telltale sign that something was wrong was in his cheeks. He was hiding something, and just as I opened my mouth to say so, Frankie plopped into the seat next to me. "Are you brooding?"

I fought back the urge to push her off the chair. I tried to ignore her and turned back to Giles who'd managed to get up and make his way to the other side of the room. Just another reason for my suspicion to remain on high alert. As soon as Nathaniel and Hector got back, I'd worry about what Giles was hiding from me.

"I'm not brooding." I hissed.

"Then why aren't you going with Hook?"

Ulrich, now that he was miraculously moving around without so much as a limp in his step, had offered to take me somewhere fun and away from the treehouse, but I wasn't ready to go off with him. Not after what had transpired between us. Which was why I was waiting on Ace to bring me something stronger to forget it all and enjoy some peace and quiet before we figured out what to do with Wendy.

"I think I'll stay here and get drunk with you instead."

Frankie laughed. "Oh, poor Arie. Are you scared of the big bad pirate?"

I shot Frankie a look, but she kept her gaze forward. Flickers of light danced against her skin, casting her face in a glow. A smile crept to my face as I lost myself in my baby sister. My first friend. Though, she wasn't a baby anymore, and she sure as hell wasn't going to poke and prod in my business. That was big sister territory.

"We have more pressing matters to concern ourselves with."

"You mean Wendy? Yeah, well she's not going anywhere, and you could use a little walk." She motioned her fingers up and down when she'd said 'walk.'

"I need to speak with Tink and get our men on this island. That can't wait."

We'd been away too long. Our supplies were already depleted upon our arrival. There was no telling how much longer they'd last.

"You don't have to talk to Tink."

I threw my hands up. "Did you not hear a word I just said?"

"You don't have to because I already did. She can't do anything until her magic is back to full strength."

"She can just siphon magic from me. It worked the first time."

Frankie shrugged. "Apparently this isn't as simple. To collect enough dust for the entire crew, it'll take a couple days. You have all the time in the seven seas, and no excuse, to take Ulrich up on his offer."

When did my baby sister become little-miss-nosey-ass? And why did she care? For the most part, I'd gotten such conflicting vibes from Frankie. One minute she was nice to me and the other she gave me the cold shoulder. I just … I wasn't sure I'd ever understand her.

A LAND OF LOST SOULS

The hair on the back of my neck stood on end, and I whirled around to find Ulrich standing in the doorway, his eyes trailing down my frame. "Meet me outside in five," he said before retreating back outside.

I scowled at Frankie, and she threw her head back and laughed. "You should see your face right now. Oh boy, sis, go have yourself some f-fun." She hiccupped and pushed me off my stool.

"Fine, but if I'm going then"—I grabbed her glass and tossed back the remnants—"you can't drink anymore. I'm cutting you off." I shot the Lost Boy who was making the drinks a look.

"Y-yes, ma'am, no drinks for her."

"You can't tell me when to quit," Frankie snapped.

"And yet I just did." I pressed my lips to the top of her head then headed toward the door.

Ulrich was standing outside waiting for me when I left the treehouse. He didn't say anything, and instead motioned for me to follow him with a simple nod of his head.

We walked in silence for a while as Ulrich led the way, his sword and hook slashing and hacking at overgrown bushes and hanging vines. We'd been traveling for so long the sun started to dip beyond the horizon. Thank the gods for small favors. I'd been dripping in sweat, and the water canteen Ulrich provided had long since dried out.

While Neverland was a beautiful sight, I missed the *Betty*. The taste of salt on my tongue and the rock of the sea beneath me. But most of all I missed the breeze, the feel of its bite on my skin during a storm and its soft caress on a warm summer's day.

Being on land for long periods of time left me longing for her, but right now was far worse than any time before. My crew sat somewhere along the edge of the island, waiting for my command. Not knowing where we were or if we're okay. I shouldn't be traipsing off into the woods with Ulrich. I should be getting back to them.

"I know what you're thinking," Hook called from ahead.

He walked backward as his gaze caught my own. How could he possibly know what I was thinking?

"Is that so?"

"You're worried about the *Betty*."

Of course he knew.

"Keenan can take care of her just fine. I left her in capable hands."

Ulrich huffed, "Right."

I picked up the nearest stick, a small one so as not to do too much damage, and chucked it at him. Apparently my aim wasn't as good as I thought at that moment because the stick *thunked* the back of Ulrich's head instead of his back where I had intended.

He yelped and whirled around. "What the hells, Arie?"

I threw my head back and laughed. "Sorry, I didn't ... I only meant ..."

Ulrich shook his head and stalked over to me. "Here I am, trying to do something nice for you, and this is what I get?"

I stopped laughing and brought my gaze back to Ulrich. A snarl on his face, yet it couldn't fool the hint of laughter I saw.

He hadn't told me where we were going or what we were doing, only that I'd enjoy it. Though that had done nothing but send butterflies fluttering through my stomach.

"Yes, Ulrich, I'm worried about the *Betty*. Happy?"

Ulrich's shoulders tightened and his hand followed suit. "Why would I be happy about that? They're my crew too. Or did you forget that?"

"Of course not," I snapped. "You're just as much a captain of that ship as I am."

The second the words left my mouth, heat rose to my cheeks. I hadn't meant to admit it let alone actually say it. There was no lie in those words, no matter how much they made me cringe. Half of the crew was that of the *Marauder* and Captain Hook, but over the course of a few months they'd become a part of my crew too.

He'd lost his ship to sirens, watched dozens of his men die, fought to save his brother from King Roland, and somehow managed to hold himself together in the process.

Rather than reply with a snarky comment, Ulrich turned his head toward me and nodded. "All right, then."

He went silent again, but only for a moment before he said, "I'm sorry if I upset you. I know you're just as stressed about all this as I am. That's why I wanted you to come with me. To thank you but to also give you a way to relax a little bit."

I hadn't a clue how Neverland had something that could cure worry and stress, but so far I had enjoyed the chance to walk and be away from the chaos for a bit.

Finally, the trees parted, leading us out onto a small cliff. I pushed my way past Ulrich and gasped. My hands clasped over my mouth as I took in the sight before me.

Seven waterfalls sat on different levels of a giant cliff, but that's not what caused me to gasp. Each waterfall glowed with its own unique color:

blue, red, green, purple, orange, yellow, and pink. Colorful water cascaded over the rock and down into a large pool of water. Light danced across the pool's surface as the water rippled against thick foam. Gooseflesh trickled down my arms, and a cool breeze slid across my skin.

Ulrich walked up beside me. "It's the rock behind the water that causes it to glow. Pascal always said that each of the falls were blessed by one of the gods. A gift that brought good luck to anyone who swam its waters. That's also probably why they're still intact unlike the rest of Neverland."

Is this why he brought me here? Did he think I needed luck?

"And you think this would be good for me?"

Ulrich shrugged and walked to the edge. "Could be, but we're not here to go into the Pool of Never."

I followed him and looked over the edge to see jagged rocks that molded into makeshift stairs protruding from the side of the cliff. Ulrich climbed down, moving and maneuvering without issue. I peered over the edge to a rock bed below. I swallowed down the bile in my throat and cursed the gods for continuously putting me in these stupid situations.

Flashbacks of dangling from a cave with Pascal at my side entered my mind. Okay, maybe it wasn't always the gods who'd put me here.

"You okay up there?" Ulrich's sly voice sent me surging forward.

Whether it was from nerves or excitement I couldn't be sure, but I climbed down nonetheless. The rock formed around my foot as though the steps were specially made just for me. I grabbed hold of another rock and sucked in a deep breath before descending.

Ulrich's words were lost to the blood pounding in my ears.

Something about the—

"Ah!" My foot slipped, and I cried out. My body clenched as I closed my eyes and braced myself for impact. I landed with a thump, much softer than I'd thought a forest floor would be.

I opened my eyes to find myself in Ulrich's arms. A smile played on his lips. I scrambled out of his hold, and he laughed.

Gods damnit. If I didn't know any better this whole saving each other's ass was turning into a game.

"I believe that now puts you in my debt." Ulrich grinned.

"Just shut up and keep going."

How had I gone years not needing someone to save me? But the second the captain boarded my ship I found myself in constant need. Heat crept to my cheeks at the thought.

I turned and looked up at the jagged rocks to see the missing step. It was several feet from the ground but not enough to leave permanent harm had I met the ground instead. I'd have been just fine.

"You mean thank you?"

I shoved him forward and did my best to hide the smirk on my face.

Cool air rolled off the water, and I lifted my face to the falls. The cascading water glowed under the moonlight, and I could've sworn the water shimmered a little extra. A wave of relaxation rolled over me, and I was content to stay there forever.

"You coming?" Ulrich called from ahead. He stood a few feet down the water, a smile stretched across his face. The moonlight bathed him in a soft glow making his hair look even darker than usual. He stood with his arms clasped behind his back and his shoulders set square, cocky.

A sense of calmness washed over me as I followed him toward the larger of the waterfalls.

The trail wound around the pool and behind the waterfall to an alcove in the cliffs. Dozens of sparkling blue rocks lit the entire cavern, casting long shadows and eerie light into every corner. It was larger than I expected, complete with dozens of smaller pools. Steam rose from the water and a light buzz sounded in the air.

I crinkled my nose. Was that sulfur?

Ulrich strode ahead and stopped at one of the pools. He turned to me, an excited glint in his eyes as he gestured for me to come closer.

"These are hot springs. They're a little hidden secret in Neverland. Pascal and I discovered them years ago and spent a lot of time up here when we needed to get away and think."

Before I could say anything more, Ulrich lifted his shirt over his head and threw it to the ground. Heat rose to my cheeks, and I abruptly glanced away. Though, he didn't seem to notice. How someone could look so good and yet be so infuriating was beyond me.

"What in the sea's sake are you doing?"

"Getting in the water; what does it look like?" he asked as he took off his shoes and socks and turned back to me. He unzipped his pants and pulled them down, leaving him in nothing but his undergarments. He raised a brow and shrugged before splashing into the water and submerging himself completely.

While the man could certainly be confusing, he was also an idiot. "Ulrich!"

He returned to the surface, a laugh plastered on his face. "What?"

"Isn't it hot?"

"Nope. It's refreshing."

I rolled my eyes. "Well, I'm not getting in there."

"Why not?" he asked. "Is the big bad monster hunter afraid?"

"Absolutely not." I lifted my chin.

"Then come join me."

"Not a chance."

Ulrich tucked his hands into his arm pits and flapped his arms like a chicken.

"Real mature." I took a step forward and then another until I stood at the water's edge. I hunched down, and put my hand in the water. It was warm, warmer than I'd ever felt natural water before, but not nearly as hot as the steam made it out to be.

"Are you just going to stand there or get in?"

I bit my lip but still didn't move. The only water I'd ever been in was the sea. But this wasn't about the water, it was about who was in it and what this meant.

"I thought we just discussed this. Don't you trust me by now?"

I did, but this wasn't about trust. Ever since the death of my fathers, I'd had a mission. I'd spent every waking moment fighting and searching that I rarely had time for these moments. Sure, I'd spent time with men and women before, shared their beds and their ale, but this didn't feel the same way as one of my casual one-night benders of fun. I didn't have time to allow myself such luxuries. I couldn't afford that type of distraction. That, and I'd seen what opening yourself up to someone did. My fathers loved one another, a love that etched itself into your soul until it consumed you. Looking at one another so deeply that there was nothing else in the Seven Seas that mattered. They depended on one another in a way that reminded me of the way my men counted on me. And wasn't that a scary thought.

I wasn't looking for that kind of commitment. Though, for all I knew, neither was Ulrich. That didn't mean I had to let my guard down. Especially with someone who was supposed to be my rival.

Someone who seemed to become something far more than that.

So, did I trust him? I cleared my throat. "Not in the slightest, but fine. I'll give it a shot."

I stripped, save for my undergarments, and left my clothes next to Ulrich's. My muscles relaxed the second I stepped into the pool. Warmth flooded over me, and I sighed in relief.

"See, trusting me isn't that bad, is it?"

I couldn't help but smile back at him. I had never been to someplace so serene before. A part of me wondered if I was simply dreaming.

This wasn't so bad, and he was right: I needed this.

Ulrich cleared his throat drawing my attention back to him. His eyes sparkled from the nearby light, and it was impossible not to be charmed by him in such an intimate space.

"I guess not."

He stepped closer. Water dripped down his skin, and a strand of hair hung over his face. I fought the urge to slide it back in place and instead kept my hands planted firmly at my sides. My breath caught in my throat as he moved to stand within inches of me.

"You know what else isn't so bad?" he said softly. My heart skipped a beat at the intensity of his gaze.

"What's that?"

Ulrich raised a brow. "Me."

I snorted. "I'm not so sure about that."

His light laughter rippled over my skin, sending sparks of electric warmth tingling through my body. He stepped back and submerged himself up to his neck.

"Oh, come on," he called out. "I'm not that bad of a guy. Give me a chance."

I arched a brow and crossed my arms, feeling the warmth of the water on my skin.

"Okay, how about I'm a halfway decent guy with a dark side."

"Halfway decent, huh?" I said, stifling a laugh.

He nodded and stepped forward; his hand slid against the edge of the pool as he stepped closer to me.

"I can be really entertaining when I want to be. What do you think? Want to take me for a spin?"

Just then, I was suddenly aware that my body was close enough for him to feel its warmth. His eyes darkened as he drew near until his breath danced against my skin.

"I don't think you could handle me," I said breathlessly.

Ulrich lifted a brow and slowly stepped back. "Try me," he said with a wicked grin.

Despite myself, I laughed and shook my head. "Was this your plan all along? Get me out here alone so you could seduce me?"

Ulrich shrugged. "Is it working?"

It was, and I wasn't sure how to feel about that. Before I could answer he laughed, and my heart stuttered. His laughter was contagious, and even though I was cautious of him, I couldn't deny the spark between us.

"What's so funny?"

He brought his hand to my cheek, and my face flushed. I couldn't help but lean into his touch. I'd been so focused on trying to escape the man that I hadn't stopped to realize how good he felt.

"Your face is redder than that waterfall out there."

I smacked his hand away, but the grin on my face remained. "You're insufferable."

"I'm insufferably wonderful."

"Is that so?"

Ulrich nodded. "I could show you how wonderful I am."

The memory of his lips on mine flooded into my mind, and my cheeks warmed. I'd been caught off guard then, but now I was prepared. Yet, did I want this? Could I want this? Deciding to tread lightly, I settled in for whatever came next.

"Like you did in the treehouse?"

Ulrich's brows furrowed in confusion. "What are you talking about?"

I shoved him back. "Don't play with me, Hook."

"I assure you I have no idea what you're talking about."

Hells. He didn't remember. How could I be so stupid? Of course he wouldn't remember. Gods only know what the medicine did to him.

"Well, then never mind."

"Wait," he said. "Are you saying that I …? Did we?"

Embarrassment flooded through me, and reality came crashing back down. I stepped away from Ulrich and scrambled out of the pool.

"No!" I shook my head, nearly certain my face was beet red. "We didn't do *that*. You just … we kind of … oh, just forget about it."

Gods, I'm such a fool.

Ulrich shook his head and climbed out after me. "I'm pretty sure I'd remember if we did anything anyway."

He stepped forward and outstretched his hand, but I had the sudden urge to flee. My heart raced, and my mind buzzed. What was I doing? I couldn't do this. I had too much at stake, too much going on to let Ulrich be a distraction or to get in my way.

My gaze darted from him to the exit. "We should go," I said softly, the words practically tripping off my tongue.

"Go? Wait, Arie—"

I raised my hand to silence him. "I appreciate you bringing me here. You were right, I needed it. But now we need to get back. I came here to find answers and help Pascal, and so far I've done a pretty shitty job of that."

Ulrich's face contorted into a mix of confusion and frustration. "You are such a pain in the ass, you know that? The second someone shows even the slightest bit of interest in you, you shut down and withdraw."

Anger bubbled up inside me. "Excuse me?"

"Just give yourself a break once and enjoy yourself," he said with a sigh. "Have you once taken even a moment to allow yourself to be happy since your fathers passed? Is that what they'd want for you?"

I surged forward and shoved Ulrich as hard as I could. "Don't you dare speak about them."

"I'm only trying to help."

"Yeah, well don't. I knew this was a mistake."

Ulrich stiffened, his face void of whatever my words made him feel. "A mistake?"

"Take me back to the Tiki Tree."

We dressed in silence, neither of us knowing what to say. The air between us was thick and heavy, and the heat had seemed to simmer inside me from our confrontation but my own inner conflict at his words still roiled around in my mind. I just wanted to get out of there.

I dared a glance at Ulrich as he grabbed his shirt. Beads of water dripped from his perfect skin, the light from the lanterns glimmered against him. Heat returned to my face—this time for an entirely different reason. He caught me staring and I quickly looked away.

"Ready?" He asked.

I nodded and followed him outside to start the long trek back to the treehouse. Every once in a while I'd hear him mumble to himself, and I thought about what to say to him. How to make this awkward situation better, but nothing came.

Ulrich obliged, though neither of us said another word as we made the long trek back to the treehouse, at least not to each other. I'd heard him mumble once or twice to himself, but that was it. I thought about what to say, about how to make this awkward situation better, but nothing came. We almost kissed, and had I not come to my senses, it may have gone further than I was willing to. Ulrich was an attractive man; I'd been practically foaming at the mouth for him on several occasions.

So why was I so hesitant to give myself to him? We were rivals, and once enemies, but he'd proven himself so much more than that since becoming a part of the *Betty*. Perhaps I was being ridiculous.

We needed to talk about this but before we could an ear-piercing scream sent both of us sprinting the rest of the way to the treehouse.

IX. THE CROCODILE

Arie

I SURGED THROUGH THE DARK FOREST AT A BREAKNECK speed. Branches clawed at my face and clothes, but the gut-wrenching scream sent my feet racing faster than ever before. When the familiar silhouette of the tree came into view, Ulrich and I raced toward it.

My breath came in frantic gasps as I ran, unable to stop my heart from racing. Though the sensations cascading through me felt nothing like my own: they were Tink's terror and panic, amplified by our bond. My legs wobbled beneath me as if I weighed a thousand pounds, but I kept running until we reached the treehouse. Worry, dread and despair careened through my veins like poison, threatening to consume me.

Some of the Lost Boys were huddled in a tight form, their backs toward one another. Moonlight filtered through the leaves in the trees, bathing them in a faint eerie light. Ace scanned the forest until he found us.

The silence was deafening until he broke it. "Are you two okay?"

I nodded. "Where's Tink? Is she okay?"

"As far as I know she's still with Pascal."

Relief washed over me as I caught sight of Frankie standing straight and tall next to Ace. Her golden hair shimmered in the fading light, and her hand was clenched tightly around a long, thin dagger. Her eyes locked on mine, and my shoulders sagged in more relief. At least she was still here. At least she was still alive. My mind flashed back to Khan. To Frankie kicking and bucking on the floor, desperately trying to get away from her captor.

Both Frankie and Tink were okay. Then why was Tink so upset? If it wasn't her that screamed, then who was it?

I craned my neck, searching the treetops for the faces of the Lost Boys. Most of them seemed to be accounted for, even the ones who I hadn't been formally introduced to. All their faces scanned the trees before us, searching for signs of wherever that screen had came from.

"Nathaniel and Hector are out there." Frankie's voice cracked, but she looked ... pissed. My sister loved those fools as much as I did. They'd practically stepped in and became father figures to Frankie. Had the scream belonged to one of them? Her white-knuckled grip and furrowed brow gave all the indications of her worry, but it was her eyes. Green laced with fear and I could have sworn, just for a brief moment, that something else lingered in them. But she blinked and it was gone. It was the same thing I'd noticed earlier back in the war room—eyes that looked nothing like hers.

"They're pirates and can handle their own," I said, unable to say more as I worked to calm my racing mind. Nathaniel and Hector were strong and able men, but what everyone didn't know was that they'd been looking for Jameson. Had he done something to them? Maybe this wasn't Wendy's doing after all.

The door to the treehouse burst open, and Pascal hurled out into the night. Tink fluttered behind him, her light a dark and fiery red as she came up to me. And taking up the rear was a weary looking Giles and *Jameson?* What the hells was he doing in the treehouse? Surely if he'd been there the whole time I'd have noticed, or Nathaniel and Hector would have reported back to me by now. I wanted to make him tell me where he'd been, and I would as soon as we figured out where that scream had come from.

Now that Tink was here, her emotions flooded through me rawer and more potent than before. Tears brimmed in my eyes as I blinked them back. I knelt to her, and she raced over to me and up onto my hand.

"We have a problem," she said and looked at Pascal.

I panned over to him, and his face paled a few shades lighter than normal.

"What is it?"

"Wendy, she has access to the treehouse, she has Pascal's—"

Murmurs rang out from the trees above, and I spun around and looked up to find …

Pascal?

There he stood, just beyond the tree line. Blond shaggy hair, a green tunic, brown pants with worn knees, and a pair of boots. I darted my gaze between the two Pascals.

What was going on?

Ace scurried away from Pascal—the one who came from the treehouse. His weapon was drawn as he pointed it from one Pascal to the other.

I set Tink down and withdrew Slayer.

She shot forward and waved her hands. "This is the real Pascal. *That*"—she pointed to the tree line—"is Wendy."

"What?" I blurted and shifted my gaze from one Pascal to the other. "What do you mean that's Wendy? I thought she couldn't get in here? And how does she look like Pascal?"

They looked exactly the same, down to the same wardrobe.

"Apparently she has something that doesn't belong to her." Tink wrinkled her nose at our Pascal.

A cackle cut over the night as Wendy emerged from her illusion. A tall and lithe build stepped forward. blond hair retracted into a short pixie cut. Her eyes brightened a few shades of blue, and her skin lightened slightly. Her gaze fixated on Pascal as she drew closer.

I gaped at Pascal and then Wendy; the tension between them was almost tangible as the air around us crackled and sparked. I shivered and glanced over to Frankie, who snarled at Wendy.

"Ah, the Lost Ones have returned." Wendy spoke through a bow, her arm flailing with a dramatic flourish before throwing her head back and letting out a chilling cackle that made my blood run cold. Chills erupted down my arms, and I fought the urge to turn tail and run. No wonder Pascal had a hard time even mentioning her name. Everything that she'd done, all the terror she'd inflicted, it was hard to believe it had been done by this crazed woman.

A LAND OF LOST SOULS

A tiny little thing I'd love to introduce to Slayer.

"She looked like you, Pascal. How is that possible?" Frankie asked.

"She has his shadow." Bells sounded as Tink shook and fairy dust floated in the air above her.

My body went rigid with her words.

"She has *what*?" I ground out.

How the hells did she get it? Better yet, how did she know we were here? Ace said Chimera probably went off and told her after attacking Ulrich, but the shadow was gone well before then. What was I missing?

"Peter, it's so good to see you alive and well." Wendy's high-pitched voice cut through our conversation.

"No thanks to you," Ace said.

"I gave him a gift. He was much more fun as the king's wizard."

Wendy had been keeping tabs on him this whole time. I shot a look at Pascal, but he didn't say a word.

"A gift?" I scoffed. "What you did was torture him until he was a mere shell of himself." I stepped out and away from the Lost Boys. "You took him and brainwashed him until you could mold him into ..."

It hit me then. The laugh, the grand entrance, the need to feel powerful. Pascal had been that person. He'd killed without remorse, he did exactly what his king told him to do. From the bits and pieces I'd gathered from my time here, it seemed as though Wendy created a miniature version of herself. Which begs the question: was someone controlling Wendy too?

"... into you," I finished.

"Ooo, you're the little pirate girl." Wendy clapped her hands together, ignoring my words as she took another step closer.

A dark dress clung to her. I squinted a bit more. No, not a dress—armor. It framed her in leather to match a pair of brown boots. Knives were strapped to her sides and a sword at her back. Dark painted lines covered her face, appearing as though she were ready for battle.

My stomach twisted in a terrible knot at that thought. If Wendy was here, her beasts had to be close. I wasn't sure we were prepared for a battle against them. Not after what I'd seen one do to Ulrich.

"I never thought you'd bring pirates home, Peter. Didn't you used to hate them?" Wendy shrugged. "I don't mind, of course. More food for my army."

More?

I glanced back at Pascal once more. His eyes sat wide and terror stricken, and his skin paled to a sickly color. His lips quivered, or was he mumbling to himself? A terrible feeling latched itself onto me, and panic surged inside.

"What are you doing here?" Ulrich stepped out from the group and stopped until he stood between her and me.

"Come now, Ricky boy," Wendy said, putting far more emphasis on the 'y', and waved a hand. "You know why I'm here. Your little pirate bitch took something that belongs to me and"—her tone turned to venom as she continued—"*I want her back.*"

She had to be joking. The Lost Boys would never willingly give up Tink … *I* would never give her up. What did she think she could do, come into the treehouse and take her by force? If that were the case, she'd already have her beasts gnawing on our bones.

I peered down at Tink, her body trembled. If she kept this up he'd go through all her fairy dust again. Adrenaline surged through me, begging me to do something drastic. I clenched my fist and fought down the urge. I wasn't used to feeling the weight of her fear in my veins, yet here it was. I inhaled deeply, releasing the air and letting my own anxiousness flow away with it. Tink's shoulders relaxed slightly, and she gave me a slight nod that I took as thanks. We were going to have to work together to understand and control this bond. Especially if her emotions were going to be this erratic.

"You want her back but Tink isn't yours to have. She's not going anywhere with you," Ulrich called back.

Wendy pursed her lips. "And you speak for everyone, do you?"

"He doesn't have to," Ace said. "You're not getting your filthy hands on Tink again."

"Do you really want to go down this road, Ace?"

"If I have to, I will.." Ace's hands shook at his side, but his voice remained stoic.

Wendy snickered and gave another flourish of her hand like she was trying to put on some sort of show. "I'm here to bargain ... a trade, if you will."

A trade? Did she have one of the Lost Boys? Or worse yet ... Did she have one of my pirates? Nathaniel or Hector maybe? Or perhaps they were simply lurking somewhere in the trees waiting to strike. Though the panic that seeped into my bones believed otherwise.

"What could you have that we'd possibly want?" Ace said.

Wendy's smirk grew as she reached her hand into her pocket and slowly withdrew something. My breath caught in my throat when I saw it—a gold chain with the small serpent trinket attached that I'd given to each of my crew members after a successful mission.

"I had no idea you kept such good-looking pets with you," Wendy purred as she remained focused on me. She twirled the chain around her finger, taunting me with its presence. "If I'd have known, perhaps I'd have taken action sooner."

My knees weakened, but Ulrich caught me before I fell. "Arie, what's wrong?"

I didn't want to tell him. I didn't want it to be true. They had only gone on a perimeter sweep. A thing they were accustomed to when not on the *Betty*. I opened my mouth to speak, but words failed me. She had them. She had Nathaniel or Hector—or both.

Wendy jumped and clapped. "Oh goody, I think the little pirate queen has figured it out. Haven't you, *little dove*?"

Oh *hells* no. Behind me, Pascal shot forward but Ace held him back. Despite how much Pascal thrashed and bucked, he managed to keep him from going any further.

"Oh, there you are wizard. I wondered if you were still in there." Wendy cheered.

The Lost Boys in the trees all drew their bows, arrows at the ready. Wendy *tsked* and shook her head.

"No need for that just yet. Now, I suggest we get to the real fun before I get bored of this game. Shall we?" Wendy snapped her fingers, and the forest around us grew eerily silent. Pascal had stopped his thrashing and the doe-eyed, scared boy returned.

Gasps and murmurs cut over the silence again, and I looked up to a sea of fear-ridden faces. Just then, a deep dread rolled over me. It crawled along my skin, seeping into it until every part of me was stricken with fear. I gulped in breath after breath, but I couldn't get enough.

A low, guttural growl came from behind Wendy, and then another before I withdrew Slayer.

"Arie? What's wrong?" Tink asked.

I gasped as Nathaniel and Hector emerged from the trees. Their hands were tied behind their backs, and blood trickled from Nathaniel's nose, but they seemed otherwise intact. I breathed a sigh of relief but kept my attention on high alert. They weren't out of trouble just yet.

"No!" Frankie cried out from behind me.

"It's okay, Frankie," Nathaniel said with a forced smile.

Panic overwhelmed me as the realization hit. We needed to get everyone out of here alive, and trading Tink wasn't in the cards. Especially now that we were bonded. Without her, we'd be done for—*I'd* be done for, and I wouldn't give up Tink's life even if we weren't bonded.

We needed a distraction. My gaze shifted to the Lost Boys above, taking note of all the assets we had at our disposal.

Just then, dark red eyes caught my own as two Neverbeasts appeared from the trees. Their large teeth snapped at the pirates' backs and ushered them forward. Both creatures let out a high-pitched howl, and I threw my hands over my ears.

"That's quite enough, you two." Wendy patted the one nearest her. "Don't you recognize them, Peter? Perhaps you should take a closer look. I'm sure you missed them while you were gone."

I turned to Pascal, who was fixed on the beasts. How would he recognize one of them? They all look the same—dark, dangerous, and deadly. And with their presence, the whole situation became a lot harder. I could use my mermaid powers on them again, but it had taken me a couple attempts to do it earlier. If I didn't do it in one try, in one quick motion, Wendy could tell them to attack before I even got the words out again.

Wendy clicked her tongue. "Of course, how could you recognize them? Jack, Jaina, say hello."

The entire forest stilled, and time itself ceased to exist. No murmurs sounded from the Lost Boys, and no one dared move. Though something else rose in its place. Blood-curdling rage. It grew thick and tangible in the air, and I fought to breathe. Those Neverbeasts were human? How the hells was that possible? Did that mean all the beasts she had were human? The ones she was supposed to have killed?

Gooseflesh slid down my arms and legs as I peered at the beasts. Their fiery-red eyes, large snouts, and elongated teeth. Long dark fur and paws larger than my hands. Underneath all that was an innocent person forced to do Wendy's bidding.

Pascal's hands balled into fists at his side, and I saw the muscles in his jaw clench. "You can't expect us to believe you didn't kill the twins."

"Oh, come on. I'm not that much of a monster. Killing all those boys and girls would have been a lot of fun, torturing them sure was, but now, seeing the looks on everyone's face? This is *so* much better." Wendy clapped her hands together and bounced on her feet.

Whatever Wendy's intentions were, I knew she wouldn't let this play out much longer. We didn't have time to come up with a well-calculated plan, but I had to do something.

I turned to Ulrich. "Keep her distracted. I'm going to try

something and—"

"Absolutely not," Ulrich whispered and grabbed my arm. "You have no idea what you're up against or how many beasts she has in those trees."

I yanked my arm free, and anger replaced my fear in waves. Who was he to tell me what I couldn't do? What if it were Clayton or Smith who were staring back at him. What if it were me? My gut wrenched at the thought of Ulrich kneeling there with fangs at his throat. I swallowed down the thought. I couldn't just sit back and watch Wendy hurt my men. There had to be a way. I glanced up into the trees at the Lost Boys and then back to Ulrich and Ace. They were the distraction I needed. A plan formulated in my mind, one that wouldn't take much effort to enact so long as everyone did their jobs.

"So, what will it be, then?" Wendy called out. "A couple of pirates for a fairy? Seems to be a good trade to me."

"I can get them both free and put a stop to this now," I whispered.

I looked at Hector and Nathaniel who were staring straight at me. Nathaniel gave me a subtle shake of his head, and Hector mouthed 'don't do it.'

"How about you just let them go and we forget about this," I snapped back. "Or I can kill you right here and now and be done with you."

Wendy laughed. "Your intimidation tactics are sweet, but unfortunately, I need the fairy. So, you can see my conundrum. Hand over Tinkerbell and the pirates will be"—she glanced at Nathaniel and then Hector—"unharmed any more than they may be right now."

"Ulrich, I have a plan, we just need to—"

"No. You can't do this alone or you'll die right along with them.

I won't let you."

Lucky for me, I wasn't his to bark orders to.

"You won't *let* me? I'm not yours, Ulrich. I don't belong to you, or to anyone for that matter. I'm going to save my men at any cost to me." My jaw clenched as I fought to keep down the need to punch him in his scruffy jaw. A flicker of something flashed in his eyes, but I didn't care. Whatever feelings I had for the pirate didn't matter. He was crossing a line.

I stepped forward, ready to do whatever necessary when Pascal stepped into my view.

"Take me instead."

Gasps sounded from the treetops as the Lost Boys looked at their undying leader, the man who had once fought Wendy and been shattered in the aftermath. He wouldn't survive another round of Wendy's wrath.

Pascal stood with his shoulders back and head held high, something I hadn't seen since … since the wizard was in control.

"Oh, Peter," Wendy interrupted. "We've already played that game."

"Then how about a pirate queen?" I stepped forward until I was blocking Pascal from Wendy. "Whatever you need with a fairy can surely be done with a—"

"Arie, no!" Bells rang out as Tink fluttered to me, but I kept my focus on Wendy. I wasn't about to hand myself over, but perhaps I could use this to my advantage.

"Let me try this one more time." Wendy's teeth were clenched together as she growled each word from between them. Her patience frayed as she continued. "I don't *want* Pascal, and I certainly don't want the pirate queen—the Mistress wouldn't be pleased."

So she was working for someone. Ursa had said I'd never stop ... someone ... and while at first, I'd thought that to be Wendy, she was too chaotic to come up with this by herself. What was I missing? A mysterious mistress without a name. A name I'd find out soon enough. Perhaps this was the same person who'd orchestrated my fathers' deaths. Once again, I was standing here with far too many questions and little to no answers.

Wendy stepped forward, her eyes suddenly much colder and darker than before. She withdrew a small dagger from the inside of her leather boot; the metal of the blade glinted in the light. Her knuckles went white as she tightened her grip around its handle and placed it against Hector's throat.

"Perhaps a demonstration is in order to prove just how serious I am."

My heart thumped, its beat matching the blood pounding in my ears. Hector struggled against Wendy's hold, but one of the beasts charged forward and clamped his teeth around his arm. Hector cried out as the beast's teeth punctured his skin. Blood oozed from the wound and dripped on the forest floor.

"No!" Frankie let out a guttural scream. I turned to her, but she wasn't looking at either of them. Instead her gaze locked with mine. "Are you really going to allow this to happen? Over a fairy?"

"Over a fairy your sister is bonded to," Ace hissed. "Or did you forget that? If Wendy takes Tink, your sister could die," His voice was low enough to not attract Wendy's attention.

"Okay we'll do either of you two have a plan, then?" Frankie gritted her teeth, and tears continued to stream down her face.

Enough of this charade. My jaw clenched, and every bit of me ached with the need to drive Slayer through Wendy's cold, black heart. I'd survived a Neverbeast before, hadn't I? Fuck what Ulrich thought—I would end this now.

I lunged, but a pair of hands wrapped around my arms.

"Arie, stop this. I can't let you do this. You'll die." Ulrich's words in my ear sent rage coursing through me.

"Let me go, damnit."

Our eyes locked, a muscle ticked in his jaw at our obvious standoff, but I wasn't going to budge.

Wendy shook her head and tapped a finger to her temple. "You know what, I tire of this game."

A second was all I'd been given before more beasts appeared through the trees, and a hush rolled over the forest. My gaze flickered between them until landing back on Wendy.

"Don't do this, Wendy," Pascal pleaded.

Wendy gave an exasperated sigh and lowered herself until her lips pressed against Hector's ear. Her lips moved but only Hector could hear her words. His features darkened for a moment showing nothing of the fear I knew was lingering behind his need to stay strong.

Nathaniel thrashed against his restraints until the beast behind him growled a warning.

"Please, Wendy." My voice cracked at my plea. "My men have done nothing to harm you."

Wendy's words turned to venom. "Nothing to harm me? Pirates harm everything they touch."

"Just as you do," Ace bit out.

"I do what I need to do to survive. You all don't even begin to understand the sacrifices I have made!" Wendy roared. "I tire of this charade."

Hector had no time to react as Wendy sliced the dagger across his throat, leaving a deep, long gash. Blood sprayed into the air, painting the surrounding foliage crimson. A strangled gasp escaped Hector's lips as he crumbled to the ground, clutching his throat.

"No!" I shrieked, hot tears coursing down my face. With every ounce of strength I had left, I fought against Ulrich's iron grip. He easily overpowered me as he tried to talk to me but I stumbled to the ground, sobbing uncontrollably. My legs were shaking, no longer able to bear my weight as I finally wrenched myself free from Ulrich's hold.

Nathanial tried to scramble to Hector, but his restraints only caused him to fall hard into the dirt. His agonizing cries tore through the night sky, and my heartbreak only intensified.

Dark furry blurs flew past me, and shouts rang in my ear, but I was lost, far too gone in my own agony to see the chaos erupting around me. Someone screamed my name—Frankie perhaps? I couldn't be sure.

I looked up to Hector's lifeless body. Memories of my fathers flooded my mind, their faces contorted in anguish, and I realized that I had failed Hector the same way I'd failed them. I was too consumed in my own world to be there in time. I'd been out with Ulrich, flirting and relaxing while Nathaniel and Hector had been caught. A hollowness rose in my chest; I had let Hector die, alone and in fear. And just as with my fathers, I was powerless to save him. I was forced to watch him succumb to his fate, unable to do anything but weep and regret.

Moments later, Wendy's piercing whistle pulled me from my agony, and I watched in horror as her beasts retreated from the treehouse. I looked around as Lost Boys cried out in pain. Blood coating their tunics and others holding on to their friends as they lay unconscious. Bodies of a few Neverbeasts lay on the ground, but not enough to put a dent in the number I'd seen in the trees earlier. Nathaniel roared in anger as he was wrenched away from Hector's body by one of the beasts. He kicked and bucked until Wendy skipped over to him. She pressed a finger to his forehead, and his body went limp.

"You have one more chance to hand over the fairy, Pirate Queen. Or my beasts will have a yummy pirate snack for dinner."

Wendy, Nathaniel, and her beasts disappeared beyond the trees, and I launched myself up onto my feet and sprinted after her. Shouts were drowned out by the sound of my pounding feet and the blood thumping in my ears. All I saw was red as I chased after her.

She wasn't getting away. She wasn't going to get away with what she'd done. Wendy was a dead woman running, and not even her beasts could stop me from her.

Laughter rang out, and I ran in its direction, putting every last bit of my energy into tracking her down. Not skipping a beat, I gripped hold of Slayer, and the leather in my grasp vibrated with the need to taste the killer's blood. After I was done with her there'd be nothing left. Nothing but the memory of what she'd done, of the people she killed and the evil she inflicted on the world. At the thought of Wendy's death, my lips tugged into a thin line and I ran harder, faster.

My throat burned, and I tasted a hint of bile on my tongue. The brush grew thicker around me, and the trees became a blur, but I refused to slow down.

"I swear to the gods I will kill you for what you've done, Wendy. You can't run from me."

Another laugh rang out. "Who said anything about running?"

"If you're not running then face me. Or are you a coward?"

Wendy stepped out from behind a tree. Fire practically danced in her eyes as I came to a stumbling halt. "No one calls me a coward. No one who wants to live anyway."

"I'm pretty sure that's what I just did."

I was being an idiot, I knew that, but a part of me couldn't care at that moment. All I saw was Hector's lifeless body as his best friend mourned with cries of pain and despair. I didn't care if I pissed off the witch. I had to kill her and get Nathaniel back. That's all that mattered.

"I'm going to pretend this little encounter didn't happen for the sake of your … unfortunate loss. But, say that to me one more time, and you'll never see Nathaniel again." Wendy snarled before waving. "Ta-ta, Pirate Queen."

I stepped forward, intent on following Wendy, when a loud roar chilled me to the bone. A towering, savage creature, its long fur matted with blood, leaped out of the darkness. I recoiled in terror and watched Wendy run away, her laughter trailing after her into the night. The beast reared back and lunged for me, but I dodged out of its way. It turned to face me again and snarled, revealing gleaming fangs that dripped saliva.

This beast was a person, a human being who was someone's son or daughter. A poor cursed soul destined to be controlled by Wendy.

So how was it my magic worked on a cursed human? I'd spoken to creatures and had the ability to manipulate the seas and skies, but this was an entirely different level of magic.

I recalled what I'd done in the cave and shouted as loudly as I could. "Stop!"

The beast paused in mid-lunge, its eyes wide and unblinking. In their depths, I saw the same flecks of gold that had shimmered in Chimera's eyes before it attacked Ulrich.

We stood that way for a while, staring at one another until a strange fog descended on my mind.

Come closer.

A chill ran through me as I whirled around, but there was no one there. I shook my head, trying to clear the fog and willed myself to focus.

I know what you are. We can help one another. Come closer.

Was the Neverbeast speaking to me?

The beast shook itself, its tail tucked and ears back in a harmless gesture, but I knew better.

I held up my hand, ready to say stop again, when voices rang out around me.

"Arie, where are you?"

Ulrich.

Before I could answer, the hulking creature launched itself forward with astonishing speed. The sheer force of its weight pinned me to the ground, and its sharp claws dug into my arms. I tried to cry out, but all that escaped was a muffled whimper.

The air grew heavy, and the world around me quieted. The beast's eyes bore into mine as if it was trying to search deep within my soul. I stared back, and for a split second, I could have sworn I saw something—a glimpse of recognition—in its depths, but it was gone before I could be sure.

"What the hell?" My voice shook with fear, and I struggled against the beast's grip. If I could just get to Slayer—

The beast lowered its head and snarled. Its hot breath brushed against my face, making me shudder. Tension hung in the air as it sniffed the space between us, and its lips curled back.

The beast let out a growl. *You smell like her, but you don't look like her.* Its voice was low and rough in my mind. *You're her daughter, aren't you?*

"What?" I asked.

"Arie!" Ulrich called out again.

Dappled light from the canopy of trees illuminated the clearing. Two figures emerged from the bushes and stopped short when they saw us. Ulrich's brown eyes were wide with fear, and Frankie stood close, her freckled face pale, but gave no sign of how she was feeling.

A deep, menacing growl reverberated through the trees as the beast bared its sharp fangs. Before it could strike, a third figure emerged from the shadows, wielding some sort of weapon. They aimed and fired, sending a dart soaring through the air until it landed in the beast's side. The creature yelped and staggered briefly before toppling onto its side.

"Don't worry it's only asleep," Ace said, brushing dirt off his pants as he approached us. "But we need to get her back to the treehouse before she wakes up."

"She?" I asked.

Ace nodded solemnly. "That's the Maiden."

X. THE MAIDEN

Arie

"HE DESERVES A PROPER BURIAL," I FORCED MYSELF to whisper, and refused to look at Hector as it was laid out behind me covered with a single sheet. Everything was so wrong. Death seemed to follow me no matter where I went or what I did and nothing I did seemed to matter anymore.

The hurt and pain in my heart escalated from a dull throb to burning, glaring pain at the knowledge that I would never hear his laugh or see his joyful smile again. No matter how much I wanted to.

And Nathaniel was still out there.

Ace nodded. "He'll be buried with respect and—"

I whirled around, anger rippling through me. "I said he needs a *proper* burial."

Ace put his hands up and nodded. "All right, all right."

I inhaled, trying to keep my anger at bay. This wasn't Ace's fault, and yet I found myself wanting to blame him and everyone else for what happened—especially me. I looked up at Ulrich, standing before the open window with tense shoulders. He had refused to listen to me, and if he had, maybe Hector would still be alive. The guilt of not being able to save Hector weighed heavily on me. I should have done something. I could have saved him if Ulrich had just trusted me to do what I do best.

Gritting my teeth, I forced myself to look away and back to the table. To someone who wouldn't make me want to scream every time I saw them.

Ace and Tink sat together, the two of them visibly shaken. Ace had taken it upon himself to work out a patrolling system with the rest of the Lost Boys, but I knew it wasn't necessary. Wendy wouldn't come back. Not after what happened. Not when she had Nathaniel. She wanted us to go to her. But why?

I'd wanted to ask Pascal but I hadn't seen him since our return. He'd mumbled to himself, something inaudible, before he had slipped past everyone and made his way up the winding staircase to his bedroom and hadn't emerged since.

"We need to—" I started to say when Frankie burst into the war room, her eyes red-rimmed and puffy.

"What we need to do is get Nathaniel back," she said with determination.

Ulrich turned around and fixed her with a piercing glare. "No one's going anywhere. Now that Wendy has Pascal's shadow it's far too dangerous. If we want to get Nathaniel back, we need to be smart."

I scoffed and stepped forward, my voice filled with indignation. "You don't get to tell her what to do. Nor do you get to tell us what's too dangerous." I shifted my gaze to Frankie, my expression softening. "We are going to need help if we're going to save him. We need our men."

"We almost have enough fairy dust to get them all here," Tink sniffed. "Should be good to go as soon as the sun comes up. May want to get some rest in the meantime."

Rest. Just the sound of the word was enticing. My entire body groaned and ached with every move. I could barely keep my eyes open and my knees from buckling beneath me. My stomach growled, and I desperately needed to bathe.

The thought of Nathaniel and what Wendy could be doing to him flooded my mind. Nathaniel was a strong and able man. He could handle himself, but against Wendy and her beasts I wasn't so sure.

"You want to sleep when he's out there probably being tortured … or cursed?" Frankie threw her hands up. "Unbelievable."

"Frankie." I stalked over to her and placed my hands on her shoulders. "I don't want to sit back and wait, but we're exhausted and outnumbered. We need to get the crew here and think this through logically. Nathaniel can handle his own. Trust me."

"Logical thinking," Ulrich huffed. "And you thought trying to take on Wendy and her beasts alone was logical too?"

I ignored Ulrich and tried to bring my baby sister close but she shrugged off my comfort. Her glare in my direction sent a thousand knives tearing through me.

"Don't touch me. You should have done something." She hissed then walked over to Ace.

She blamed me. Of course she did. So did I.

She had thought of him as a brother and a teacher, so it was no surprise that his death had been harder on her than most. But he'd also been one of my best friends. A true confidant. His death felt like Victor's and Malakai's passing all over again, and now Hector's vacant stare and shocked expression would be etched into the back of my mind just as my fathers were.

"We do need to talk about what we're going to do about the beast," Ace said as wrapped his arms around Frankie. "That room isn't made to hold the Maiden if she wakes up and wants out."

"I don't understand why we're keeping her here at all." Ulrich stalked to the table to join us. "She's one of Wendy's beasts who, at any given moment, will strike."

"But it could be someone we know. You heard her, those beasts by her side were Jack and Jaina—"

Ulrich laughed. "You believe her? Come on, Ace, she's a liar."

I understood his words, but I was far too angry to agree with him. We'd spent years fighting monsters, but I wasn't so sure the Maiden was one. She'd spoken to me. I'd been able to command sea life, speak to them in their minds and ask for their aid. But never had one talked back to me.

She knew Ursa. Or at least, she knew I was her daughter. How was that possible? Had Ursa been to Neverland? I'd considered she was working with Wendy before—and still did after her charade about curses. Perhaps that was how the Maiden knew my mother. Though the beast's words had sounded surprised to see me, it seemed she had known me too, or at least knew of me.

Either way, if I didn't get my ass to bed, I was going to fall asleep right here on the war room table.

"Ace, how long will the sleeping effects last for?" I asked.

"A few hours longer. I can have Pibbs and Chuckles hit her again if she wakes up before then."

"Good. It'll do us all some good to get some rest. We'll get together in a few hours and figure out what's next."

Ace, Tink, and Frankie made their exit. I rose from my chair to do the same when Ulrich's hand wrapped around my arm.

"Arie, can we talk?"

I ripped my arm from his grip. "I need to rest. I suggest you do the same."

Hurt washed over him, but I didn't have the energy to care, nor the want to care. I was far too tired, far too angry. He'd prevented me from saving Hector.

I wasn't sure I would ever be able to forgive him for that.

A soft knock sounded at my door, and I rolled over, pulling the pillow over my head to muffle the sound. The knock came again, louder this time, and I muttered curses under my breath, dreading the possibility that it might be Ulrich.

"What?" I grumbled.

The door creaked open, and a sliver of light spilled into the room. "Is there space here for me?" a small voice asked.

I jolted upright to find Frankie standing in the doorway, her face weighed down by sadness. A tinge of my own grief washed over me as she stood there, just as she did when we were kids. We had been so close for many years before everything changed, and I never thought she'd come to me for comfort again. Especially after the look she'd given me today.

While I was grateful for it, how could I make this moment mean something when all I wanted to do was go back in time? To erase the hurt on her face and the deaths that plagued our dreams. We both stayed silent, not daring to look at one another. Instead, I scooted over, waited for her to climb in, then pulled the covers around us.

I wrapped my arm around her and placed my chin on top of her head. The awkward sleeping position made me uncomfortable, but it was better than being alone. Even though I couldn't bring myself to say it out loud, Frankie's presence was calming me down just as much as it was for her.

The gentle beat of her heart against my chest and the sound of her soft breathing gradually lulled me into a peaceful drowsiness.

That was until she spoke, and I felt the coldness of reality seep into my veins.

"I keep seeing him when I close my eyes."

Her voice trembled, and I knew that all the pain she had been suppressing had finally been unleashed. She sobbed under my weight, and I fought to keep my own voice steady.

I sighed heavily, knowing all too well what images plagued her mind. "I do too."

"A part of me wants to blame you for what happened to him."

I swallowed the lump in my throat. "You'd have every right to be mad at me."

She shook her head. "Wendy would have killed one of them before any of us could have done something. I think we both know that."

My little sister, the voice of reason.

"We have to avenge him." Frankie's voice cracked.

"And we will. I promise."

"I know I'm probably far too old to be getting consoled by you, but—"

"No matter how *old* we may be, I am always here for you." I promised her a long time ago that I'd always be there. And when it mattered most, I had left her to fulfill my own vengeance. I had forgotten my promise, my commitment to her, and instead abandoned her to hunt and kill for longer than I planned.

When I assured her I'd come back, it was with the intention of being gone for mere months at most, yet here we were with so much time having passed, so much so that she had to track me down, an endeavor that almost got her killed.

From this moment, having her wrapped in my arms, I knew I would never break another promise to her if it was the last thing I ever did. We would get Nathaniel back, we would stop Wendy, and after that nothing would keep me from finding out the truth about Viktor and Malakai.

Frankie didn't say anything else, and with that I and hoped we would both have a dreamless sleep.

Morning came far too quickly. The sun seeped in through the window, casting the room in a faint glow. I rubbed my still-sleepy eyes and sat up.

Frankie's soft snores brought a smile to my face. Without making too much noise, I rolled out of bed, threw on a new shirt and pants, and stuffed Slayer in its home at my side before making my way downstairs.

To my delight, everyone was either still asleep or on patrol, which gave me time to have a little one on one conversation with the Maiden.

No one would have believed me had I told them a Neverbeast had spoken to me. Maybe Ulrich would have, but I was in no mood nor had any desire to speak to him. Pascal would, but I had a rising suspicion he wouldn't be seen for a while. Not just because of the sun, but because of the Neverbeast.

That scar on Pascal's face had to have come from one of them— the fear in his face when Wendy arrived and they appeared, the way he simply froze and shook in their presence. Though for a second, when he'd offered himself up, I thought I'd spotted something off in Pascal's face. Something that appeared more akin to the wizard than the one previously known as Peter.

I put a cork in that and bottled it for later. If he wanted to talk about it, he would in his own time. Right now, I needed to figure out what this Neverbeast knew about my mother, and perhaps with Slayer's help, I could find out which Neverbeast sank its bloody teeth into my friend.

The room where the Maiden was being held was guarded by a

sleeping Chuckles. Drool slid down his chin, and his loud snores were enough to wake up the entire treehouse had it not been for the fact he was in an entirely different wing.

I still didn't understand how a tree could have different wings and corridors.

Sliding the keys from Chuckles's pocket took far more concentration than I hoped for. I slid a hand into his lap and he shifted. I froze but slipped the keys from him before he woke. I unlocked the door and walked into the room.

The room was dark, only illuminated by a small lantern on the opposite side. I cleared my throat and withdrew Slayer.

You don't need that. I have no intention of hurting you. Yet.

The Maiden's voice cut through the silence and I cleared my throat.

"And why is that exactly?" I asked and took another step into the room as I searched for the beast. I hadn't any idea how big the room was, or what else could be lurking in its depths, so I remained as close to the light, and the door, as I could.

I have my reasons. Unless you came here to finish the job your mother never did?

"What are you talking about?"

Your mother is the reason I'm a beast. Your mother is the reason I'm stuck in this place when I need to be back with ... my people.

"I'm not sure I'm following, but rest assured, you don't have to worry about my mother."

She only had to worry about me.

Bright red eyes appeared in the darkness as the beast stepped closer.

And why is that?

"Because I killed her."

A deep, throaty laugh assaulted my mind, and I winced. I wasn't sure how killing my own mother was funny, but I didn't question it. My mother was a true evil that had plagued the seas with her wretchedness for far too long. It was a good thing she was dead.

Oh, that's the best thing I've heard in a long time. And you, little mermaid, what are your intentions?

Why in sea's sake did she want to know anything about me? And how did she know I was a mermaid? Had my mother told her about me? Hells, did that mean Wendy knew about me?

It didn't matter. She'd been there in the forest. She may have not been the beast who killed Hector but I had no qualms with taking it out on this one.

"I want justice for Hector. For my fathers. And for those Wendy has tortured and killed."

The Maiden stepped forward until her entire frame melted from the shadow, and her formidable size became even more evident. Her head reached my shoulders, and her thick black fur made her appear even larger. Her legs were muscular and strong like they were carved out of marble. I wouldn't have been surprised if one swipe of her paw could have snapped my neck.

Every single person Dee has encountered has been wronged by her. She's evil at her core. But, if you killed your own mother, I suppose killing Wendy would be a piece of cake in comparison.

Ursa's Leviathan shape flooded my mind. Long tentacles and big beady eyes. Wendy was a child compared to Ursa.

"Dee?"

Er ... yes, it's a nickname Wendy gave herself, but that's not important. I'll tell you what. You help me with a little something and I'll tell you everything you need to know about Wendy. How to get into her fortress, where your pirate is surely being kept, how to strike her where it hurts. All of it.

Temptation and curiosity caught me in its grasp. I wanted to know whatever I could to gain leverage over that murderous wench, and having a Neverbeast in my debt could prove useful. And if it didn't work, I'd just kill her.

"Why would I do any of that after what one of your kind did?"

You think we have a choice? You think any of us want to help Wendy? We want her dead just as much as you do. But our bond to her keeps that from happening.

"What do you want me to do?" I'd given myself up far more than I'd wanted to recently. In order to save people I cared about I would willingly do it again. Even if it meant helping this beast.

Break the binds that tie me to Wendy.

Was that possible? I'd never broken a curse before—

The curse can never be broken, but the binds that tie me to her and to this body can be broken by a mermaid. Now will you help me?

The last of her words were sharp and packed with pain. How long had this poor woman been trapped in this beast form? Was she another one of the Lost Girls?

"Why should I trust you?"

You shouldn't. You shouldn't trust anyone. That way no one can ever hurt you.

Sorrow laced her words, and as much as I wanted to agree with her considering what Ulrich had done, I couldn't. The men on my crew, my sister, I even trusted Pascal. And wasn't that something? People could be trusted, you just had to have the ability to tell the difference between the two.

"How does this work exactly? I'm not going to have to bind you to me, am I?"

You can take the bonds if that is what you want, but just know that if I ever find another mermaid to sever the bond between us, I'd find you and kill you.

The Maiden took a step forward, and I pointed my dagger at her, waiting for any sudden movement.

Put that damn thing away. I already told you I wouldn't harm you.

"You also said not to trust anyone, and you just threatened my life."

She laughed. *True enough. I promise to keep my teeth in my mouth. But for the bonds to be severed, we need to be in close proximity. You'll have to touch me.*

I swallowed and nodded. That made sense, but I wasn't putting Slayer away. When my father, King Rylan, had opened my mermaid half, I'd taken the trident in my hands and in a matter of seconds the magic coursed through me and tore down the barrier keeping it closed off.

I nodded, lowered Slayer, and allowed her to come closer.

Her dark fur swayed, and her claws clicked against the hardwood. She reached out to me, her head lowered, and I slipped my fingers in her fur. I hesitated for only a moment before the power surged through me. A waterfall of energy that shot through my veins and connected us both.

The Maiden relaxed against my hand, and heat rose between us. It rolled over my skin, cascading over every inch of my body until it was all I could feel. Warmth and power.

What are you doing? the Maiden hissed. *If you don't calm down, you're going to kill us both. Don't you know how your own magic works?*

I pulled my hand away, and the power dissipated, leaving me gasping for breath.

"Whoa."

Are you stupid? Weren't you taught how to manipulate your magic?

I raised a brow. "A witch's magic can't be manipulated."

That much I knew for certain. I'd spent years trying to work on my power and never once could I do anything more than what it wanted me to. The sea and sky were always there, always a dominant force. All I had to do was wield it.

For sea's sake, not your witch half. You're supposed to use your mermaid magic. Shut off the witchy stuff and open the other. Your mother did it just fine. Did she not teach you anything?

I laughed. "The only thing she taught me was how terrible of a person she was. She collected thousands of souls, consumed them, and created a monster in the process."

Why was I telling her all of this?

Interesting. So did you know her at all?

I shook my head. "I was raised by my fathers. Malakai and Viktor—"

Wait, who?

"Malakai and Viktor of Bellavier."

Holy hells, this is something. You were raised by Malakonius and Vikterian? This changes everything. Look, all you need to do is—

"You knew them? You ... Do you know who killed them?"

The question came before I had a chance to stop myself. She knew them. Finally, someone with real possible connections. For the first time since leaving my home, I felt real honest hope, hope that maybe not all was lost, that I could finally figure out more than just the bare bones of what I'd found in my travels. Which was nothing besides who they really were.

I knew them well. They were good men, and I wasn't sure I'd ever seen love like theirs before. I'm sorry for your loss. Unfortunately, I don't know much about what happened. I was already Wendy's prisoner when they died. But I have my suspicions. And I know you want to pry and ask me more, but right now we need to break these bonds before Wendy realizes I haven't returned, before she calls me back to her.

I didn't want to let this go. I wanted to point Slayer at her and demand she spill everything she knew and only then would I help her. But she was still a Neverbeast, and I wasn't sure I was up for the challenge right then. Not when she held possible answers I'd been seeking for far too long.

"Fine. We do this, but then once we're done with Wendy, you'll tell me about those suspicions?"

The Maiden nodded. *I will. Now let's break these bonds.*

"Okay, but I'd rather not kill us in the process."

Right. You need to compartmentalize the two magics. Close your eyes and focus on the part of you that matters right now.

Why was it always the need to focus?

Doing as she asked, I inhaled and felt the Maiden's warmth fill me again as her fur curled around my fingers.

Rain pounded in my head, thunder roared in the distance, and the smell of brine consumed my nostrils.

Focus.

I steeled myself against the oncoming storm and focused my sights on the mission. I opened my eyes to find that I was no longer inside the treehouse. A grassy hill stood between two large granite boulders. Perched on top of the hill was a golden trident beaming with power and light. Instinct took hold as it pulled me closer. I hiked up the steep incline and reached out for my destination.

Suddenly, an inky blackness consumed my vision, and terror ripped through me, causing me to cry out and clutch my chest.

I faintly heard the Maiden's voice in my mind.

This is the curse. You must cut the bonds. That darkness isn't real.

Right. The darkness wasn't real.

Drawing on my inner strength, I grabbed hold of the darkness that covered me and ripped it away, shred after shred until I stood in front of the trident once more.

With a newfound vigor, I plucked it from between the rocks as if it were a delicate flower fully bloomed; a beacon of light illuminated the surrounding area.

Power surged through me, and I heard her command.

Good. Now find the binds and cut them.

But looking around, there was nothing but wide-open space.

"Where are they? I can't see them."

Bring the trident to you.

Doing as she asked, the light of the trident enveloped me in its warm glow.

Focus on the trident's magic, the same magic that flows through you. Do you feel the warmth?

I nodded, and before she could explain more, I felt it. Warm air wrapped around me.

I didn't have to look far. I followed the trail to the strands of silver. As I stepped closer, the darkness revealed itself—threads of black and silver that stretched out in every direction.

Hesitantly, I reached out, not sure where to begin untangling such a complex web. But as soon as my fingers brushed against one thread, it lit up.

The Maiden purred. *Yes, that's it.*

Drawing on my strength, I began to cut the threads with the end of the trident. One by one they snapped apart until finally there was nothing left but a pile of unraveled strings at my feet.

Now open your eyes.

I opened them and was back in the treehouse, standing before one of the most breathtaking women I'd ever seen.

Brown eyes replaced red, and dark beautiful skin sat stark naked in front of me. I couldn't stop myself as my gaze trailed down her frame. Curves that had my lips begging to trail down every inch of them.

It had been far too long since I felt the touch of a woman, or a man for that matter. Far too long indeed.

I cleared my throat. "I'll go get you some clothes."

"No need, I'll be fine."

From one breath to the next, the Maiden shifted back to the beast and then back to human again.

"You can control it now?"

She laughed, bright and warm. "It feels good to be me again, and yes, I can. The binds kept me how Wendy wanted me. The only way I could change is if she allowed it. But now that the bonds are broken, I can do as I please."

"Okay, but you still need to wear clothes. I may enjoy the scenery, but it might startle some of the others."

The Maiden shrugged. "Fine. After you."

"Oh no, nice try." I stripped out of my shirt and handed it over since I still had on a brasier. "Put that on for now. We have a lot more to discuss before I even think about letting you out of here."

"Right. What do you want to know?"

"My fathers—"

Marian shook her head. "Wendy is what's important right now. Once she's taken care of, we can talk more about them. What do you already know about Wendy and what she's doing?"

Reluctantly, I pushed down the questions about my fathers and told her about Tink, about wanting to open the gates, and the very little intel we've had so far.

"Wendy's practically out of fairy dust. She used most of it for her own gain. Fairy dust can be used in many ways. Good or bad. It can heal, transport, create, and even kill. For Wendy, it has done it all."

Fairy dust was a weapon. For sea's fucking sake what else was going to happen or be brought to light? Still, something didn't make sense.

"How did she run out of fairy dust when Tink is able to regenerate her dust?"

"Wendy didn't want to wait for that to happen. For a time, she captured fairies and used them, but then the need for power outweighed that. She grew vengeful and greedy. She still has a few in her midst, but they're far too sickly to do anything."

I thought about the shape Tink was in when we found her. Skin and bone, frail, and barely able to flutter her wings without extreme effort. If this was how Tink looked after being with Wendy for a short amount of time, I couldn't even imagine what had happened to the others who'd been with her for longer. Bile rose in the back of my throat.

"That's why she wants Tink back?"

"That, and Tink is the mother of all fairies. She's the first one created by Pan. When Wendy found that out, thanks to torturing another fairy, she knew she had everything she needed with Tink. It took her a long time to get her, and when she did …"

The Maiden's words trailed off, and she wrapped her arms around herself. "She will go to whatever lengths she can to get Tink back. Including killing and torturing your people. All your people."

My eyes widened.

The *Black Betty*.

"She knows more of my people are here?"

"I overheard the conversation she had with Chimera—the only beast of hers she allows to be in their human form. She said something about a shadow and how *he* was going to fall right into her trap. And later she said something about how the pirates don't stand a chance."

She stole Pascal's shadow *and* had time to plan a trap. A gut-wrenching realization hit me square in the stomach. "When was this?"

"A few days before your arrival I guess."

How was that possible? Had Wendy known we were coming?

No one else besides those on my ship and King Rylan knew we were headed to Neverland. *Hells*, had someone betrayed us? Wendy knew far too much, and none of this made sense. What would she gain from having Pascal's shadow other than using his face against him? Once again, I had far too many questions and not enough answers. That seemed to be a pattern I was quickly getting irritated over.

"My crew is back on my ship. Wendy won't be able to get to them."

"With Chimera she can. You're not the only sea witch in the world, little mermaid. Chimera is one of the best I've ever seen."

Another sea witch? Hells-fucking-tastic. Was Chimera why I was unable to stop the storm? That would make sense as to why it stopped the second Wendy got what she wanted. I needed a drink and to get back to the *Betty* before I lost everything.

"What's her end game?"

"Her end game is whatever her mistress says it is. Everything she does is by the grace of her mistress. Pascal wasn't contacted by Wendy's mother; Wendy killed both of her parents after the abuse and torture inflicted on her as a child. The Mistress brought her on as an apprentice, used and brainwashed her into the chaotic person she is now. It was the Mistress who really saved her."

"How do you know all of this?"

"I spent many years as Wendy's *pet*. She's a talker. Unfortunately, Wendy played with my memory, and I don't remember who the Mistress is, or a lot about my past for that matter." The Maiden paused. "Wendy knows how to pick and choose the things she wants you to remember and those she deems worthy of forgetting. All I know is she's determined to get to the Celestial Plains, and it's not good if she succeeds."

Muffled voices sounded from behind the door, and I whipped around just as Ace and Chuckles barged through.

"What the hell is going ... who is that and where's your shirt, Arie?" Ace asked.

I looked down and shrugged. "She needed it more, and it's the Maiden."

"My name is actually Marian."

"Where's the beast?" Chuckles said as he searched the room.

"I am the beast," Marian snapped. "And you'd be wise not to call me that again."

"Look, there's time to explain later," I said. "Right now we need to get Tink and get my men on the island before Wendy gets to them first. I'm not losing any more of my crew. Now, if you don't mind, Marian and I are going to get dressed."

"There's something you need to see first." Ace rubbed a hand on the back of his neck, refusing to meet my gaze. "And here, take this." He threw his shirt over his head and tossed it to me.

"What is it?" I asked as I worked my way into his shirt.

Chuckles peered around Ace. "You're going to want to see this for yourself."

XI. TIGER LILY

Pascal

IT WASN'T SUPPOSED TO BE LIKE THIS.

I thought getting my memories and my soul back would allow me to be stronger, to come back to Neverland and face Wendy. Instead, since the moment we arrived in Neverland, I'd been a blubbering mess. A mess that didn't stand a chance against her. Seeing her had brought back suppressed memories and a fear I hadn't felt since the second she took Taigra from me.

I was weak, and in doing so I'd done the only thing I thought possible. Perhaps it was the wrong move.

"Are you saying you want control back?" the wizard asked, seemingly unfazed by the situation as he took another bite from his chicken leg.

I'd given my other half control over our mind when Wendy had shown up, seeing her had broken me all over again and I couldn't face her. I didn't want to face anyone right then. I thought I would have been able to deal with being in her presence and instead, I'd been too stunned to do anything. Just like when I'd seen Taigra's motionless body on the forest floor. Unable to do anything but grieve.

Flashes of long forgotten memories flooded back until the one I hated the most came to the forefront.

The sun's golden rays poured through the canopy of ancient trees, basking me in its warmth. But despite the spectacle before me, I felt a chill deep within. One that I couldn't shake. I knew the Lost Council was wrong; Wendy was my friend. There was no way she was responsible for such a heinous crime.

I remembered bringing her to Neverland—she hadn't needed any fairy dust to be accepted to the island. Neverland had a way of knowing people's true natures, and Wendy had passed with flying colors.

Had I missed something?

If the rumors were true, Neverland would know. I would know.

The forest hummed around me. Birds sang in the trees above, and crickets chirped on the ground below. Leaves rustled, probably from nearby critters, and when I closed my eyes, I begged the forest for guidance.

"Show me what I came here to see. Show me what truth I have been too blind to see."

It answered with deafening silence save for foliage that parted to reveal a widened trail ahead. The sounds of the forest hushed to a dull whisper as I stepped forward.

The clearing came closer and with it I saw someone lying among a field of red and purple flowers. A crimson cloak covered them, possibly shielding them from the beating sun. I stepped closer and kept my feet as light as possible so as not to startle whoever lay beneath the clothing.

I strained to see the swirl of design on the cloak. And then I saw it. The letters 'LB' staring back at me. My hands shook as I raced forward. I ripped away the fabric, and my breath caught in a strangled gasp.

Taigra—my tiger lily—lay motionless, her glossy black hair splayed around her pale face now dull and lifeless. Flecks of dirt and dried blood stained her clothes and muddied her skin. Trembling, I reached out to touch her still form, and a wave of raw pain washed over me. I swallowed down the thick knot in my throat and lifted my chin as I took in the extent of her injuries.

A surge of grief rose as my mind struggled to believe that the person I wanted to spend the rest of my life with was gone. I cradled Taigra's body close to me, desperate for some sign of life as tears streamed down my face. But there was nothing—nothing but this relentless reality that refused to be undone.

This wasn't real. None of this was real.

I closed my eyes and begged the gods to make this nothing more than a dream—a nightmare. But when I opened them, my lily still lay in my arms, cold and dead.

Something in the grass caught my attention. I squinted, trying to make out what it was. Light glinted against silver, and I leaned over to pick it up. A small dagger. Dried blood coated its blade, and I dropped my gaze to the handle. Ornate swirls, decadent markings, and an engraving of 'LB' on the butt end.

I'd given this to Wendy on her first night in Neverland. A scared, lonely girl who wanted her mother. A mother who only wanted what was best for her daughter. I told her it would keep her safe, it would be the first line of defense against any evil that came her way.

"What did she do to you, my love," I crooned as I dipped my head.

I never wanted to believe that Wendy was capable of such evil and yet here it lay before me—the evidence of her treachery undeniable. My heart grew heavy with grief as sorrow threatened to swallow me whole.

I shook the memory away, felt my breath leave my lungs as the pain of losing Taigra assaulted me all over again. When I'd seen Taigra's lifeless form, something had awoken within me. I hadn't gone back to the treehouse, hadn't consulted with the fairies or spoken with the mermaids. I did the only thing my enraged self could do.

I went to the source.

But I'd lost.

Wendy tore me apart in every direction until there was nothing left. And she could still tear me apart with just her presence. I don't know what I'd been thinking. I should have known she'd still affect me in such a way, and yet ... I'd wanted to see her, I'd wanted to see the look on her face when she took her last breath. Because I had planned on killing her. The second I got close enough I was going to do it.

But then my entire body had betrayed me as she'd stood there and laughed and taunted and killed. And now she had my shadow. She had found some way to trick me and take the most valuable piece of me. At any moment she could waltz through the front door and take over everything I hold dear.

So why didn't she? What was holding her back from just taking everything and claiming it as hers?

Would Neverland know the difference?

"So, what are you going to do about it?"

Me? I will do nothing because I am nothing. I'm useless. But you, you can do something. You can stop her.

"Is that why you let me take control?"

Because the other part of me, the part that had been under the king's rule, had been ruthless. The wizard killed, tortured, and did it all without remorse. I needed that. Neverland needed that.

We couldn't allow anyone else I cared for to die.

Hector's face flooded into my mind, and then Taigra's. A face I thought I'd never remember. Dark silky skin with a glow like the moon. Big dark eyes full of adventure. My chest ached with her loss, and for the man who I'd started to call friend.

You have to do what needs to be done. No matter what it takes.

"Are you sure? Because if you're not sure—"

Just get it done, I thought, before relinquishing all control to the darker, twisted side of my broken soul.

XII. SHIPWRECKED

Arie

PASCAL WAS SITTING UPRIGHT IN HIS BED, A TRAY OF food spread around him as he stuffed his face with whatever he could. Biscuits, chicken, mead, berries, and potatoes. Only the dim light from a couple of candles allowed me to see his face. To see the intensity in it. He looked over at me, a crooked smile on his face, and raised a chicken leg into the air.

"Little dove! I was wondering when I was going to see you. Care for some chicken?"

Apparently this was what Ace wanted me to see. There was a hollowness in Pascal's eyes, a shift in what I'd seen since he got his memories back. I'd seen it when Wendy appeared, only for a fraction of a second, but it was there. And here it was again. A part of me didn't want to believe this was happening, that Pascal had gone back to the state he was in as King Roland's wizard.

"I know what you're thinking, and don't worry. Peter is fine—he's tucked away and will stay that way until he can learn to control himself better. Poor lad, his noodle isn't ticking on all waves."

"Peter is fine? What in seven seas are you talking about?"

Pascal spoke through a mouth full of food. "Would you rather me call me Pascal? Though I suppose calling me Peter when Peter wants to be called Pascal makes sense. Though talking about myself in such a way seems rather pointless, don't you think?"

Okay now I was really confused.

"And right, I forgot he didn't tell you about any of this. When you put us back together, which was so kind of you by the way"—he winked before continuing—"it didn't exactly work the way we thought it did. Sure, all the memories are back, and things appear to be a bit clearer. But somehow there are two of us now. One Pascal and one Peter—two minds in one. Only, this is one mind split into two."

"You have got to be kidding me? You're telling me this entire time you've been holding that information back? Why?"

"Peter felt it was necessary. Plus, I wanted to see what happened when this all played out. I just hadn't expected him to lose himself the second Wendy came into the picture. Oh, and did I hear right? You have the Maiden in the treehouse?"

I'd left her in the room and Ace and Chuckles guarding the door. For now, that was the safest option until we could figure out more. I wasn't sure how to explain what I'd done, and until I had a chance to talk with Tink I wanted to leave it all in the dark.

"How did you know?"

"We can sense her. We feel her presence." Pascal leaned his head back against the wall. "She's the one who tortured us, you know. The one who did this." He lifted a finger and trailed it along the scar across his face. "It's not entirely her fault, but Peter isn't going to be able to control himself around her. You can thank Wendy for that."

It appeared I could thank Wendy for a lot of the chaos that had gone on around here.

"Fine. But you stay in this room. I don't need to explain to everyone else why you're suddenly not yourself. Again."

Pascal laughed. "Where do you presume I am to go when the sun is high in the sky, little dove? Though, you could stay with me. I don't mind the company."

I rolled my eyes and shook my head as I closed the door behind me. This was just great. There were far too many problems and not enough solutions or time to deal with them all.

"Are you all right, Arie?" Tink stood down the hall, her small frame illuminating the walls around her. Worry beamed from her.

"I'm fine. Look, we need to get to the *Black Betty* now. They could be in danger."

Tink nodded. "Ulrich and Frankie are already waiting for you in the war room."

Ulrich. Just the sound of his name sent anger rushing through me. I still wasn't too keen on seeing him, or speaking to him for that matter. But he was a skilled pirate, and there were dozens of his men on that ship too.

Just as I expected, there was far more than just Ulrich and Frankie in the war room. Everyone besides Marian and Chuckles were there. I didn't have time to explain every last detail, so I gave them the quick version.

"You're keeping that thing alive?" Viscera snapped and pushed his way to the front of the small crowd. "That thing needs to be put down. Do you know how many of those beasts killed our people?"

"Didn't you hear Wendy?" Pibbs spoke up. "She turned Jack and Jaina into those things. If Arie found a way to save one of them, she can save them all."

I held up my hand. "I'm going to try, but listen. Wendy is out for blood. She's after my people. I'm not asking any of you to risk anything for me and mine, but I have to get them back here. Plus, if we're going to stop Wendy then we need all the help we can get. Including murderous, evil pirate scum."

Viscera's face paled at that last bit. I didn't need to recite his own words to get the point across, but the way he looked between Frankie and myself made it worthwhile.

"How do we know you'll come back?" Teddy asked. "How do we know you won't just get back to your ship and leave us to deal with her?"

Rage surged through me, threatening to burst and lash out at him. I gritted my teeth and clenched my fists, trying to keep a lid on my temper.

"Because I'm a monster hunter. Because I will not stop until she is dead by my hand, her screams ringing in my ears as payment for all the damage she has done." My breath quickened, and my anger worsened with each word. "I will make her bleed and beg for mercy, but even then, mercy will not be mine to give. She has taken innocent lives, tortured innocent souls, and caused so much suffering and pain. It's time someone returned the favor."

"Okay, fine. We believe you and will wait for your return," Doc said as he stroked his beard.

Viscera took a step forward, but Ulrich stepped in front of him and shook his head.

"Arie isn't going to go back on her word."

"Are you sure about that?" Viscera hissed. "It sure seems like she wants to use her dagger on you after Wendy took off. How do you know she won't stick that thing in your back?"

"Arie can be mad at me, she can hate me and even refuse to speak to me, but none of that matters because I know she will do the right thing. I know she will fight until her dying breath. Because that's what Arie does. That's who she is."

A lump formed in my throat, and I fought to swallow. Damn him for defending me. I opened my mouth to tell him just how I felt about it when Frankie's hand rested on mine.

"Not now."

She was mad at him too. I could see it in her eyes. She'd looked at me the same way back in Khan. After years of being apart she resented me and hated me for leaving her behind. At least now that anger was pointed at someone else.

"We can get into this later," I said. "But right now, we have to get to my ship before Wendy does."

I had no idea if Wendy was really after my people or if this was some trap, but I couldn't take the risk. Keenan was a great sailor, but he was out-skilled against a sea witch. One that could possibly be much stronger than even me.

"Tink, are we ready?" I looked down at the fairy, and she nodded. "Good, then let's go. I don't want to waste any more time."

Frankie, Ulrich, Tink, and I stood outside the treehouse. Ace assured me that no one would mess with Marian and that he would check on Pascal from time to time. He'd also ensure that no one would touch Hector's body or bury him without me saying so. Once we got everyone back, we'd give him a proper send off.

Tink flew up and landed on my shoulders. "Arie, now that we are bonded, this is going to feel much different than it did before. Your energy is going to be used just as much as mine when we do this."

I remembered what they'd said about the bond. How it would affect me and that I was stuck with it. So far, Tink had proven she was a valuable ally, and it hadn't hurt me yet. Though I admit I haven't been able to speak through our bond or feel any emotion from her. Perhaps that was what she meant when she said it would take time for it to settle in.

"Stand together and grab onto one another," Tink instructed, her voice gentle yet firm.

We grabbed hold of one another, and I felt a little bubble of trepidation build inside of me. Tink cupped her tiny hands around her mouth and blew glittering dust into the air. It swirled around us, settling on each of our heads as a magical tingle coursed through my veins.

Tink waved her hand in front of us and spoke a single word that must have been the native language I'd heard the Lost Boys speak. Instantly, the air around us began to swirl like mini tornadoes, picking up speed until we were surrounded by a brilliant white light that blocked out everything else around us. A moment later, the light faded away and we stood on board the *Black Betty*.

The sky was clear, but dark gray clouds threatened rain in the distance as I looked across the horizon. Around us men shouted and worked furiously, none of them even registering our return.

Tink fluttered from my shoulders to Ulrich's.

"Keep her safe—I need to figure out what's going on," I said before trailing off to find Keenan. He stood at the bow, barking orders at the crew while trying to keep himself upright.

"Kay!"

He whirled around, and I saw relief wash over him. "Hells, thank the gods you're here. We're under attack!"

Keenan pointed down toward the sea, and something dark and big swam underneath.

"A sea serpent?"

Keenan nodded. "And a gnarly one at that. It just sprung up out of nowhere."

"How did you all get here?" Smith said, his breath coming in rapid succession.

"Smith!" Ulrich shouted and grabbed hold of him.

"Hook, it's good to see—is that a fairy?"

"We can catch up about that later. We need to focus on that serpent first."

Smith nodded and turned to Keenan. "The men are ready, but I'm afraid there isn't enough gun powder to take that thing down."

A sly smile tugged at Keenan's lips. "The captain is back; we'll be fine."

I wasn't so sure about that. Wendy had a sea witch on retainer, and for all I knew it was controlling this monster. I looked around and spotted a group of men gathering at the very end of the ship. An idea suddenly came to me, and I raced in their direction.

"Where's Sanders?" I asked one of the men.

"Below deck. They're working on reinforcements."

"I'll get him," Frankie said and took off.

A sea serpent head the size of a small ship burst from the water and snapped at the *Black Betty*. All men working around the main mast screamed and ran, leaving only us at its mercy. Smith and Keenan held their ground and fired round after round as large bullets ricocheted off the serpent's scales.

"Keep doing that and it'll only piss him off." I pointed at the gunpowder barrels and Keenan grabbed ahold of one.

"Where should I take it?"

"Remember that time near Grimm's Meadow?"

Understanding lit Keenan's face as he barked orders to other men. They wrapped the barrel up with rope and began placing them on both sides of the ship.

I rushed over to Smith and shouted, "We need more powder! Now!"

Smith nodded, and I held onto the mainmast. Ulrich looked at me, pleading with me for something to do. "When I give you the signal, light the fuses and throw them overboard."

Ulrich nodded and took my place by the mainmast as I climbed.

"Are you sure this is a good idea? Tink has enough dust to get us all back."

"Do you want us to be stranded on Neverland?" Losing *Black Betty* meant losing the only means necessary to track down the bastards who killed my parents. The only means to finding the truth and getting back to Atlantis. My men didn't want to live on an island long enough to build a new ship. This was it for us.

A long tentacle shot out of the water, and one of the men blasted it with a cannon. A loud cry erupted in the air around us as the tentacle slipped back into the water.

I peered out into the vast sea, looking for any sign of the sea witch. *There*!

My gaze landed on a small boat with one occupant. It was too far to get a good look, but I saw him. Chimera.

Suddenly clouds moved closer in every direction, casting us in darkness as the men continued to gather what barrels we had left.

"Frankie!" I called out as she and Sanders appeared from below deck. My sister pushed through the crowd until she was within hearing distance. "I need you to take my place and keep things moving."

We'd only ever done this once before—a trick that had almost killed all of us—but it was the only chance we had. When Frankie stood opposite me, I worked quickly to bring her into the fold.

"In case what I do next doesn't work, you will need to tell the boys when to light the fuses and where to throw them. Climb up the mast, and the second you see shadows in the water, give the order."

Frankie narrowed her eyes. "And what will you be doing in the meantime?"

I pointed toward the small boat. "Hopefully, if I can get to him in time, I can stop the connection between the serpent and the Neverbeast, and the serpent will be easier to take down."

Frankie grabbed my arm. "You can't be serious. How are you going to get over there with the serpent in the water?"

"You're just going to have to trust me."

Another tentacle flew out of the water, this time landing hard on the deck as pieces of wood splintered through the air. Yet the men pressed on, each of them working tirelessly to keep the *Betty* afloat.

I looked at my crew, at the men and women who'd been my family. "Follow Frankie's lead, and do not let up until the damn beast is dead!"

"Aye!" Keenan called out and lifted his sword in the air. "And straight on till morning."

The crew burst out in agreement, and I rushed over to the ship's rail. A hand grabbed ahold of me, and I whirled around to find Ulrich and Tink.

A part of me wanted to yell at him, to tell him to let me go and do my job, but then he surprised me with his words.

"Be safe."

I gave a stiff nod before jumping off the boat and into the water.

I sank into my gift, bringing forth the mermaid. Slits formed around my neck, and a tail replaced where my legs were. I gave the *Betty* one last look and prayed the serpent wouldn't come my way. Though I had a rising suspicion it wanted only the *Betty*.

My vision narrowed to a pinpoint, the only thing in focus being the small vessel ahead. Chimera, now a full-fledged man, stood at the bow, arms outstretched and a shockwave of magical energy radiating off him. I swam with urgency until my limbs were burning, determined to reach him before he could cast a spell to stop me. I surged out of the water and collided with Chimera, sending both of us splashing back into the sea. We fought in its depths, swirling and slashing with everything I had.

Until pain seared into my tail and I cried out.

My hand closed around something cold and hard. *Slayer*. Everything stopped as realization slammed into me. He'd used my own knife against me. How the hells had he gotten it? Without hesitation, I pulled it out of my tail and held it up. A wildfire of fury bubbled within me, intensifying my own powers until energy surged through my veins. It pushed away the pain of the wound and allowed me to renew my attack on Chimera.

I surged forward and grabbed him around the throat before slamming him into the side of the boat hard enough that his head cracked against it.

Something grabbed hold of my tail and pulled me away from Chimera. A tentacle wrapped around me and, with Slayer still in my hand, I sliced into the sea serpent and sent it scurrying back to the ship.

I turned back around just in time to see Chimera climbing back on his boat.

Chimera let out a loud roar that pierced my ears, reminding me that there wasn't much time left if I wanted everyone to survive this battle. I had to stop him now or there would be no going back.

"It's too late!" Chimera threw his head back and laughed. I whirled around to find the serpent back at the *Betty* and screams carried from it. I cried out just as something hit me from behind and everything faded to black.

XIII. A KING'S GIFT

Arie

I AWOKE WITH A START.

My head throbbed as I took in my surroundings. Disoriented and confused, I struggled to make sense of this strange place. Water surrounded me. Blue and silver light filtered through the depths, casting an ethereal glow on everything it touched. I blinked, trying to adjust my eyes to the unfamiliar setting.

I was underwater.

The water around me seemed to be held at bay by some kind of dome, and sea life swam past, their fins and tails shimmering in the glowing light.

A woman appeared in the depths. Summoned by some unseen force, her body illuminated in the same bright blue as the water that surrounded us, cascading down her curves with an almost hypnotic grace. Her eyes sparkled with a hint of mystery, and her lips curved into a gentle smile.

I gasped, feeling a mixture of awe and terror as she entered through the dome and recognition hit me.

Kai, the Sea Goddess.

She glided up to me, standing several feet taller, and gracefully knelt. Her hands rested lightly on my shoulder, a touch that was both calming and comforting. I stared up at her, overwhelmed by her beauty. She wore a long, flowing blue dress that spilled out behind her in waves and contrasted well against tanned skin. A delicate glass crown was placed upon her head, each point expertly shaped to resemble a delicate spike that tapered to a point and sparkled.

She smiled at me, and I found myself smiling back. Without warning she stood up, taking my hand in hers as she helped me up and led me around the dome of water. We moved through the depths, the water becoming shallower until we finally arrived at a small island composed of white sand and beautiful rock-like formations. Rocks that had seemed to crystallize into tiny bits of coral.

We sat down on the warm sand. My toes—now bare of boots and socks—dug in, the beads of sand soft between my toes. I basked in the warmth of the sun and listened to the waves lap along the shore. I knew I wasn't supposed to be here. Something was happening, but my mind seemed far too free to care about anything else at this exact moment.

"I thought you'd never come," I admitted.

"I know," Kai said, her honeyed voice rich and beautiful against my ears. "I wanted to come sooner, but I couldn't."

"Couldn't?"

She was a *goddess* for sea's sake. If she wanted to be somewhere, I was sure nothing could stop her.

"I'm not allowed anywhere near Neverland."

"Why not?" I bit my lip at my question, hoping she didn't mind my interrogation.

Kai sighed. "Pan is upset with me. I hurt him. Unintentionally, but I hurt him, nonetheless. We haven't spoken or seen each other in a long time, but I'm sure the ban still holds true."

"Ban?"

"Yes, a barrier that keeps out trespassers. Neverland is Pan's territory. Just as Atlantis is mine."

I froze. "Atlantis is …"

"It was my first home." Kai shifted so the sunlight covered her face. "The place where I first created the merpeople. All the gods have their own island—and people—that aid as a link to their power. We can keep whoever we want out with a little magic."

I thought about that. How only merpeople could enter Atlantis and those of worthy souls could enter Neverland. But hadn't Pascal found a way to get around that with fairy dust? Did that mean something in Atlantis had the same effect?

"Wait, so how are you here now?"

She turned and faced me. "Your father."

I looked up at her, amazement filling me. My father helped her. I started to ask for an explanation when my hand warmed and something solid appeared in my grasp.

The Trident of Atlantis.

Its long shaft fit perfectly in my hand, and the three prongs glinted in the sun. Power seemed to emanate from it, and I could feel a presence surrounding me, grasping me in a warm embrace. At that moment, the world righted itself, as though every moment before had been dull and lifeless. I'd felt nothing but raw energy and a rightness the first time I'd opened myself up to the trident. Now it was here again to aid me.

"It's a gift from your father. And a connection to you that allowed me to enter your mind."

"What? Won't he need it? And couldn't he have brought it to me?"

Why did that sound like I was some little girl hoping her daddy would show up and save the day?

"Unfortunately, no. He can speak in your mind thanks to your mermaid heritage, but he doesn't have the ability to do this." She nodded to the trident.

"And what exactly am I supposed to do with that? Wendy is in Neverland. The trident is a fair weapon, but it does me better in the sea than it will there."

Kai's lips tugged into a grin. "Atlas's trident always seemed to have a mind of its own." Kai shrugged. "Once it has fulfilled its purpose, it will return to Atlantis."

What in sea's sake was that supposed to mean? Though, having the trident back in my hands did feel strangely good, as though I needed the trident as some sort of safety net. I winced and patted Slayer to apologize. Slayer was my weapon of choice, but Atlas's trident was a part of me—of my heritage.

"You have to get back; your people need you, and I have already stayed too long. Take your father's gift and make that wretched Wendy pay for what she's done."

I nodded. "I will."

"Oh, and Arie?" Kai's lips curled into a devilish grin. "I'd refrain from calling me a worthless salty bitch in the future."

A bright light blinded me, and as it vanished, so did the Goddess of Sea and Sky.

My eyes fluttered open, and everything came rushing back. Chimera's voice cut through my ringing ears.

"It's too late."

My hand shot out of the water, the trident connecting with the bunt end of a sword. I twirled around in the water, my tail swishing against the current, and I watched Chimera's face turn a pasty white. He looked down at the trident in my hands, his jaw dropping in the process.

"She didn't tell me you were his—"

I raised the trident high above my head and brought it down with all my might, but Chimera jumped back into the water.

What the hells was he thinking? He'd seen that I was a mermaid, so he thought going back into the water was a smart idea?

He's a sea witch.

Kai's voice flooded into my mind, and I swore. He could

command the water.

I dove and searched for him, my eyes darting around until landing on a large serpent with sharp teeth and a whirling vortex beneath it. Though this looked nothing like the monster attacking the ship. *Shit.* Could Chimera turn into a damn serpent too? It lunged forward before I could figure it out and sunk his teeth into my arm. Pain ripped through me. Screaming, I desperately fought to keep hold of the trident.

With my free hand, I slammed it into the serpent's side, sending it spiraling backwards. I swam away, trying to put as much distance between us as possible. A hand wrapped around my ankle and tugged me downward. I reared back to find half-man, half-serpent. What the hells? His arms were free leaving the rest of him to resemble the serpent. I'd never seen anything like it.

Jabbing the end of the trident into Chimera's shoulder, he cried out and bubbles surged from his mouth. I twisted my body, using force to kick him off me. Chimera flew backwards. He recovered quickly and charged forward. Clutching the trident, I spun away and stuck the prongs into his tail.

His whirlpool grew as he turned away from me and back toward the small boat.

Chimera resurfaced, returning to his human shape. I launched myself into action and chased after him. The clouds darkened and thunder rolled in as he called upon a storm with his arms outstretched. With each crashing wave threatening to drag me under, I gripped onto the boat's edge and launched myself up into it. With all the strength I had left, I thrust the trident hard into his torso.

With a deafening shriek, he stumbled backwards, tripping and landing in the boat with a thud. His body writhed in pain, each shallow breath gradually drawing slower. He gurgled and gasped for air, and a gush of blood spilled from his mouth.

The salty spray of the sea sent a chill up my spine as I willed my mermaid tail to form into legs. As I towered over him, his eyes widened with fear.

"I'm glad to know that I'll be the last thing you see before death," I said coldly. I thought about Hector, about Ulrich, about all the people who will be better off when this monster is slain.

He may have been human, he may have been commanded by Wendy, but there was no denying the murderous look in his eyes. This man wasn't one of the innocent souls of the Lost Boys.

With a deep breath and all my strength, I pushed the trident in one powerful thrust until I heard a chilling crack of bones breaking and Chimera's final breath slipping away.

Finally, the clouds dissipated, revealing the sun beginning to dip past the horizon. I gripped the trident in my hand and turned around. Shit, I nearly forgot.

The *Black Betty* was in flames.

Its sails were ablaze, and the billowing smoke blackened the sky above. The crackle and roar of the inferno filled the air, with sparks flying in all directions. I searched the waters for my crew, but if they were within the burning sea, I couldn't tell.

Frankie. I fell to my knees, dropping the trident, and Slayer, in the small boat in the process. She couldn't be dead. I refused to allow my mind to go there again. My sister had been put in harm's way far too many times since coming with me.

And now this.

I was going to kill Wendy. Strip her down and feast on her bones if I had to. She doesn't have a clue who she's messing with, but she would, and there wouldn't be enough beasts in her arsenal to stop the reckoning coming for her.

I clutched the trident back into my hand, or what I thought was the trident. I peered over to where it lay in the boat to find it had shifted back to a necklace. The same way it had after King Rylan had gifted it to me to use against Ursa.

The raging flames slowly consumed the *Betty*, and I watched in sorrow as my home, the one place that I called my sanctuary, slowly sank beneath the waves. We had been the fiercest pirates on the Seven Seas, and now, in a single night, our reign had ended. I swallowed, and my pulse raced at the thought. A ship can always be rebuilt, but there would never be another ship like *Black Betty*.

Raising my hands in the air, I called upon the wind to bring me closer. I had to search for my men. *For Frankie*. Had the serpent devoured them—or perhaps the flames?

Thoughts raced through my mind of Frankie and Keenan, of Ulrich and Tink, and all the others—and even Wendy. Out there somewhere planning her next scheme. I vowed to make her pay for this. I focused my energy on the wind and felt its power at my back as it pushed me forward with greater strength.

I would end this. For Pascal. For Hector. And for my ship and my crew.

A LAND OF LOST SOULS

In the distance, I spotted something. Hope surged through me as much as the wind that propelled me along. Could it be? Was it really them?

As I drew closer, cheers sounded from beyond the wreckage. They were alive.

Relief washed over me, enough to send tears to my eyes. I barely held them in as the cheers increased.

What could they possibly have to celebrate about? Our ship was gone. There was nothing left of my home. My books and scrolls, every map from here to the Enchanted Realm. Dozens of precious trinkets and dozens of trophies. All of it was materialistic of course, but that didn't stop the ache that crushed me from what was now lost.

I shoved down the pain as I always had and let a smile tug on my lips.

"Arie, thank gods you're all right." My sister waved at me. "You should have seen it. Ulrich was amazing."

I scanned the boats until my eyes met the broody captain's. Fear and worry covered his face, but only for a second before being replaced with the same blank expression he usually wore. He nodded once in my direction before returning to his task of rowing.

"What happened to the serpent?"

"Hook happened," Sanders replied. "Frankie was shouting for us to drop the barrels, and Hook was firing flaming arrows to get them to blow." He gestured wildly with his hands as he continued. "But the bastard wouldn't go down, so Hook dove in after it. Almost thought we lost him until he popped back out of the sea. The serpent didn't stand a chance. It was glorious."

Glorious? Losing the *Betty* was glorious? I bit my tongue from lashing out and instead glanced at Ulrich, who held my gaze. His recklessness had nearly cost him his life yet again. What the fuck was he thinking?

First risking his life against Chimera, and now this? Did the man have a death wish? He wasn't a mermaid, or a sea witch, so what made him think going in after that thing was smart?

I looked away, back to the sea. Ulrich was strong and brave, but too reckless for his own good.

He wasn't invincible, I reminded myself. No matter how much he thought he was.

What would I have done if I'd lost him?

The thought took me by surprise, not that I cared, even if my racing heart and aching chest said otherwise.

"Ulrich!" I shouted. "Are you out of your damn mind? You could have died."

He only shrugged as he continued to row. His shoulders were tense, and he refused to meet my eyes again. "Only seems fair to return the favor."

"I had worked out a plan. Frankie had things under control and Keenan—"

"It was the only way," Keenan interrupted. "The serpent was moving too quickly, and the fuses were taking too long. We had it under control."

I couldn't stop the laugh that escaped. "Under control? You call causing the *Betty* to sink, under control?"

"You." My gaze pierced through Ulrich. "You're okay with this? You who lost your own ship?"

Anger flashed in Ulrich's eyes, and Frankie chimed in. "No one is happy about the ship, Arie. We did what we had to do to survive. Something you should know plenty about." He looked over at Frankie.

The sting hit me hard, digging deep at the underlying words from my sister. I thought we'd finally moved past that. I'd apologized repeatedly for leaving her behind and not bringing her on the ship. But she should understand by now why I had. Never had I meant for it to be a punishment, or as a means to leave her behind. Frankie was the last bit of family I had until I met Rylan. Even still, she was my baby sister, blood or not.

"*Betty* is at the bottom of the sea, Wendy somehow continues to have the upper hand on us, and Hector is dead. And you all think this is *fun*?"

Silence loomed in the air at my words. I clasped a hand over my mouth as all attention landed on me.

"H-Hector is ... dead?" Keenan asked.

"Nice, Arie." Frankie pressed a hand to her face.

I let out a sigh. I hadn't meant to say that, hadn't wanted to mention Hector until we were back on shore and I had a moment to figure out what to say. I was so tired of failing everyone, of losing everything. I placed my hands over my face and let the tears fly.

Ulrich spoke up. "We can speak about Hector when we are back on shore. But yes, Hector is gone."

Gasps and cries of anger spread through my men. Sorrow nipped at me and I swallowed it down.

"Wendy is going to pay for her sins." I lifted my head from my hands and stood. "I swear to you right here and now, we will not stop until we watch *her* world burn."

My men cheered once more, and I called the wind to push us on. Fluttering bells sounded before Tink landed in my boat.

"I feel your sorrow, I feel what you're going through, and I promise things will get better. We will stop Wendy and get back what's ours."

I nodded but refused to say anything more and instead watched as the sun finished its descent over the horizon, casting us in darkness.

XIV. PYRE OF LIGHT

Arie

I PRESSED MY HAND TO THE CLOTH, AS I LISTENED TO Ulrich fill our crews in on what happened. Hector lay stiff beneath my hand, and I fought back the need to cry. Now wasn't the time to lose myself. I had to hold it together for the rest of the crew.

The air in the room grew heavy with tension as questions were hurled my way. The men around me seemed to be moments away from exploding with rage. I expected this and braced myself for the onslaught of their hatred, but it still stung.

After all, it was up to the captain to keep everyone safe. It was up to their leader to lead them to glory and not to their death. It was their friend's duty to have their backs.

I had done none of it.

Instead, we were getting ready to send our friend's soul to the afterlife and prepare for battle. I heaved a sigh and looked at my men. Someone here had informed Wendy of our plans. It was the only way she would have known where my ship was, when we were getting to Neverland, and when Hector and Nathaniel were out patrolling.

A traitor.

My mouth grew dry as the word echoed in my mind. I clenched my fists, feeling the red-hot anger boil within me. Someone within my own ranks had been working with Wendy the whole time. A knot of worry tightened in my chest as I considered who it could be.

And now both Hector and the *Betty* had paid for that treachery.

"So, you didn't even try to save them?" Keenan spat, pulling me back into the conversation.

"Of course, we did," Ulrich snapped back. "There's no reasoning with Wendy. She had her beasts and—"

"Have you seen these beasts, Cap?"

I nodded to my friend. "They're …"

I paused, unable to come up with a way to explain how dangerous Neverbeasts were, and how one of them was locked away somewhere in the treehouse. The last thing we needed was another death to clean up. And I was pretty certain it wouldn't be Marian's.

Though, to my relief, I didn't have to.

"They're beasts straight from hell." To my surprise, it was Jameson who spoke. "Deadly and ruthless, they only listen to whoever controls them. They kill whatever they can, and whoever they can, without a second thought. They're born from witchcraft, and they are not something to take lightly."

"You've seen them before?" Ace asked.

Jameson gave a stiff nod but didn't offer any further information.

"So, what, we just sit back and allow this Wendy girl to get away with it?" Keenan took a step forward, his finger pointed at Ace. "If any of you had anything to do with this—"

"Enough!" I slammed my hand on the war room table.

The room fell into an eerie silence. I dug my fingers into the table to keep my temper at ease. "I know you're angry, and you have every right to be, but this is not the time to talk about it. We need to focus on mourning our friend." My words were thick, searing my insides as salty tears rolled down my face. "Do any of you think this is what he would have wanted? Are we really going to argue over this? Nathaniel is still out there, and if we want any chance of getting him back, we need to keep our heads on straight."

Soft murmurs and apologies sounded from the crew, but it was lost to me once more as I brought my focus back to Hector's form.

"Are the preparations ready?" I asked.

"Yes," Ace replied and placed a hand on my shoulder. I stiffened at his touch. We'd been pretty indifferent to one another, what with him trying to kill me upon our first meeting, but I saw the person underneath that hard exterior. I saw the same thing in all the boys who occupied this tree.

Loyalty.

They reminded me of my crew. We weren't just people who sailed together and took down monsters, we were a family who would do anything for one another. And that's what I saw every time I looked at Ace.

I saw myself.

"Good. Then let's begin."

I stood and watched as the flames of the pyre flickered in the dark. The night was hot and still, sending shivers coursing down my back. Anguish thickened in the air as I looked at my crew; they stood in a half-circle around the pyre, their faces reflecting in the firelight. Some were solemn, others in tears, and a few of them bowed their heads in silence.

Pride swelled within me at my brothers and sisters, the ones who had ridden with me into battle, who stood by me through the hard times.

My legs shook as I stepped forward and cleared my throat. "We stand before our fallen brother to honor his bravery and his loyalty to this family. He was a tough son-of-a-bitch and a man any of us were lucky enough to have at our backs. He-he was ... I ..."

I couldn't do this. I didn't have the strength to do this.

Just as I tried to turn away, a hand grasped my own, and I traced the length of the arm until I came face to face with ... *Ulrich?* Of all people, why did it have to be him? He didn't say anything, didn't even look at me, just stood there holding my hand. His warmth seeped through my skin, and for a brief moment everything else around us faded.

I swallowed down the sob that wanted to escape and continued on.

"We all know who Hector was to this family, and he will never be forgotten. Tonight, we celebrate his life and tomorrow"—I took in a deep breath, allowing my power and rage to fuel my words—"tomorrow, we will take down the bitch responsible. In his name, we will not surrender!"

Around me, everyone cheered and lifted their weapons above their heads as they chanted Hector's name.

Ulrich's hand slipped out of mine and I instantly missed the warmth. I'd been so angry with him and said things I wasn't sure I could take back. Not that I really would, but Ulrich didn't deserve my wrath. I may have been upset with him for risking lives but I wasn't angry. I wanted to be mad at him, it would have been easier, but he wasn't responsible for Wendy, or for the *Betty*, or even Hector. None of this was his fault, and yet here I was making an ass out of myself treating him poorly.

Now wasn't the time to talk about it, but I was going to have to speak with him soon.

Instead, I focused on Hector. My friend who taught me to wield some of the finest weaponry. Who played cards like it was no one's business, and he was one of the best mates I'd ever had.

A mate I'd never see again.

I caught sight of Frankie, her arm linked in Keenan's and her head rested on his shoulder. Frankie's eyes and nose were red, but something Keenan was telling her brought a smile to her face. I grinned at the sight. Bringing my sister on board had been a good decision, and I would forever be grateful to Hector and Nathaniel for taking her under their wings. And now it was good to know that Keenan seemed to take a kinship to her as well.

Pascal stood on the other side of her, his head bowed as he mumbled between his lips, but truth be told, I was surprised to see him out here. Granted he'd come around to Hector, and he should be a part of the funeral, but I'd hoped he'd at least stay out of sight considering what was going on. The simple thought of the wizard being in control again sent unease through me. Pascal was unpredictable, and now that the Peter part of him wasn't in control, I had no idea what to expect. All I knew for certain was that I needed to keep an eye on him and figure out how to get his shadow, and mind, back before it was too late.

We all stood there around Hector's pyre long after the flames died out. The crew told stories about him—their first encounters or some of the fun hunts we went on. Before long, even I was joining in, recalling the time he and I somehow managed to get ourselves captured by rival pirates. We had to fight our way out, just the two of us. It was probably one of the best moments of my life as captain of the *Betty*.

Before long, people said their goodbyes and headed back to the treehouse for the celebration of life. I stayed where I was, unable to allow myself the luxury of celebrating just yet. We'd done this before, after the death of every crew member, but this time, in this place and under these circumstances, it just didn't feel right to celebrate.

Hector could come back and haunt me all he wanted for not celebrating him, but right then, all I wanted was to stand there and pray to the gods to give me the strength and the will to continue.

I rested a hand on the now cold pyre and blinked away tears. "Until we meet again, my friend."

"Are you going to join everyone else?" Ulrich's voice called from behind me.

I shook my head. "I think they'll be just fine without me. Plus, I've never been good with goodbyes and going in there feels like goodbye."

"Mind if I join you, then? I hate goodbyes too."

"Fine by me." I shrugged and lifted my head. Though my insides screamed at him to go away because I wasn't good at apologies either.

But he deserved one, and now everyone was gone, and we were alone, and there was no telling when we'd be alone again before setting off to kill Wendy.

"You know, I don't normally have to do this, and when I have to admit … certain things … I find it's hard to get the words out. It's just I'm—"

"Stubborn, hard-headed, a pain in the ass?"

I raised a brow. "I was going to say I'm not good at saying … saying I'm …"

"You're what?" He gestured for me to continue. A gleam in his eyes.

Is he enjoying this?

Swallowing down my annoyance, I blurted, "I'm sorry. I shouldn't have blamed you for holding me back from Wendy, but I am pissed that you did it. That you felt you couldn't trust me, and that you risked your damn life again."

"Wait, so let me get this straight." Ulrich's icy tone lowered. "You're upset with me over trying to keep you alive? So, it's okay for *you* to risk your life time and time again, but it's not okay for others? Don't you think that's a bit hypocritical, Arie?"

Hells, he was infuriating.

"I didn't risk my life, *someone* decided to take that option from me. I had a plan for Wendy, just as I had a plan with the serpent, but you felt you could take control of the situation and do as you please."

"Take control? There was nothing to take control of. I assessed both situations and did my best to handle them accordingly. There was no telling how many beasts were out there. If you tried to save Hector or Nathaniel, you would have died with them. Why is that so hard for you to understand?"

"What's hard for me to understand is how you felt the need to dismiss my idea without even asking me what I was doing. You made it plain and simple that you didn't care about their lives. We wasted valuable time when we could have saved them both right then and there."

"You don't know that." He stepped forward, his body so close to me that I could smell him. Mint and musk and … Ulrich. My breath hitched in my throat at the way his dark, mysterious eyes practically sank into me, looking deep within my soul. "How would you have been able to stop dozens of beasts from attacking?"

I threw my hands up and whirled around. I couldn't be that close to him. Not right then. "Did you not hear what happened in the cave? How we were able to stop the ones from attacking and made it out safely. I even broke Wendy's hold on the Maiden for gods' sake."

"You did what?"

Right. There hadn't been time to tell everyone what I'd done to Marian. To my delight she'd kept herself scarce while the funeral went on, but I knew I was going to have to tell everyone about her eventually.

I waved a hand at him. "It doesn't matter. None of this does. Had you just listened and trusted me, we wouldn't be having this conversation."

Ulrich gritted his teeth. "Maybe you should try putting some faith in others before you start talking about trust."

"Why are you so insufferable?" I hissed.

"Oh, I'm sorry, *Captain*, are you upset that someone just wants what's best for you? That someone cares? Your life matters to a lot of people. Hector and Nathaniel both knew what they were getting into when they accepted your invitation to join your crew. Just do yourself a favor and let other people help you."

Words failed me. I didn't know whether to be pissed or taken aback by his statement. But I didn't need anyone to take care of me. I'd been doing it by myself for a long time before he came aboard my ship. It wasn't about to change just because he wanted it to.

"You also knew what you signed up for when you accepted my invitation after sirens attacked your ship. You don't get to dictate what I do, Ulrich. You're not the captain of the *Betty*—"

"And now neither are you," he bit back, his brows furrowed, chest heaving with anger.

I flinched at his words, the reality of them hitting me like an avalanche, burying me until there was nothing left but silence.

His face sombered, and he mumbled, "I'm sorry, I shouldn't have said that."

"And yet, you did."

Swallowing down the lump in my throat, I turned and left him standing next to the smoldering pyre. Hurt and anger mixing in my core. After this Wendy business was done, I was going to find a way to leave this hell of an island and continue this mission without him, without anyone.

Ending the life of all those who wronged me was all I thought about as everyone else celebrated Hector's life.

The treehouse hummed with chatter. Hector's name rang through the room as the crew continued to tell stories—good and bad. I'd have given anything to join in, but the ache within me grew just at the mere mention of him. I peered around the crew searching for Frankie when I found her and Ace in a rather close embrace. Laughter consumed my sister's face, and Ace looked at her the same way Malakai and Viktor used to look at one another, giving her all his attention in a way that Clayton never did.

A part of me was glad Ulrich's brother decided to stay in Khan. Clayton didn't want to come back to Neverland, but he also wasn't the right one for my sister. It had hurt Ulrich but he also knew that his baby brother needed to find his own path. Much like Frankie had.

Ace turned in my direction and flagged me down with a wave of his hand. I stalked over, and he lowered his voice.

"Marian needs to see you," was all he said before returning his attention to my sister.

Though, Frankie's attention was all on me.

"Are you okay?" she asked. "And I mean other than the loss of our friend?"

Shouldn't I have been asking her that? She had developed an

inseparable bond with Nathaniel and Hector since coming aboard the *Betty*. Thank the gods above she had Ace to offer her strength and comfort, and to make her smile in a way I'd never seen before, otherwise I was afraid she'd already be off to hunt down Wendy.

"I'm fine. Are you okay?"

Frankie sighed heavily. "I'm trying to distract myself with other things. Today we should honor those we lost, but tomorrow ... tomorrow is for revenge."

"That it is." I nodded and glanced at Ace. "Keep her safe, all right?"

The corners of his mouth quirked up in a half-smile. "You got it."

I left the two of them and went to find Marian, my footsteps echoing in the hallway as I made my way to her room. Tomorrow may be a day for vengeance, but tonight I wanted to ensure we stood a chance.

When I reached the door, I knocked twice before it opened to reveal Marian leaning against the frame. The firelight caught in her eyes, turning them into a flickering golden color.

"Arie, good you're back," she said, moving aside to let me in. "Have you laid your friend to rest?"

"Yes," I replied, my stomach churning at the thought. "Now it's time to discuss what comes next. I also brought back reinforcements."

Marian nodded slowly. "I fear that even with reinforcements, it may not be enough against the other beasts." She began pacing around the room. "I've had some time to think about this, and I may have an idea on how to get around them."

"What about the pipes? The instrument Ace used to keep all the Neverbeasts asleep when we rescued Tink."

Marian shook her head. "That works to only keep already sleeping beasts asleep and isn't always effective. We won't be able to defeat the army Wendy has gathered with that. But I think there's another way."

She smiled, her eyes dancing with a newfound vigor as she began pacing around the room.

I watched her for a moment before asking, "What do you have in mind?"

"Well, what happens when the roots are cut from a plant?"

I furrowed my brows, still unsure of what she was getting at. "It dies, eventually."

Marian smirked. "Exactly."

Realization flooded through me. Taking out Wendy's beasts was as simple as cutting the ties that linked them to her; Wendy was the connector to each one of them—the root of a plant. Removing the source would take out every last beast in one swoop. It's a good thing I already planned on slicing that bitch to pieces.

I nodded slowly, beginning to understand the brilliance of her plan. "Oh, this could work."

"Wendy enjoys the thrill of a show. So, let's put on a guise and give her the thrill of a lifetime."

The plan was clever and daring—much like Marian herself—and it was perfect. There was much more to figure out, but this was a good start.

"Let's go introduce you to everyone else before we start planning," I said, making my way toward the door.

"Are you sure that's a good idea? Pascal—"

"I'll worry about Pascal. But we can't keep you hidden, and everyone needs to know that there is a way to stop the beasts from killing us all. Obviously once they see what we did, they'll come to understand that you—and the rest of the beasts—are just more of Wendy's victims."

It took some more convincing before Marian agreed to come out with me. Everyone stood in the main room, all huddled in different groups lost in conversation. No one realized our entry until one of the Lost Boys approached.

"Who is this fine beauty?"

Marian lowered her voice. It was sweet and seductive and sent shivers down my spine. "Someone who would chew you into a million pieces, spit you out, and leave you broken for the next beauty."

The Lost Boy paled and took a few steps back. I turned my gaze to Marian whose eyes sparkled with golden flecks.

"Sh-she's one of them."

Everyone scurried away from where Marian and I stood, except my crew who pointed their pistols or swords in our direction. Well, in Marian's anyway.

"Wait, it's not what you think." Ace surged forward, leaving Frankie behind, and stood between us and the crowd.

"He's right." Tink's bells sounded from behind me, but I didn't move. She lightly landed on my shoulder and cleared her throat. "Arie was able to sever the tie that held this woman to Wendy's control."

"We have a new understanding of what the beasts are and how we can save them," I added.

"*Save them?*" Ulrich stepped through the crowd, and I bit my tongue from telling him to go away. "You want to save them after what one of them did to Hector? You can't be serious?"

"This one's cute," Marian said and licked her lips. A surge of jealousy rose within me, and I swallowed to keep it far, far away from me. If Marian wanted him, she could have him for all I cared. What good was a man who didn't trust me anyway?

Though I couldn't help the snip in my tone as I spoke. "We have a lot to discuss before we start planning our attack. Everyone will meet in the war room in ten minutes."

Ace approached and placed a hand on my shoulder. "You have a plan?"

"It's in the works. Where's Pascal?"

I searched the room of people, but my friend was nowhere to be seen. Had he seen us approach and ran off when he saw Marian?

"I saw him go outside not that long ago. He might still be out there."

"All right, I'll go check on him. Would you?" I gestured to Marian, and without skipping a beat Ace nodded and offered Marian his arm to escort her to the war room. Frankie's eyes lowered into slits, but I motioned for her to come with me before she started a fight with Marian.

"Help me find Pascal."

We exited the treehouse into the inky, starlit forest. A breeze kicked up leaves and wafted the smell of wet earth and pine into our faces. Up above, the sky was illuminated with twinkling stars that seemed to dance against the dark night.

In the distance, a muffled sound broke out from the silence, and Frankie and I shot each other a look before sprinting toward the grove.

Behind a large maple stood Teddy, bound and gagged and tied to the tree. Frankie rushed to his side and ripped through the rope with a knife as I tore away the cloth from his mouth. He gasped before throwing himself into Frankie's embrace, stuttering out his thanks. He gave a grunt before throwing himself into Frankie's arms and thanking her.

"What happened to you?" Frankie asked softly.

"Pascal ... he looked ... he didn't recognize me." Teddy stood up straight and inhaled. He was by far the youngest and smallest of the Lost Boys, but I had to give him credit for his lack of fear.

"Did he say where he was going?"

Pascal had left the treehouse without telling us. Damn him. Was he going after Wendy without us?

This was not good.

Teddy ran a hand through his hair and sighed. "He said he was off to see a man about a shadow."

XV. SON OF A GOD

Pascal

PETER HAD GONE DARK INSIDE OUR HEAD, SO THAT left me to figure out what to do. After seeing Hector's lifeless form on the pyre, I'd decided it was time to act. Afterall, hadn't Peter told me to take control and do what needed to be done?

So, I took it upon myself to do just that. What I hadn't expected was Teddy to be outside, or for him to try and stop me from going alone. Peter may not have appreciated what I did to Teddy, tying him up and leaving him to the mercy of whoever came out to get him down, but he was in my way. It didn't help that it had been so long since I'd strung someone up.

Not that our little dove would be happy, but she'd understand the importance of what I had to do.

I took off down the path that led to Lily's Cove. But Wendy wasn't my intended destination just then. Father, whether he wanted to be a part of Neverland anymore or not, needed to come out of the Celestial Plains and explain himself. How had Wendy been able to look like him, speak like him, and we didn't know it? Father was a God for sea's sake. Surely he'd have counter measures in place for such things.

It was possible that this was just an illusion orchestrated by Wendy. Though that didn't explain how she had known we were on our way. That was a problem for a later time.

Wendy hadn't always been a powerful witch. She had the ability inside her, of course, but seeing her standing there with Hector and Nathaniel on their knees and Jack and Jaina turned into those beasts, she had come far since our departure. At this point anything was possible, even masquerading as the God of Life and Death.

I shuddered.

Sucking in a deep breath, I allowed the cool air to fill my lungs as I veered off the main trail and took the way I'd gone so many times. Where Peter had gone so many times?

Trying to decipher between myself: the wizard, and Peter was starting to get confusing and frustrating. He'd wanted everyone to call him Pascal, but that seemed far too weird when I'd been called that across Khan. The king's ruthless and terrifying wizard.

When Peter handed me control, I never thought he'd give me *everything*. It was … *lonely*. I'd grown used to having another presence in our mind. Even when that other part of my mind was blocked before

Arie freed it, I'd always felt something, like there was an itch I couldn't scratch. But now? Now there was nothing but complete and utter silence. As if Peter had vanished.

I shivered again and pulled the hood of my cloak over my head.

The oak tree wasn't much farther, but there was no telling how long of a head start I'd given myself. Knowing Arie, she'd track me down before I even had the chance to speak to Pan.

Finally, the large oak tree came into view. It was a giant among giants, bigger than the treehouse, though this one had a tendency of appearing only at night when those with prying eyes couldn't see it from afar. Neverland seemed to still hold some of its magic after all. Its branches were laden with a multitude of deep green leaves. Its trunk was rough and covered in scaled bark, and deep grooves reached up along it in delicate swirls.

I placed both hands against it. Its bark was smooth and hard against my touch, not so much like wood, but more akin to scales. Heat wrapped around my fingers, sending a warmth through me that countered the chill of the night.

This tree had been mine and my father's spot when I was nothing more than a little tike. Father brought me here and would spend hours telling me stories about how he created Neverland, how he loved everything it represented, and most importantly, how he yearned for a chance to leave it one day.

I never understood until much later why he wanted to leave. Not until I learned who Kai, the Goddess of Sea and Sky, was.

But now he needed to tell me what the *fuck* was going on.

"Father," I whispered. "I don't know why you've decided to not come to Neverland when it's dying. I don't know why you've allowed Wendy so much leeway in your own home. And I really don't know why you've taken it upon yourself to cower in the middle of a thunderstorm, but right now you're needed. Come out and speak to me."

I closed my eyes and pushed power and magic into the tree, allowing the connection between myself and Neverland to put force between my words. There was no telling whether Pan would answer my call, but I settled in for the wait. If Arie showed up, I'd take that as a sign the big man wasn't coming and forget him altogether.

I sat on the ground and leaned my head against the tree. My fingers dug into the ground, and a spark of calmness washed over me. In the entire time I'd been the king's wizard, I'd felt many things: lust, joy, wickedness. But I'd never felt *serenity*. And that's exactly what the land was giving me. Was this how it felt to be whole? It had been so long since I knew what that word meant. Neverland must have felt it too because before I knew it, roots wrapped around my arms and legs and leaves from above draped over me in a protective shell. A shell that said, 'welcome home,'

"I missed you too, old friend."

A flash of light broke my tranquility, and I shielded my eyes from it.

"Peter," a voice called out.

The light dissipated, leaving me under the scrutiny of the moonlight, and ... Pan.

His figure stretched several feet above me, and his power weaved through the forest like the breeze, crawling along my skin and heavy against my rib cage. He wore a long, deep green cloak that draped down to the ground and its hood cast a shadow over his face.

"Hello, father."

He tilted his head and raised a brow. The scars on my face and the eye I'd lost gave all the notions of a battered and broken man. "You're not *my* Peter."

I huffed. "You don't recognize your own son? I suppose that's because we're utterly broken, and you've decided to hide away and let it all happen."

Realization lit in his face as he surveyed me. His frame seemed to shimmer as if he was nothing more than a glimmer of light.

But that would mean ... *No*. He wouldn't do that. *Would he?*

"This is more of Wendy's doing?" he asked.

"*More* of Wendy's doing? What do you mean?"

Pan gave me a somber look and rubbed the back of his neck. "You don't understand what's at stake, Son. There are more things afoot than you could imagine, and I must be vigilant and careful. There's much you don't know and—"

"Then fucking tell us." I shot up from the ground and pointed a finger at him. My rage boiling to the surface at his cryptic words. "What is so damn important that you left us to be tortured and beaten and broken until there was nothing left but ..." *But me.*

I blinked back tears to keep my composure. Peter wasn't here to keep me in check, and I wasn't about to give Father any benefit of the doubt here. He'd given up on Neverland, on me, and I wouldn't let him forget it.

"Us?" Pan asked. I wasn't sure I wanted to tell him if he, a god, couldn't figure out what was wrong with us. But thankfully he continued before I could come up with an answer. "I couldn't leave the Plains. If Wendy and her mistress knew I was in Neverland, everything would be over. I shouldn't even be here now."

I scoffed. "You're not really here. Don't you think I recognize the magic at play here? For once in your life stop sugar coating everything and be *real*."

Pan's gaze grew hot. "Fine, but lower your voice. We don't need unwanted attention. Wendy's beasts could be anywhere. She's trying to seek entrance into the Plains. She's amassing power beyond anything I've seen before, though Wendy is nothing more than a pawn in her mistress's game. A middle woman who is nothing more than for show. She has enough fairy dust and power to take down the gate that holds the Celestial Plains at bay."

"We were told Wendy is low on fairy dust."

Pan froze. "If that's the case then perhaps Wendy is far more out of the Mistress's control than I thought. Wendy has always been a bit harder to keep tabs on. As you well know, she likes to take things into her own hands and do things her own way. What she did to you and those poor Lost Ones, turning them into Neverbeasts, none of it was the Mistress's plan. At least, that's what I've gathered, and it doesn't mean it rings true. However, this will make it harder for anyone to gain entry to the Plains—not impossible, just harder."

"Why does this mistress want to get into the Celestial Plains?"

Father's shoulders sank, and he looked away. I fished through the many memories we had of him, but none of them were of him looking so bleak. He was a power, a god who controlled the souls of the Plains. A man who had the ability to give life and death to any he pleased. If even he was scared, what kind of influence and power did this mistress have?

"She wants to kill me."

I doubled over in laughter. I couldn't help it. Did he think we believed that? "This mistress wants to kill you, the God of *Life* and *Death*? Oh, that's rich."

Pan focused his gaze on me. "You're different than I remember the last time we spoke."

Fury rose within my core, every fiber of my being scorched with the flames. Different? Had he not seen what I'd been through, what I'd done to survive? Could he really not see what was wrong? "This is what happens when you're strapped to a table and tortured by rats, when you're mauled by giant beasts with deadly fangs, when you're too messed up and have to force yourself to forget who you are." I pointed to the scars on my face and then to the eye that was now white and filmed over. "My soul was ripped to pieces and consumed by a devil of a woman and then I was sold to a king who used me for his own devices. So please, *Father*, tell me how different I really am."

Pan flinched, but the anger remained. "There's no amount of power in this world that can take away the anguish I feel over what Wendy did to you."

"I don't want your pity, or your apology." Okay, maybe I did just a little, but that felt more like a Peter thing than me. "What I want is to know how to stop Wendy from doing this to anyone else. What I want is to cut off the head of the monster responsible. But I can't stop what

I don't know is coming. So, tell me."

He nodded. "Okay. What exactly do you want to know?"

"For starters you can tell me how the hell Wendy was able to trick me into giving her my shadow."

"Witches are powerful beings, but ones who work with the darkest of magics tend to have many tricks up their sleeves. It shouldn't be possible for her to have done that, but perhaps it has something to do with what she did to you before you left Neverland."

The image of Pan had come to us in our mind, and hadn't Wendy manipulated that same thing? Taken it and twisted it until it molded into the wizard I'd become? Had she somehow connected herself to my mind? Had that been how she was able to keep tabs on me this whole time? I shook my head and settled on my next question.

"This mistress—who is she?"

Pan moved to sit next to the tree and placed his hands in his lap. He leaned his head against the tree and closed his eyes. My throat grew dry, and my chest tightened at the sight. It felt wrong to be so angry with him just then, but I wasn't going to forgive him so easily. Not after he did nothing to help me. Instead, I sat in the grass across from him.

He opened his eyes and brought them to mine. "Wendy's mistress is a witch named Germaine. Though I believe now she goes by Queen Gemma."

My entire world stopped and my breath caught in my throat at the name I'd heard so many times before. During my time with King Roland, I remembered he'd worked out an alliance with the Queen of the Enchanted Realm. Whispers and rumors had run rampant in Khan about her and how she ascended the throne after the death of the VonWhite family. Rumors that she was the one who slaughtered the king and queen and their two sons.

If the queen was involved in all of this, then Ulrich could still be in danger. Maybe this meant it was finally time to tell him about his past. That he was the rightful heir to the Kingdom of Chione and the ruler of the Enchanted Realm. That he was the last of the VonWhite line.

"Do you know of her?" he asked.

"Unfortunately. This queen, she wants you dead?"

His shoulders slumped and he nodded. Wrinkles had etched themselves around his eyes and above his brow, making him look surprisingly ... human. "I've taken many lives in my very long existence, both young and old, and some can't accept that death is part of life. No matter how much I help the living, I'm still blamed for the dead."

He paused for a moment and stretched out his hands, the blotches on his skin telling stories of a long life lived. "Germaine was one of those who never understood this balance. After her parents died in a horse-riding accident and her lover passed away from an incurable disease, she chose to seek vengeance on me instead of grieving."

"She wants to kill you for doing your job. For taking the souls of people who died of their own stupidity, or for the natural order of things. Doesn't that seem a bit ridiculous?"

"Would you not kill to bring Taigra back?" His voice softened as he spoke her name, and it was like a knife in my heart—in Peter's.

Taigra had been more than just a friend, she had been a confidant, a rock to ground us when we felt alone in this world—the love of

Peter's life, of my life. My father had abandoned me too many times to count, but Taigra had always been there for me.

"You know, I never blamed you for her death," I whispered.

"No, but Germaine blames me for what happened. Rather than allowing herself to grieve, she schemed and plotted and did everything she could to find a way to get them back. With my death and her access to the Celestial Plains, she could bring back whomever she wanted."

I ran a hand through my hair, which was suddenly slick with sweat. Could he really do that? Could he bring someone back from the dead?

"So why don't you just let her have what she wants and let it go?"

"It's not possible. It would be like having a hollow shell of a person; they would be unable to love, to feel, to eat or sleep. What kind of life would that be? Souls are essential to the balance of the universe—they must come and go for it to thrive. If we take away this natural order, if we allow souls to linger in this realm ..." He didn't need to finish. I knew where he was going with it.

Ursa had taken and consumed dozens of souls, and it had turned her into a deadly monster. I'd been there when it happened. I'd seen the destruction she had caused. The idea of having an entire world of that kind of chaos was enough to make me shudder.

Gemma and Wendy needed to be stopped.

"So, what do we do? How do we stop them?"

"Are you not the son of a god? Are you not Peter, the leader of the Lost Souls of Neverland? Surely, you of all people can figure out how to stop them. You have all the tools you need."

"Could you be any more cryptic? And how do you expect me to

do anything when Wendy has my shadow?"

"Your shadow isn't all that you are."

He stood, and with one deliberate and slow step at a time, he walked toward me until he was kneeling and his face was level with mine. His gaze held my own, and his lips were slightly pressed together. Before I could say anything, he rested a hand on my head. His fingers were warm and heavy as I fought to keep myself from leaning into his touch.

My toes and feet tingled as a low electric current coursed through my veins, traveling up my legs and into my torso. Tensed muscles trembled under the strain, and my head pounded against the force of whatever this was.

Power seemed to build inside me, like a balloon ready to burst, and I held my breath waiting for pain to come that never did.

My eyes snapped open, my body hummed, and the air cracked with electricity. And instantly I felt ... whole.

Pan let go and stepped away from me, his face unreadable. "Take this gift and use it well. You will need it in the coming days. Be strong."

I sat there stunned, unable to say anything as I watched him step away. I tried to hide the disappointment on my face, the bits of anger that wanted to seep out from my core and rain down on me. He was leaving? Abandoning me yet again simply because he was afraid. That's all this was. He didn't want to take down Gemma and Wendy—he'd rather leave that to me.

Something warm swelled in my chest, and the thoughts dissipated leaving me with a feeling I couldn't quite put my finger on. And then it hit me.

Are you there?

Nothing.

Hello?

Still nothing.

"What did you do to me?"

"I did nothing that wasn't already there."

But it was clear what he'd done. My soul and mind were no longer split in two. I was myself again. I was whole and powerful—the son of a god.

Light surrounded us again as my father made his descent back into the Celestial Plains. "Peter?"

For the first time since getting my memory and soul back, hearing that name didn't send a shiver of guilt and fear through me. I'd blamed him for everything. For leaving me and not caring enough to help when I needed him. But deep down I knew that wasn't the case at all. Pan had always been a god, and he would always be a god. His primary job was to protect Neverland and the Celestial Plans, and if he thought locking himself away to keep that all safe was the right choice, I understood that, and I'd accept it.

"Yes?"

"I may not be here physically but know that I am always here." He placed a hand over his heart. "And I am always watching." Pausing, he looked up and sighed. "There's something else you should see before I go. As I said, I do keep watch, and it appears you have some interesting things going on with your pirate friends."

I narrowed my eyes as the vision pierced my mind. Two figures, one with their back to me and the other's face was one I'd seen many times. They spoke in hushed tones, but it didn't stop me from hearing exactly what I'd been wondering since getting to Neverland.

Traitor.

That couldn't be right. *Him* of all people?

"How did you know?" I asked.

My father gave me one last look. "I told you, I'm always watching. I see everything that happens in Neverland."

I wasn't sure if that made me feel better or not. The fact that he'd seen what happened to me, had known what was done to me.

A sudden shout from behind made me spin around as Arie's frame rushed toward me, her expression full of concern.

"Pascal? What were you thinking just up and leaving? You had us all worried. Do you even realize what could have happened if Wendy and her beasts had found you?"

The fear in her voice stirred a strange sensation in my gut, tinged with the same odd feeling as before. What was this? I turned around but my father was gone.

"Oh, don't you fret," I said, turning back around to give Arie a reassuring smile. "I can handle myself."

"I'm sure you can." Arie raised a brow. "Pascal, are you feeling okay?"

How could I tell her that my father had put me back together? That I was, for the most part, whole again? I wasn't even sure I believed it myself.

"I'm fine. There's something I need to tell you though."

Arie needed to know the truth. She deserved to know that there was no wizard and there was no Pascal. There was just *me*. And yet, when I opened my mouth to tell her nothing happened, I swallowed down the lump in my throat and settled for the information about Wendy.

"So Marian was right, the Mistress is behind this. And she's a queen. You're certain?" she asked.

"I've never questioned my father before, and he's always been right."

Arie stood near me, her red hair pulled back and away from her face.

"Look," she said, "we need to get back before they send out a search party. It's time to start planning our next move."

We walked in silence for quite some time, my mind spinning with the encounter I'd had with my father and what he'd said to me. The name he'd given me, a name who wouldn't see the light of day. She needed to know. There was no way around it. I thought about checking it out for myself, after all, I wasn't known for torturing souls for nothing, but that wasn't right.

I wasn't the wizard anymore. He was gone. *No.* That wasn't right either. That part of me, the wizard, was always some part of me. It was just buried in the deepest part of my soul and it took a wicked witch to bring it forward. It was time to embrace the wizard—to embrace every dark and light side of me.

The lights of the treehouse came into view, and some of Arie's crew stood outside around a fire, their faces lit and their laughter loud as we approached. My gaze flickered between Arie and her men as they greeted one another before it landed on the one nearest her. The one who'd caused all this pain and suffering.

I shook my head, trying to come to terms with what I was about to do, and who I was about to accuse. If my father was wrong about this, I wasn't sure anyone could come back from another unnecessary death. But my father hadn't ever been wrong before.

"Arie," I said, my voice solid and unwavering. "There's something else you need to know. Something you're going to want to hear."

Everyone around the fire turned to me, but Arie was the only one I saw.

"You have a traitor within your ranks, and he's standing before this very fire."

XVI. LOST SOULS

Arie

"HOW CERTAIN ARE YOU?" KEENAN ASKED, HIS FINGERS interlocked atop the table. His gaze bore into the wood, waiting for my response. I thought back to Pascal's words and the way the traitor had paled in response.

Could I trust my instincts—the gut feeling that Pascal had been right? I had no hard evidence to back up my belief, only the traitor's fear that had been etched into his face when Pascal voiced his name.

Frankie interjected, her voice steady and sure. "It makes sense. Nathaniel and Hector had commented a few times that he had been acting weird lately. He's kept himself pretty scarce since we got on the island too."

I nodded and agreed with her assessment. The only way to find out for sure was to bring him in and get the truth.

"Smith mentioned he seemed a bit odd too," Ulrich chimed in. "Always appearing nervous and almost paranoid, but I hadn't suspected it to be this."

Ulrich, Keenan, Frankie, and I stood in one of the more cramped rooms of the treehouse, the musty smell of mold and dust cloying in our nostrils. Pascal was conspicuously absent, but I didn't have time to ponder it. Ace, on the other hand, had been more on board with this plan than I expected, and I found myself appreciating him more and more during our stay in Neverland. Especially after he'd outfitted us with enough means for extracting a confession from our traitorous crewmate. I could feel my resolve hardening, ready to take whatever steps necessary to protect those closest to me.

"All right, let's get this over with." I stepped over to the door and rapped my knuckles against it.

The door opened, and the traitor stood in front of me, his face taut and eyes wide. I could feel the looming dread that hung heavy in the air. Daniel, a burly lower member of my crew, had a firm grip on his arm. I gestured toward an empty chair with a wave of my hand, and Daniel pushed the traitor, who still refused to look at me, forward. I slipped into the chair across from him and settled in for the game.

"I'm going to give you a chance to explain yourself, Giles," I said.

Giles. I still couldn't believe it. When we first met, Keenan and I had found him amid a shipwreck, floating on a piece of broken plank and on the brink of dehydration and surely death. He'd given us some story about his captain trying his hand at monster hunting. He'd been the crew's sailing master and their only survivor.

We should have left him there.

Giles stuttered and mumbled something about Pascal being out to get him and that he'd never betray me, but I didn't believe a single word he said.

"Let's try this one more time," I said as I unsheathed Slayer from its scabbard and let it glisten in the candlelight. "Tell me why you betrayed us."

Giles whimpered as he stared down at Slayer. "Please, Captain, don't do this."

I leaned forward in my chair, my voice tinged with resolve. "I'm not doing anything ... yet."

He shook his head and begged me for mercy. But I wouldn't show him any pity if he wasn't willing to tell me what I wanted to know. I stood up and stepped toward him, dagger in hand, and his eyes widened in fear.

I locked eyes with Keenan, and then Ulrich, and nodded at Giles. "Hold him. Frankie, find something to cover his mouth for a moment. We don't need the others to hear just yet."

Keenan and Ulrich lurched forward and grabbed hold of him. He squirmed and bucked, but they held firm as Frankie stuffed a cloth into his mouth.

"I don't want to do this. I get no joy out of this, but you have to understand." I lowered my voice. "I can't allow this to stand."

My mind flashed to Pascal, wondering if he'd given Wendy this same look. Was I no better than her?

Hector's face replaced Pascal's, and without hesitation I pressed Slayer's point to Giles's arm. I sliced into it, leaving four distinct marks carved into his skin as each point of contact oozed crimson blood. He screamed through the cloth, but I ignored him and moved closer to press the flat end of the blade against his neck. Frankie ripped the cloth from his mouth.

"Now," I said coolly. "Tell me what I want to know. Who else is in on this?"

Giles shook his head wildly in defiance, so I pressed harder against the vein bulging from his neck. One flick of my wrist and this would all be over. But I needed to know who sent him. Giles may have betrayed us, but there was no way he was in on this alone.

What could he possibly be afraid of that kept his lips sealed?

"This person you're trying to protect is worth dying over?" Ulrich gritted his teeth. "Arie has done nothing but show you kindness, has done whatever she can to ensure you have a roof over your head and a belly full of ale."

"Was it Ursa?" I asked. She'd set so much in motion it seemed the logical choice, but to my dismay, Giles shook his head. Of course, he could be lying.

The name Pascal had given me flooded into my mind. The Queen of the Enchanted Realm who'd been the mastermind behind not only Wendy, but Ursa too.

"Was it a woman by the name of Gemma, or perhaps Germaine?"

Ulrich shot me a look. "The Queen of the Enchanted Realm?"

I ignored him and bent down until Giles's face was level with my own. "Was it her?"

He slumped down in the chair, and Frankie grabbed a fist full of his hair. She appeared unfazed by any of this. As though she'd had done this before. Once again something sparked in her eyes that dissipated when she blinked. "You may as well get this over with. You won't see the morning sun unless you do."

I pushed the sharp end of the blade just below his Adam's apple, and he winced.

Nodding, he muttered, "Yes, okay, yes it was her. Please just stop. I didn't have a choice!"

"You always have a choice," I spat back at him.

Giles shook his head in disbelief, tears streaming down his cold cheeks. "She didn't give me one. She has my ..." He gulped audibly and clamped his mouth shut.

My grip on the blade intensified, and I leaned closer as I hissed out my demand. "What does she have?"

Giles's voice trembled with his reply. "She has my wife. She said she would turn her into one of those gods-forsaken beasts if I don't do everything she demands of me."

I searched his eyes, hoping to see a flicker of a lie, but instead found ... emptiness. A look I'd seen often in the mirror. Lowering Slayer, I returned to my chair. Frankie, Ulrich, and Keenan retreated to the other side of the space, and I thought about what I was going to do.

Did I believe him? He seemed afraid enough, but for all I knew that had more to do with Slayer's presence. Or it was just some ruse to make me think he's just an innocent bystander. A pawn in a much bigger game. Either way he couldn't be trusted.

It appeared Queen Gemma had been playing the long game. If this started all the way back when Giles first arrived ... A weight of understanding hit me like a ton of bricks.

Had Gemma been the one to kill Malakai and Viktor? Maybe not by her hands, but by hiring someone to do it. Didn't the Brotherhood work under her rule? If she had ties to Ursa and to Wendy, there was no telling how far her influence reached. Which had me wondering ... Was Jameson only here because of her? Was he spying on me?

I felt sick. Perhaps I was just overreacting, but something in my gut told me I was on the right track.

"Arie, what is it?" Frankie asked.

"Get him out of my sight. Have Ace find a place to hold him and have a guard on the door at all times of the day."

Giles's face sagged with visible relief. "Oh, thank you, Captain. I—"

I bolted from my chair and thrust Slayer toward him, pointing it in direct line with his torso. "Do not mistake this for mercy," I hissed. "One wrong move and I won't think twice before running you through."

Daniel grabbed hold of Giles and ushered him out of the room just as Ace peered in. "Everyone's waiting in the war room. Are you ready?"

Was I ready to face a room full of people waiting to hear about their potential death? Would this plan of ours even work? I guessed there was only one way to find out.

Everyone stood around the war room, grim faces and nervous glances shot my way. A group of misfits, lost souls who were looking to me for direction. If we were going to make it out of this alive, we needed to inspire a little courage in them, and I wasn't sure my face screamed that right then.

We had a daunting task ahead of us, and if we didn't come together as one, we'd be lost to Neverland and Wendy's band of beasts.

"My brothers, my sisters," I began, "and friends new and old. The struggle against Wendy and her beasts has been hard and long fought, but those in Neverland have found a way to persevere. And now more than ever we need to keep going. Together, we can stop this plague from spreading to Neverland's core."

I paused, looking around the room. The weight of their stares grew heavy, but I held firm. "Marian and I—"

"You mean the beast you brought into our home," Viscera called out.

The Lost Boys hadn't been happy to hear about what I'd done. Most of them had looked to Ace who seemed more inclined to allow me to take the lead. I wasn't sure that was a good idea considering every person in this room besides the pirates looked as though they wanted to murder me right then and there. But if we were going to make this plan work, it was important for them to see what happened when a bond was broken.

"You mean your fellow Lost Ones?"

Viscera huffed. "Says Wendy."

I ignored Viscera as murmurs cut over the crowd. "We have figured out a way to possibly stop Wendy and her beasts all at once. If we can sever the link between her and the beasts, then all this stops."

The room grew silent. No one said a word, but their eyes had regained a spark of hope. I nodded and continued. "I know there are risks involved, but we cannot allow fear to stifle our will. We cannot allow ourselves to back down from this fight. We must be bold, and we must be brave."

I looked around the room once more and saw the determination in their faces.

"We will find a way to distract the beasts, but we must do it quickly and quietly, utilizing the element of surprise to our advantage."

"And you think this will work?" Doc asked.

"We know it will." Marian left the shadows to stand next to me. "How do you all think I'm able to stand here and speak with you all as a human? Until Arie saved me, you all thought the beasts were nothing more than vicious monsters. Now you know that a bunch of them are your friends and family."

"She's right." Ace rose from his chair and placed his hands on the table. "You heard what Wendy said about Jack and Jaina. You all knew Wendy before she went off on her own. She never lied, if anything she told the cold, hard truth. And now we have to save them all. The only way to do that is through Wendy."

"So it's settled, then. We will do whatever it takes to defeat Wendy and set the innocent free." Marian and I looked at each other, and I could feel the same fire there that I had seen in her when we first met.

"There's one more thing." I cleared my throat, unsure how to tell this entire room of people that Giles had betrayed us. I planned to keep it a secret and only tell those who needed to know, but then wouldn't I be doing the very thing others were doing to me? Keeping secrets, lying, betraying. Giles had broken an unspeakable vow. Frankie was surely keeping something from me—I'd been suspicious, but seeing her in that interrogation only further proved something was going on with her. And then there was Ulrich.

No. I had to tell them, and so I did.

An uproar of anger swept through the war room as pirates and Lost Boys voiced their opinions. Most of them wanted his head on a spike, but I couldn't allow that. I wanted it, more than anything, but his words refused to leave me. His wife was being held against her will. I had no way of knowing whether it was the truth, but until I knew for sure he was my prisoner.

"Giles has been a part of this for a long time. There's a chance he knows things we don't. So, while I appreciate your anger, right now we have a larger evil ahead of us. Until things settle down, we will keep Giles close and at arm's reach. No one is to go to him, speak to him or about him, until I see fit."

A chorus of agreement sounded from the people around me, and I sighed in relief.

"Good, now let's get to work." Marian gave me a half smile and retreated to her corner of the room.

The rest nodded in agreement, and soon plans were being made. I had to be honest, hearing the eager determination in their voices was comforting. It gave me a much-needed boost of confidence that maybe this plan of ours was going to work after all.

We spent our last remaining hours working out every last detail. Marian and I would lead a team of Lost Boys and *Betty* crewmates to distract the beasts. I had wanted to be there to watch Wendy's life leave her, but as much as it pained me to admit, Ulrich had made a good point. I was the greatest defense against her beasts. Ulrich and the rest would take to finding Wendy and any beasts that remained at her side and take her down before things got too bad.

While everyone strapped themselves with various weapons and supplies, I took it upon myself to head to the kitchen and help prepare some food for the trip. Lily's Cove was a full day's walk, and we were going to have to stop at some point.

Pascal stood in the middle of the room, his back to me as he sliced up pieces of meat. He'd been quiet since his return from speaking with his father, a meeting I wish I'd been invited to. I'd have loved to give the god a piece of my mind. He may not have taken Pascal's shadow, but he abandoned him, nonetheless. He could have stopped Wendy from the very beginning and instead he cowered behind his gate to ensure Gemma didn't get her claws in the souls of the dead. While I was sure it was an important task, it shouldn't have even gotten this far.

Pascal's shoulders stiffened. "Hello, Arie."

His voice sounded mellow and unfazed. Had the other half finally come back out of his hole?

"Pascal." I strode up to the table and collected the pieces of meat he cut and placed them in the container he'd gotten out.

We remained quiet for several moments before he continued. "I know you must think I'm a coward for what I did—for hiding away."

Yep. The other Pascal was back.

"You did what you thought was necessary, though I am curious. What changed your mind?" I asked then tossed a piece of meat into my mouth. The savory taste on my tongue was euphoric as I closed my eyes to enjoy every last bite.

Pascal shook his head. "Nothing changed my mind. My father decided to just ... put me back together."

My eyes shot open, and I coughed and wheezed to get out the meat that was now lodged in my throat. Pascal patted my back until I could speak. "What do you mean? What about the wizard?"

Pascal shrugged. "I am the wizard just as I am Peter. I've been thinking about this a lot. When Wendy tortured me, a part of me shut down and hid away. It wasn't the soul being ripped from me. It was a safety mechanism. I've always been the wizard, as I've always been Peter. There's always been a darker side to me and that's what Wendy wanted to see. She wanted to break me, and when she did, she got tired of me. She found out what she needed to and then threw me away. And rather than let that broken piece free. I created the wizard and locked the other half away."

My head spun. Pan had taken both pieces of a broken puzzle and put them back together. Was that possible? I suppose it was, but how certain was I?

"When my soul returned, so did I. The pieces that were made from Wendy's torture just needed to be glued back together."

"And how do you feel now?"

Pascal shrugged. "I'm not sure how to answer that, but maybe in time I will be able to move on from it." He turned to me and laughed. "You look like you've seen a ghost."

I shook my head. "I'm just letting this information sink in. Are you sure you're okay?"

He placed a hand on my shoulder and nodded. "For now. I'm not such a lost soul anymore, so I'll be okay eventually."

"Are you prepared to take on Wendy, then?"

I knew he couldn't go out into the sunlight, but surely there was a way to get him there. Would fairy dust do the trick? It had taken us from here to the ship and back, surely it could get one person to Lily's Cove.

Pascal locked eyes with me once more and a determination rose in his face. "Tink and I have discussed a way to get me there once night has fallen. I will rendezvous with you at the campsite just as the sun sets."

Someone cleared their throat behind us, and I whirled around. Ulrich stood in the doorway. I had to tilt my head back to take in the full sight of him. He was wearing his leathers, tight around his muscular body in all the right places. The white of his shirt beneath illuminated his tanned skin, and I'd be lying if I said I hadn't noticed. Knives were strapped to his sides and across his torso, and a pistol sat in its holster on his belt. His scent wafted over me as he stepped inside, a subtle mix of musk and mint that had always stayed with me since we'd first met. His dark eyes glinted with amusement as he caught me staring, and I blushed and turned back around. I was supposed to be mad at him, not undressing him with my eyes.

He'd been an ass during Hector's funeral and had dismissed me as a captain. I had to remember that.

"Pascal." Ulrich strolled up to the table. "Would you mind giving Arie and me a minute to speak in private?"

I shook my head. "I don't think—"

"Of course, but someone needs to finish cutting up this meat." Pascal handed the knife to me, and Ulrich eyed me wearily.

I raised a brow. "If I wanted to stab you, I would have done so many times with Slayer."

"Yes," Ulrich said, "but you're holding a knife, so I figured it was best to assume the worst."

We both laughed, and the tension between us dissipated slightly. We stood with only inches between us, and I could feel the heat radiating from his body. The air around us thickened, and for a moment I forgot that I was furious with him.

I shifted uncomfortably, unsure how to respond.

"Look, I know you're upset with me." He stared at the floor, not quite meeting my eyes. His hands were clenched around the locket at his neck. I thought back to the first time he'd shown it to me. A picture of Clayton and a reminder of his mission to save him. Ulrich took a deep breath and continued. "But I want you to know that I do trust you. You're a great captain, and I should never have said the things I said. I think I was just scared to let you take on Wendy by yourself."

"I wasn't planning on taking her on by myself. Had you trusted me, you'd have known that," I bit out. Frustration found its way back to me, and I sliced viciously at the meat. I was certain by the time I was done it would look more like a sloping heap of disaster, but I didn't care.

"Just like when you didn't trust me to take care of things on the *Betty*."

I pointed the knife at him. "And where exactly is she? Oh, right, at the bottom of the gods forsaken sea!"

"I admit it didn't exactly go as planned—"

"Exactly as planned?" I shot him a look.

"*But* everyone made it out in one piece."

I had to give him that. He'd managed to save my crew while I'd been battling with Chimera. He'd saved those who weren't even his to save and he'd done a lot of that since he'd joined my crew. But was that enough to forgive him?

As if he read my mind, he shook his head and said, "I will never forgive myself for not trying harder to save Hector. He was a good man and he deserved better. But do you think that maybe you could see things from my point of view? That I was simply trying to ensure that more deaths didn't happen. You've seen what Wendy's capable of, and there was no telling what else was lurking in the trees behind her."

Ulrich ran a hand through his hair and started to pace. He was just as beside himself as I was about this entire mess. I wanted to tell him that everything was going to be okay, but how could I possibly know that? Now we were about to head off to take on Wendy and there wasn't a soul in this entire treehouse who knew if we'd make it back alive or not.

I sighed and placed the knife on the table. "I know you were trying to help, and I don't blame you for that. But if we're going to continue this friendship and partnership, then we're going to have to learn to trust one another, and I'm not sure I can do that."

"You're not sure that you can trust me?"

I shrugged.

I hated the thought of putting any sort of trust in anyone at this point. Not when I could just do things myself and ensure it's done right, but I knew that wasn't always the right choice to make. Before all this madness was over, I knew I was going to have to lean on others. But why did it have to be him? Better yet, why did I have to be attracted to a pain-in-the-ass pirate captain?

"You're right. We do need to figure out how to do this together, if not just for survival then for the good of our people. If you can't trust me, then maybe we shouldn't work together after this."

His words were like ice against my rib cage, and I pressed my hands onto the table to steady myself. Is that what I wanted? It would make things easier. Putting distance between us would also help this infuriating pit in my stomach that formed every time he entered the room, or the way my heart fluttered.

"But I don't think that's what either of us want." He took a step closer. "I never thought I'd be admitting this to you, but somewhere during this mission of ours, I've found myself caring about you. I won't apologize for it, or for the fact that it's become a weakness—"

"Oh, so I'm a weakness?"

Ulrich threw his hands up in the air. "For sea's sake, Arie, will you—"

I threw my head back and laughed. "I'm sorry, I couldn't help myself."

"And you say I'm the insufferable one."

He cared about me. Captain Hook, the notorious pirate captain who slayed monsters and feared nothing, cared about *me*. And as much as it pained me to admit, I knew I cared about him too. He'd made a couple of poor judgment calls, but it didn't deter me from feeling the truth in his words, nor the fact that we'd both said many things we couldn't take back. But perhaps we could work at mending the wounds we'd given one another.

Clearing my throat, I said, "I'm sorry, you were saying?"

"I'm saying"—his hand moved closer to mine and our fingers lightly brushed against each other sending an electric current of sparks through my body—"that I'm sorry. You're a big girl who can take care of herself, and I have to learn how to deal with that. I'm so used to being the one who takes charge and does what needs to be done that sometimes it's hard to sit back and let others do that for me."

Heat flooded my cheeks. "Well, I'm sorry for not trusting you either. It's not something I'm exactly good at."

"For good reason," Ulrich said.

Our eyes met, and he leaned in closer. I wanted to move away at the same time my body felt heavy and weighed down with lead, unable to move no matter how hard I tried.

"Your mother turned out to be a monster, a friend turned out to be a betrayer, and you've spent your entire life fighting a war that was never yours to begin with."

He brushed a strand of hair from my face, and my entire body froze. What was he doing, and why wasn't I stopping him?

"But maybe it's time to let someone else in. Maybe it's time to truly believe that someone can be trusted if you just open that part of you. I won't pry, and I won't force you, but hells, Arie." He paused and took a step closer until there was nothing between us but a sliver of air. "I want you. I've wanted you since the moment I saw you take on the monsters you're so good at hunting."

His lips lowered, and everything around me silenced as I fought to breathe. This wasn't happening again. Back at the waterfall he didn't even know we'd kissed, and now he was so close again. Did I truly want this? Did I want to subject myself to opening up to a man who may be the very end of me? A part of me wanted to, but another part, the part in the far back of my mind, screamed at me to run as it always did. I was a runner. I ran when my fathers were killed, I ran from my sister who needed me, and I ran whenever I started to feel something *more*.

Maybe it was time to stop running.

His lips were only inches from mine when a voice interrupted us. "We're ready to head out, Cap—"

I cleared my throat and backed away as disappointment flooded Ulrich's face.

"You don't want me, Ulrich," I whispered. "I'm far too broken to be loved."

I peered around him and found Keenan in the doorway. "Good, then let's move out."

XVII. NEVER ENDINGS

Pascal

MY FATHER'S POWER SWAM WITHIN ME, MIXING WITHIN my own magic as it coursed through every vein and every muscle. I felt unstoppable. Strong, like I could do anything I set my mind to—a force to be reckoned with and the master of my own destiny. I hadn't expected him to piece me back together *and* grant me a little extra strength, but it left me feeling *whole*.

Yet, now that we were about to take on Wendy and her beasts, for some reason all I could think about was Taigra and how much it hurt that she was gone. She'd already be on the front lines, gearing up with the rest of the pirates and Lost Boys and Girls to fight whatever battle came our way.

Dark eyes stared back at me through the window, and my mind flooded with the memory of Taigra. I'd thought I'd done everything in my power to keep her safe, and instead I'd been the reason for her demise. She'd wanted a life away from the one she'd been dealt and in doing so said yes to a daring new life. She said yes to me. Her sweet, honeyed voice echoed in my mind.

I choose you, Peter. From now until the end of our days. I choose you.

"You're the reason I'm still fighting, and I won't stop until she pays for what she did to you. I swear it," I told the emptiness around me.

Stepping away from the window, I reached out to pick up the glass vial next to me. Fine golden-hued dust brimmed within it—the small grains sparkled and shimmered. I uncorked the top and spilled a small amount into my palm before placing the vial back down. The grains were cool and soft as I pinched some between my thumb and forefinger. A sense of calmness washed over me, and I let the dust fall back to my palm.

I pictured my destination and held up my hand, drawing in a ragged breath and feeling the dust from my palm tickle my nostrils. With a gust of air, I blew the dust out in front of me, and my world spun.

The campsite was just outside of Lily's Cove. Taigra's home. My mind wavered again to visions of her lifeless form as it laid in front of me, her eyes clouded and her dark skin cold and pale. Wendy's laugh echoed in my mind, and I swallowed hard, taking time to remember I was in charge of my own mind now. I could do this. I strode through the last bit of foliage to find the campsite swimming with Lost Boys and pirates. A sight I never thought I'd see. Pirates were always destined to be the downfall of Neverland, or so that was what the legend said. One that dated back to the first pirates to find Neverland. They were treasure hunters in every sense of the word, and they stopped at nothing to get what they wanted. At least, that was until I met Arie and her band of misfits.

Now here they stood, setting up and getting ready for a probable death. Arie was certain this plan could work, but something nagged at me. It all seemed far too easy. Arie was expecting things to go wrong, that Wendy would lead us into a trap, and while that was certain, she wasn't worried.

People greeted me as I made my way to where Arie and Frankie stood in proximity and appeared to be in a heated conversation—one I probably shouldn't have eavesdropped on.

Arie hissed. "You have to tell me what has been going on with you. I know you're not telling me everything about what you did during your time away. I've noticed the way you act sometimes, the look in your eyes." Arie stiffened and whirled around, her gaze fixed on mine. "Pascal! Thank the gods. Will you please tell my sister that it would be in her best interest to stop lying to me."

Frankie threw her hands up. "Can we just get through—"

"She doesn't want to tell you because she thinks you'll think poorly of her." I shouldn't have said anything, but the words poured from my lips before I could clamp them shut.

Arie narrowed her eyes at me. "What do you know?"

I shrugged. "Not for me to tell. Now, when are we going the rest of the way to the cove?"

"No," Arie snapped. "Not until some trust is shown. There's been far too many secrets being kept, and I'm tired of having to wonder whether I should be expecting another catastrophe."

"Can we focus on what's important first?" Frankie snapped back. "When things settle down, I promise we will have a conversation. Okay?"

Arie let out a breath and straightened, giving up for the time being.

"Pascal, there you are," Ulrich called from behind me, Tink stood on his shoulder. "Are you ready to finally end this?"

I sighed in relief, glad he hadn't commented on my mind too. Maybe Arie had kept that to herself, to which I was grateful. Even though I felt more myself than I had in a long time, my shadow was a constant void, and I'd do whatever it took to get it back. Wendy would pay for everything she'd ever done, all the darkness she'd tainted onto the world, in my home.

Yes. I was *very* ready.

"As soon as Arie makes the announcement," I told Ulrich.

Arie, her gaze still fixed on her sister, groaned. "Fine, but this isn't over."

Frankie rolled her eyes. "Of course it's not; gods-forbid you let something go."

Arie started to say something when Smith ran up to the four of us. "Hook, we've uh … got a problem."

"Another problem?" Arie gritted her teeth.

"What is it, Smith?" Ulrich said at the same time.

Smith nervously played with the hem of his coat before his gaze flickered between the two captains. "Follow me."

He led us away from the main campsite to a more remote section where I knew they'd be keeping Giles. I hadn't been there when Arie interrogated him, so I had no idea why they decided to bring him along instead of keeping him locked in a secure room back at the treehouse. A question I didn't think was necessary to ask at that moment.

The small clearing came into view and with it ... disaster.

Giles laid on the ground, his neck twisted at an unnatural angle and his eyes still wide open in shock. One of Ulrich's men was next to him, unconscious and bleeding from what appeared to be a minor head wound.

I let out a deep sigh as I knelt beside Giles. He was gone, but it wasn't enough. Giles would never pay for the atrocities he'd committed against Arie and her crew, or anyone else for that matter. Despite being one of us during this time of chaos, he'd betrayed our trust and had brought upon his own demise.

Giles's neck was broken. Someone had used stealth to their advantage and had taken him out before he could say too much. Frankie approached the two bodies and knelt beside me. Her fingers grazed Giles's neck and understanding lit in her face. Her gaze flicked to me.

Yes, it appears we both knew who did this.

"You know who did this, don't you, little assassin?" I whispered for her ears only.

Frankie's jaw dropped. "So, you do know."

I nodded stiffly. "I know a lot about the Brotherhood. I know how they work, how they act, and how they were trained. While you are missing some key pieces, I can tell you were a part of their organization for some time. I see the flicker of darkness in your eyes from time to time, the same darkness that inhabits the souls of all the Brotherhood. However, you didn't do this, of course." I pointed to Giles.

"You can't tell Arie," Frankie pleaded.

"I know. You will do that for yourself in time." I stood up and turned to Arie, speaking louder for everyone to hear. "I believe this was the work of one of the Brotherhood. This was a clean break and quick. A signature of the assassins."

Recognition flashed in Arie's face. There was only one other person with us who was a member of the Brotherhood, an assassin that had been placed in our care by a mysterious man with the initials RH. Curiosity got the best of me as I wondered why Robin, a man who hated the queen and everything she stood for, would send Jameson to aid Arie. Did he even know what he'd done? After this, I'd be sure to send him a letter, or perhaps show him a visit.

"Has anyone seen Jameson?" Arie asked.

"The last time I saw him was in the war room," Ulrich replied. "I can ask around and—"

"No," Arie hissed. "No one can know. We keep this between us."

"What happened to not keeping secrets?" Frankie chimed in.

"It's too much of a risk. We don't know for sure, and until Ulrich's man can be questioned, we need to keep this quiet. No secrets are being kept. We're just withholding information for the time being."

I understood why Arie wanted to take precautions, but I had a feeling it was more than that. No assassin, no matter how trained, would have left a body behind if they wanted to remain anonymous. Jameson wanted Giles to be found and wanted Arie to know it was him.

"If this was Jameson's work, it's probable that he's already taken off and warned Wendy we're coming. We've lost our element of surprise," Frankie said.

I shook my head. "I don't think there ever was an element of surprise on our side. Just a plan that may or may not work. All we can do is stick to it and pray it works."

"He's right," Ulrich agreed, running a hand over his beard. "We'll stick to the plan. Jameson doesn't know everything. Nathaniel may be in more danger, but Wendy is too smart to kill him now after everything."

"Fine." Arie sighed. "Then let's get the crews ready and move out. We've already wasted enough time."

Moments later, we headed out to Lily's Cove. I led the way, taking the trail I'd been down hundreds of times before. The trees had grown taller and thicker, blocking out much of the night sky. Despite that, I could still make out Taigra's home in the distance.

"Is that it?" Frankie asked as she peered forward.

I nodded, unable to bring myself to speak. My throat ran dry, and my stomach turned at the thought of Wendy being here, of her sleeping in Taigra's bed and walking around the same halls as she once did.

We continued in silence until finally, as we crested a hill, we saw Lily's Cove. It truly was a beautiful sight—blue waters sparkled and glittered even in the moon's glow, lush trees that provided welcoming shade and shelter from the heat, and a large house built on a cliff that had an incredible view.

For a moment I allowed myself a second to take it all in, then my gaze scanned for any sign of Wendy and her band of beasts. Thankfully, there was none, though that didn't mean they weren't out there awaiting our arrival.

Arie motioned us off into our groups, and we said our goodbyes. Arie and Ulrich stood next to one another, so close that most would be unable to hear their exchange. But thanks to being back to my new and powerful self, I could. I'd known Ulrich for a long time—a tortured soul and one who didn't understand love. Who had grown up only knowing the love of friendship. He loved the Lost Boys just as we did him, but I wondered if he'd understood the true meaning of love. That was until he met Arie. He watched her closely before speaking.

"You may say that you're broken, Arie and that's fine because I accept that. I accept all of you and I will do whatever it takes to help put those broken pieces back together. I will do whatever it takes to prove I'm not the bad guy."

He walked away leaving her looking more stunned than I ever saw her before. Her eyes met mine and instantly the Arie I knew was back.

She and her group headed back through the woods and down the trail that led to the top of the cliff, whereas Ulrich, myself, and our group headed down toward the cave. There was a hidden entrance, one I was sure Wendy had discovered at some point, but with luck she hadn't found the hidden access I'd created for emergencies.

Entering the dark, dank tunnel of the cave, I ran a finger along the rough stone wall until I found a metal loop. I pulled down a lantern, and it caught fire with a spark of sulfur. I gestured for the others to follow me as the light illuminated winding passages in every direction.

We moved forward cautiously, the silence only broken by our footsteps echoing off the walls. After a short while, we finally reached a large chamber with smooth walls and a faint smell of sulfur in the air. Ulrich took point, grabbing hold of a metal loop embedded in the wall and pulled down another lantern to light up more passages beyond us.

"How far do these tunnels run?" one of the men behind us asked.

"Some will take you to the opposite side of Neverland and some lead to nowhere at all. A lot of this is nothing more than an illusion, magic meant to keep unwanted people from entering. Lucky for you, I was the one who built them."

Taigra had been so afraid of the world when she arrived. I'd taken every precaution I could to ensure she no longer needed to be afraid. This place had been her sanctuary, her safety net, and then it became her complete and utter ending. I shifted my weight and concentrated on what I needed to do.

Just as I found the next tunnel we needed to enter, a deafening roar sent shivers down my spine.

Neverbeasts.

This was not good. I'd figured there was a chance we'd run into some of her beasts, but hope had failed me yet again.

With little warning, three of Wendy's beasts materialized from the shadows. Terror ran through my veins like ice cold water. Three large beasts, their coats a patchwork of mud and bark, snarled at me. As though I wasn't surrounded by other men and their main purpose for being here was me. The thick fur of their coats, the sharpness of their pointed claws, and their beady red eyes seemed to strip away any courage I'd managed to muster.

I wanted to run from them but was too stunned. I dropped the lantern I'd been holding, fear outweighing my will to do anything but remain as I was.

My heart continued to beat wildly against my rib cage as the Neverbeasts stepped closer. I couldn't move, couldn't breathe. Behind me, Ulrich yelled something inaudible, but I couldn't make out his words.

The beast in the middle took a step forward, its large head bowed and its elongated teeth snapping with ferocious intensity. Deep-red eyes glowed as they trailed over me, seeming to size me up for a delicious meal.

My father's voice rattled in my head. *The shadows you fear are nothing more than obstacles you must overcome. Believe in yourself and you will find a way.*

A hand wrapped around my shoulder and tugged me back just as the beast lunged. Everyone scattered away from the angered creature as Ulrich brandished a sword to ward it off. The other two beasts followed suit, snarling and snapping at us.

"What do we do, Hook?" Smith asked.

Before Ulrich could reply, the beasts lunged all at once. The men ran in terror, fumbling for their weapons. Ulrich cast a glance at the last surviving light as it hit the ground with a sickening crash, plunging us into darkness. Screams and cries of desperation pierced the night as the beasts attacked.

Chaos ensued around me. Men and beast fought paw to sword. Blood splattered the walls and floors as I worked out what to do. I created these tunnels and in doing so they answered to me. Perhaps if

A LAND OF LOST SOULS

I used that to my advantage …

"I've got an idea," I called out. "Everyone just stay where you are."

I hadn't been able to use my magic much. Being split in two everything was hazy and difficult to decipher but now I was whole again.

I mustered every ounce of energy I had and called on the power within. A strong gust surged through the tunnels, carrying with it a swirling vortex of dust, pebbles, and debris. The walls morphed and shifted, creating a complex and winding labyrinth that would confuse even the most intrepid of travelers.

The Neverbeasts roared with rage as they raced through the maze, desperate to sink their claws into me. I had trained my whole life for moments like this. Well, whenever Father decided he'd show up and teach me, anyway. This trick had been one of the first he'd introduced me to.

Concentrating hard, I shifted in and out of view, appearing in one place only to vanish in the next. I couldn't move but for a few paces at a time, especially in complete darkness, but I didn't need to move far for this to work. I stopped at the edge of a tunnel, and the beasts closed in on me. I recited the ancient incantation that would seal them in from both sides. The magic clicked into place. With a mighty thud, one of the creatures slammed into the barrier, howling furiously as it was consumed by a searing purple light.

They growled, snapping their jaws in the air but none of them tried to escape.

I reappeared in the main tunnel where everyone awaited my return. "Is everyone okay?"

"Would be nice if we could see," someone called out.

"Feel the walls; there should be more unlit lanterns around," I responded.

Shortly after, a lantern flickered to life and illuminated the faces of our group.

The men around us were battered, bloodied, and bruised, but no worse for wear. Save for the couple that had lost their lives. Ulrich swore to come back for them when this was all over.

Hopefully Arie was fairing far better than we were.

"The tunnel that leads to the main house is just a few passageways up. Let's keep moving and stick close together."

We made our way through the last of the tunnels until it pooled us out into a larger room. A single door stood in our way. Beyond that opening was Wendy and I'd waited a long time for her. To watch the life drain from her eyes, to see her heart ripped from her, and her lungs unable to gasp for air. I wanted to call upon the very beasts she controlled and watch as their claws sink into her flesh and gnaw on her bones.

Wendy was mine, and no one could stop me now.

"Wendy will have put Nathaniel down in the cellar rooms somewhere," I said and turned around to face the group. "You find him and get him out of here before Wendy can do him any more harm."

"You're going off to face Wendy alone?" Ulrich shook his head. "That's not a good idea."

"I have to face Wendy alone, Ulrich. At least for now. Find Nathaniel, get him out, and then come find me." Hopefully by then Wendy will be dead and this will all be over.

"Pascal, you can't really think we'll just let you do this on your own."

"I know you will, Ulrich. Because you of all people can understand why I have to do this. All I'm asking for is a little time. Then you can burst through the door and do as you please. I just need to make sure this hasn't all been for nothing. Wendy loves her traps, and I would never forgive myself if I led you all into one."

Ulrich hesitated but finally gave a stiff nod. "Be safe."

I nodded and left the group as they muttered their disapproval, but I didn't have time to address their concerns. Not when Wendy was moments away from death, not when my revenge would finally be completed and Taigra's name could finally be put to rest.

I pushed open the door and stepped into a long hallway lined with lanterns, the fluttering light casting a soft yellow glow over the tapestries and paintings gracing the walls. Taigra's artwork adorned nearly every available surface—her signature, lush brushstrokes were unmistakable. Despite Wendy's attempts to rid the place of Taigra's legacy, I was grateful that some of her hard work remained intact.

The stairs at the end of the hall twirled upward in an almost gentle embrace, more reminders that there were still parts of this place that hadn't been tainted by Wendy's touch.

As I took the last few steps down the hallway, I could feel Wendy's presence buzzing in the air. It crawled along my skin and seeped into my bones. The memory of her torture was at the forefront of my mind as I entered a large entry hall, only to be engulfed by a scene of utter destruction. Tables overturned, chairs broken into pieces and thrown across the room, curtains ripped down and stuffed between broken window frames, and smoke stains smeared along the walls. Even in the dim light of the room, I could tell it had been done with precision and rage—or perhaps jealousy.

Still, I made my way through the remnants of the once beautiful home, half expecting a beast to jump out at any moment, until I stopped at a pair of grand oak doors. Beyond them was Taigra's library and the one place I knew Wendy would be.

I pushed open the creaking doors and was met with a pungent smell of something wild and musty. Books littered the floor, some with pages ripped out and scattered into pieces as though one of her beasts had used them as chew toys. Wendy sat in the center, her back pressed against a Neverbeast's fur as it snuggled around her. It let out a low rumble upon my approach. Wendy held a book in her hands and flipped through it without acknowledging me.

From the moment we left camp, I thought about what I wanted to say to Wendy. I thought about what kind of things were important and things that didn't matter. She'd taken my shadow, killed Hector, took Nathaniel, and she'd cursed so many Lost Ones. She'd tortured me and broken me down. And yet the only thing I really wanted to do was end her life before she could utter a single word.

Wendy lowered her book and smiled. "Peter, have you come to kill me?"

"Where's Nathaniel?" I asked.

"Oh, you mean the big burly gingerbread man? He's around." Wendy stood, and the beast stumbled to its feet and shook out its fur. "Where's your little pirate queen?"

I shrugged. "She's around."

Wendy laughed. "She sure is."

What did she mean by that? Dread washed over me for a split second. Did something happen?

"You know, I'm rather surprised to see you here." She threw her book into one of the many piles and hitched a hip on the only desk still intact. "I figured stepping into your dead lover's home would be ... triggering."

My vision blurred with rage as I took a step forward, my hand tightly gripping the hilt of my dagger. Wendy's lips curved into an amused smirk, and that one look stoked the fire building within me. My arm whipped forward, blade glinting in the light, and a primal scream tore through me as I hacked and slashed at her. The blade bit into her flesh with a sickening sound, and I felt a surge of satisfaction as red droplets rolled down her cheek and splashed onto the ground.

Rather than cry for mercy, Wendy laughed. *Laughed*. A deep chuckle that shook her slim frame and sent tremors of hatred through me. The sight of her own blood dripping down her arms and chin only seemed to fuel her mirth. She simply reached up and wiped it from her chin, reveling in the pain I'd inflicted.

The Neverbeast had been snarling from the sidelines the entire time. It was as if it knew the fate of this fight and was ready to strike on command, yet that order never came. Wendy instead turned to the beast and spoke in a measured tone. "Go do what needs to be done. I can handle it from here, Jack."

Jack?

An ache tugged at my chest. That beast had been Jack, my friend and brother in spirit if not by blood. It was like he didn't even recognize me. Before I could call out to him, Jack lunged into action and disappeared out the door I'd come in, leaving me alone with Wendy.

"Is that all you've got, Petey?" she said as I lunged forward. In a flash, a sword appeared in her hands, clashing with my dagger in a symphony of steel. I tried to focus on the fight but my emotions kept getting the better of me, like she was taunting me with every parry and thrust, pushing my buttons to make me lose control.

Our weapons locked together, and she scrutinized me with a look of smug superiority. "You know you can't win this fight," Wendy said quietly through ragged breaths. "Give up while you still can, or it will only end badly for you."

My dagger felt like a lifeline in my white-knuckled fist as I bared my teeth in rage. I wouldn't let her have this last laugh—not today, not ever.

Our blades clashed again. Time lost all meaning as we struggled, until I had her pinned against the wall with my blade against her throat. Fear flashed in her eyes, and for a split second I was back to the first time we ever met.

"It ends now, Wendy. For everything you've ever fucking done to me," I shouted, raising the blade above me, when an explosion of noise blew through the room.

Marian blasted through the door and slammed into me, sending us crashing into a pile of books. I scrambled to my feet just as Wendy took off toward the door only to be met by Ulrich. She stopped dead in her tracks and scurried backward.

"What was that for?" I bellowed, my face flushed with rage.

Marian turned to me. "I'm sorry, but you can't kill her, Pascal. Not yet anyway."

"It's about time you showed up. I've been calling ... wait a minute." Wendy's brows rose. "Your bond has been severed. How is that possible?"

I turned to Marian. "I thought you said she'd know when that happened?"

Marian narrowed her eyes at Wendy. "She should have. Dee, is there something you want to tell us?"

Wendy waved a hand at Marian. "Of course I knew, I was just … uhhh … confused that's all."

A sense of unease came over me as I looked between Wendy and Marian. Marian's face lit up. What had she figured out?

"And what do you mean I can't kill her?" I asked. "You know what she's done, who she's hurt. And you want to let her live?" I said through gritted teeth, my clenched fists trembling with fury.

"You can't kill her because … because Arie has been taken, and we need her to tell us where."

Blood drained from my face. Taken? How the hells did that happen? She had pirates and Lost Boys on her side, her sister and Marian. How was this possible? Uncontainable rage surged through every part of my body. I picked up a nearby chair and chucked it across the room. It slammed against the wall, splintering into dozens of pieces.

I turned to Wendy, to the one who'd started this whole mess. I'd witnessed her evil firsthand, felt it every time the breeze caressed the scars on my skin.

Wendy opened her mouth to speak, but Marian appeared next to her and grabbed hold of her hair. "It's not your turn to speak, witch."

"How did this happen?" I seethed, hostility radiating from my body.

"Jameson," Ulrich growled, eyes burning with rage as wild as mine.

"I was just getting Nathaniel out when Marian found us."

Jameson? The one who had somehow been working behind the scenes and orchestrating a betrayal. Was this his plan all along? I returned my gaze to Wendy and knew without a shadow of a doubt that we would get nothing out of her. Which meant she was no use to us.

Marian tugged on Wendy's hair. "Where is she?"

"Wendy isn't one who breaks easily." I stalked over to Wendy and Marian. "She'll never tell you what you want to know."

"So how are we going to find Arie?" Ulrich asked.

A small twinkle of bells sounded from beyond the door, and a few seconds later Tink appeared. "I believe I can help with that. I may not be able to find her exact location, but the bond allows me to know what direction she's in."

Marian clicked her tongue. "So, what you're saying is there's no real reason to keep her alive?"

"Huh, I guess not." I smiled widely.

Wendy pursed her lips and unleashed an ear-shattering whistle. It echoed off the walls and shocked a collective gasp from the room. Everyone held their ears, wincing as the shrieking noise continued to pierce the air. Amidst the chaos, Wendy's lips stretched into a mischievous grin.

"You're all going to want to start running."

Marian erupted into a laughter that seemed to take over her entire body, shaking and choking on her tears. After catching her breath, she cleared her throat and grinned at Wendy. "Oh, you actually thought Chimera was coming. I'm sorry to burst whatever ego bubble you have going on, but he's dead."

Wendy paled and shook her head in disbelief. "Y-you're lying."

"How did you not feel it?" Ulrich asked. "Didn't you say she should have been able to tell."

Something flickered in Marian's face. "Because Chimera and I were never hers to begin with. I nearly forgot that we were Queen Gemma's beasts. The first ones to come to Neverland. The others, the Lost Ones, are hers. Is that why you always had a harder time controlling the two of us? I just thought it was because we were stronger than them. I guess it doesn't matter anymore."

"What did you do?" she shrieked. "I swear to Pan himself I will slit your fucking throat where you stand."

"Oh, I wish I could take credit for killing that insufferable ass, but unfortunately, that was Arie's doing."

What?

I looked at Ulrich whose smile was larger than I'd ever seen before. Was that a look of ... pride?

Wendy's nostrils flared, and her face contorted with anger and hate. Two silver daggers glimmered in her hands, and she let out a deafening screech as she lashed at Marian. The air around them thickened, and suddenly Marian's body morphed from one breath to the next; her body grew, and her skin was replaced by long shaggy fur. Her dark eyes shimmered to a deep crimson, and when she opened her maw wide to let out a low growl, Wendy lunged.

The two of them clashed in midair, Wendy slicing and stabbing, and Marian who fought back with claws and teeth.

They were an impressive force to watch, both relentless in their desire to rip one another apart. Marian's teeth sank into Wendy's arm, eliciting an agonizing cry from her lips as her blade shredded across Marian's face. The beast scrambled back, her tongue lolling to one side and her teeth bared.

But then something unexpected happened: Marian shifted back into her human form.

"Hook, if you wouldn't mind." Marian nodded to Wendy.

Ulrich, without skipping a beat, walked up and held Wendy. Her bleeding arm dripped on his boots.

"As fun as this is, and as much as I want to be the one to kill you, I think it's only fair to share in this wonderful opportunity."

Marian walked to the door and pressed her fingers to her lips and whistled, nearly the same whistle as Wendy's, only this one was short and sweet. Much nicer on my fragile ears.

Who was Marian talking about? Ulrich and I were here, as was she. Did she mean one of Arie's pirates? I imagined since Ulrich was here that he'd managed to find the pirate, but I couldn't be too sure. He'd failed to say much of anything since standing there and watching this all play out. Why did it feel like I was the only one not in on this plan?

Suddenly, claws clicked against the floor from the hallway, pulling me from my thoughts.

Dozens of claws.

Neverbeasts slowly piled into the room, their eyes burning with hunger as they approached Wendy. My body froze as I watched. I knew these beasts weren't here for me, but seeing them here reminded me of my own battle against them. Mainly Marian, though seeing her in her human form eased some of that fear. I swallowed the unease that rose in my throat. I had to remember that I wasn't the one strapped to a table or being held against my will. I wasn't the one about to be devoured by my own beasts.

I had broken free of Wendy's hold, and I had survived.

"We haven't killed Wendy, how are they listening to you?" I asked.

"Your pirate queen is far more powerful than I imagined. Before Jameson showed up she managed to sever all the bonds at once."

Wendy closed her eyes and paled. "N-no, that's impossible. I would have felt it." Her eyes shot open and her mouth dropped as she shot me a look. "You distracted me."

"And a mighty good distraction it was." Marian beamed. "Now, I think it's time we end this, don't you, Pascal?"

I shook my head. "There's one more thing I need from her. Where's my shadow, Wendy?"

She whirled around, her face twisted in fear as she stammered an answer. "P-Peter, you can't let her d-do this. Please, if I give you back your shadow, you'll show mercy, right? We were friends once. I loved you. I still love you. Please."

I stepped closer to her, my eyes hard and unyielding, knowing full well this would be the first and only time I'd ever go against my word. I just hoped the gods forgave me. "You're right. We were good friends. I suppose I could be merciful if I wanted to be. If those are your terms, then I will do what is necessary."

Ulrich shot me a look but let me continue.

Wendy hesitated for a moment then let out a long breath and slid her fingertips into the neckline of her shirt. She pulled out a small glass vial with a cork stopper that dangled from a thin silver chain. Inside the vial, my shadow swirled with delight and recognition.

"You were much more fun after I broke you," Wendy hissed, and then smiled up at me.

"And you'll be much more fun when your body is nothing more than a pile of ashes and your name is a distant memory."

Grasping the vial in my hand, I uncorked it, and my shadow flowed out and swirled around me. I tilted my head back and felt the wave of relief as it connected with me.

And then Neverland sang with my return. The trees whispered in my ears, the waters churned, and a gentle breeze tugged at my hair, welcoming me back. I would never have to be alone with my own thoughts so long as they were here with me. Neverland's air around me—I was home again. Truly and completely home.

I shifted my gaze to Marian and gave her a nod. "She's all yours."

Wendy wailed and cursed at me, but I was already walking toward the door.

As much as I wanted to be the one to end Wendy and feel my blade sink into her, the people she'd cursed and forced to do her bidding deserved this far more than I did. I'd gotten my revenge on Wendy. She thought she'd broken me until there was nothing left to mend, but I picked up those pieces—and with a little help, I'd found my way back. I'd done what she thought impossible. I was free.

Marian lifted her chin, a smug look on her face as she uttered one single word. "Attack."

Coming Soon:

A Kingdom of Wicked Souls
Dark and Twisted Tales Book three

An evil queen.

A captured sea witch.

And a pirate captain willing to do whatever it takes to save the one he loves.

Arie is trapped—again—and Queen Gemma is quick to prove herself more ruthless than any king. Desperate to break free, Arie must resort to any means necessary. Even if it requires making deals and playing the dutiful puppet in the queen's game.

As Arie fights for her life, Ulrich finds himself on a warpath to save her. He's up against terrible odds, even more so when he discovers the truth about his past. Seeking out a mysterious hooded man and his band of assassins, they must work together to stop the queen and save as many innocent souls as they can.

The clock is ticking as Queen Gemma's plans begin to unfold. Will either of them be able to stop her before her dark ambitions bleed through the streets of the Enchanted Realm? Or will they finally fall victim to her wicked plans?

AUTHOR'S NOTE

This book took SO much out of me, but here we are at the end of another story and onto the next. A Land of Lost Souls was a really fun book to write, but it was also a struggle. I had a hard time really immersing myself in the plot of this book but the more I wrote the more it all came together. The ending was one that I messed with for SO long and I just hope it paid off. For those of you who are mad at me for what I did in this book... I'M NOT SORRY! But at least Wendy paid for it in the most epic way... right?

Anyway, now that it's over, I want to take a moment to thank those who rose to the occasion and helped me in tremendous ways! If it weren't for them, this book would still be a complete mess.

Rae – My critique partner, best friend, and biggest supporter. I'm sorry for the chaos that is me, but I also thank you for sticking with me and being a part of my life! Without you none of this would be possible.

FingDing – My love. Your support means more than you will ever know. Thank you for taking on the chaos monsters for me while I worked to finish this. You're my rock, my life, and the best thing that's ever happened to me. I love you!

Nastasia – Your editing skill and expertise always help me to forge the best work possible. You may have been given a handful when I sent this book to you but you rose to the occasion like the badass that you are!

My Betas – Krista, Sarah, and Gisselle. You guys freaking ROCK and dealt with this story when it was just a shell of what it is now. Your feedback was appreciated beyond measure.

My wolf pack – Your continuous support is always appreciated, and I love you all! I hope you all enjoyed this book as much as I did writing it … after much frustrations of course!

Last but not least to myself – YOU KICKED ASS! Keep on keeping on and remember the force is always with you!

About the Author

Jay R. Wolf is an author of dark and urban fantasy, a wife and mother of three, and a huge geek.

She is from a small town in Michigan and moved to the big city to pursue her dream of acing. Though her dream of racing cars is in the wind, she finds herself in a comfy lifestyle in the Mile High city where writing fantasy has become a passion.

Her other hobbies include long walks in ancient forests where the wild things roam, gaming against evil foes, and catching fish in the great lakes.

Want to know more?
Website: www.authorjayrwolf.com
Facebook/Instagram @authorjayrwolf

www.ingramcontent.com/pod-product-compliance
Lightning Source LLC
LaVergne TN
LVHW040208200625
814264LV00028B/562